FORTRESS OF THE KING

MEDICI MAFIA BOOK 1

MACKENZY FOX

DAKOTAH FOX

MEDICI MAFIA
BOOK ONE

FORTRESS OF THE KING

DAKOTAH FOX
MACKENZY FOX

AUTHOR'S NOTE

CONTENT WARNING: Fortress of the King is an adults only dark mafia romance centered around the Medici Boston underworld crime family. It contains scenes which may disturb some readers including but not limited to: kidnapping, mentions of domestic violence and human trafficking, torture scenes (only to the bad guys!) foul language, bondage, and lots of steamy loves scenes. Reader discretion is advised, for adults 18+

Cover by: @peachykeenas (Savannah Richey)
Formatting by: @peachykeenas (Savannah Richey)
Line Editing by: Lunar Rose Editing

For those out there who dare to dream x

BLURB

I TRIED TO WARN HER.

From the moment I laid eyes on Rayne Michaelson I knew she had to be mine.

She's heaven sent. An Angel. She's nothing like me.

They call me the King of Boston.

There is nothing the Medici crime family cannot obtain.

Wealth. Property. Fast cars. Women. *Anything.*

Nothing is off limits. Except her.

She's a mystery. A ghost. And she holds secrets of her own.

The problem isn't the web she weaves all around me, but the fact that I'll stop at nothing to seek my vengeance on those that want to hurt her or those who get in my way.

The trouble is, what if she's the enemy all along?

PROLOGUE

THE RAIN TEAMS DOWN IN TRUE FEBRUARY STYLE, THE GRAY clouds above looming like they will burst open any minute, threatening the already dreary day with little comfort or even a speck of solace.

The man who raised me, my Uncle Mario, the first Don in a long list of Medicis after my father, God rest his soul, stands beside me. He's stoic and unreadable, watching the Pallbearers place his son's coffin over the gravesite as we gather around.

I know the death of Roberto has hit my uncle hard, his only son, heir to the Medici crime family, and soon to be king of Boston, when Mario steps aside.

Not many of the family know that Roberto wasn't just being groomed to take over because he's the next in line, but because Mario's health has been ailing for quite some time, and he needs to put provisions in place. Both the eldest sons in the family work their way through the ranks, learning the business from the ground up.

The good. The bad. The ugly.

The downright debauchery.

And now I'm reluctantly next in line.

My Uncle is as strong as an ox, he always has been a formidable presence and a man to be feared. I know if anyone can beat this cancer, it's him.

In truth, I never wanted this job. I never saw it in my future. While Roberto and I were both destined to run this empire side by side; I was always more comfortable being in the background. Running my security business, the Fortress, and partnering with the family in building the biggest casino in Boston. It is a work in progress, and it sends a statement to the rest of the city that this is Medici turf, and we will rule no matter what.

I stare directly across the gravesite, wondering where it all went so very wrong.

Roberto's wife, Allegra, stands at the foot of the grave as the coffin is interred into the ground, watching as her husband's shiny, black casket is lowered into the black hole.

Stricken, she throws a handful of dirt onto the coffin as the Priest chants his benediction.

She's dressed head to toe in black, her face hidden by her mantilla, forever the widow of the

man that would never rule.

We've been friends since childhood, though I know from the time we were old enough to understand what hormones were, she was sweet on me. We got together earlier in college, one night after we'd had too much to drink, and from then on, we had casual sex on and off. It fizzled out; I was too young and didn't want commitment and I wasn't in love with her. I ended things, but we remained close.

She's family, and I've no romantic liaisons with her. Over time, she grew more like a sister, who gets under my skin and whom I love in equal ways, much like my blood sister Valentina, who's younger and far more naïve.

Allegra's head moves to glance at me as I stare at her. I don't see her face but her shoulders shake from her sorrow as she brings a tissue up to her nose. Her eyes are covered, and I realize she will never be able to see the world as she did before.

Death changes you. This, I know.

I saw my father gunned down when I was fifteen years old, young enough to not quite understand why someone would do that to my papa, yet old enough to relive the horror every single night when I sleep.

The nameless faces remain in the forefront of my mind when I need to punish myself for not being able to save him, for seeing him like that; vulnerable and weak when he was none of those things. He was the hardest man I knew, tough and disciplined, while also remaining the fairest. And when he lay bleeding in my arms, my world shifted.

I lost everything that day, and I vowed to make his enemies pay. A vow that one day I would grow up to be just as feared as he was, that the mere mention of my name would send men trembling and packing.

His death made me the cold-hearted monster I am today.

If not for my dear, sweet mother, I would probably be in hell right now, or at least in purgatory, repenting for my sins as I clink my glass with the devil himself.

I've feared nothing since that day, and I trust very few people.

Allegra looks away and back to the pit before her.

She and Roberto had been married five years ago. She's a beautiful woman; there's no denying it. However, I could never betray Roberto like that. He'd been in love with her for years as we grew up, and his affections never strayed.

The trouble was, she gave me her heart long before, and I didn't reciprocate. I couldn't.

I would never have been a good husband to her back then so early on in life. I like other women too much, and I prefer to enjoy them rather than pretend monogamy is my thing.

Maybe for the right woman, I could be, with someone who's just like me, but those women are few and far between. The old saying is true; women make men weak. And there is no room for me to indulge in weakness other than to get laid.

I feel the tension radiating off the man next to me. It jolts me out of my reverie.

"I want them found," Mario mutters in Italian.

I nod.

"I want them in the basement, ready for me to cut out their hearts."

"It's already in place. Whoever did this won't get to enjoy another breath, of that I can assure you."

We may not know exactly who this was yet, but the fact remains: we will, and they will pay.

I always get my mark. *I always win.*

I place a hand on his shoulder. I'm one of the few people whom he trusts. He loves me like a son, just like his beloved Roberto.

He nods once. "I never had any doubt."

I have even more reason to worry about him now. He's aged overnight. His salt and pepper hair is now white, his skin grayer than usual, and his hands shake whenever he holds a whiskey glass. That's new.

He'll never say it, but he loved his son. I know he made him proud.

And it tugs at my heart, what little I have left of it, that I may not have his approval.

We have much to discuss, and I know what conversations are coming. I dread the words that haunt my soul when I know the burdens that are about to be bestowed on me; I've known my whole life that this could happen.

But this is what I have to do.

The reluctant King.

I never wanted to rule.

God help those whoever crosses the Medicis, that's all I can say. If they think Mario and my father were tyrants, they haven't met me yet. They don't know how depraved I can be.

I take no prisoners, and I won't accept weakness, just like they taught me.

The rain beats down harder as the sky finally breaks, almost like it's a sign, and I make peace with it. There are no choices in this family, I learned that long ago.

I know now what I have to do.

1

ANGELO

"Angelo Medici?"

I glance up from my newspaper slowly, unhappy with the intrusion and the fact that my quiet time at Render Coffee House has been disturbed.

The beautiful woman looks down at me with bright, shining eyes and a big smile.

Well, well.

Perhaps all is not lost after all.

My bodyguard moves toward her, but I spare him a quick glance, and he backs off, stepping back into the shadows.

She seems to know me, but that isn't hard since everybody knows who I am.

The fact that she has the gall to interrupt me, however, is what surprises me the most. Most don't, or won't, if they know what's good for them. She's either incredibly brave or just plain stupid.

Those that know me in my world say I'm a tyrant. Some would say a beast; it's just the degree of the monster which varies. Today, I must have summoned some patience.

I arch an eyebrow at her interruption.

"Claire." She holds a hand to her chest like it's meant to mean something to me. "Claire Holdwright. I work at the gallery."

Big fucking whoop.

Holdwright.

I wonder if we fucked?

The gallery is one of my many business ventures in the city, though I'm more of a silent partner with my brothers as shareholders. I'm just here for the art, the opulence, and I enjoy acquiring beautiful things.

Hmm. Surely, I'd remember those long legs wrapped around me. Although I've never fucked a person in my employment or someone who works for one of my companies, that's just not good for business.

I don't do well with names, either. I'm better with faces.

I also don't like women who like to chat, and Claire Holdwright seems like a chatter.

My temper starts to flare; she shouldn't be talking to me like we're old friends. However, because she's beautiful, I momentarily let it slide, and also because a slight movement in my peripheral ensnares my immediate attention.

The woman standing to her right captures my gaze, and my eyes lock on hers. It's almost as if they're unwilling to look away yet have no choice in the matter.

Christ, she's fucking beautiful. Angelic.

In my world, very few things surprise me. Very few things keep my attention, but there's nothing like a beautiful woman I don't know with long, golden hair, pale flawless skin, and gorgeous legs to grab me by the balls and shake.

She definitely shakes.

Like a predator sniffing out its prey, I'm suddenly alert and interested, though I let none of it show on my face. My mask has long been in place, I've been in this game a while, and I play the part of a king well enough to own, divide and conquer it.

I want to own her, even if just for a night.

Like a siren's call, she doesn't look away. Instead, those green, penetrable eyes stare right back at me, like she isn't afraid of the monster deep inside me, like all of the bad shit I've ever done no longer exists because she's my atonement.

Clearly, this fucking coffee is spiked. I should slap myself.

I've always been a romantic at heart but never, until now, a fucking idiot.

"I'm so happy that you're going to be contributing to the charity auction at the gallery. This year's donations are phenomenal, thanks to your generosity, of course," Claire goes on because I've not said a word. She beams down at me like I'm Jesus himself.

If only she knew. I'm the fucking devil.

My world is spinning as the vivid green of the woman's eyes linger over me, and I'm thrilled when she's the one to break the connection.

There's hope for her yet.

I have to fucking know who she is.

My eyes cast over her petite frame. She's well dressed in an expensive short dress with long sleeves; it's fitted and business-like, but it outlines every goddamn curve on her beautiful body. Her high heels make her appear taller than she is, and I find myself imagining her legs wrapped around me while I fuck her senseless.

I shift in my seat uncomfortably.

The slight arch of her eyebrow tells me she knows who I am, but none of the usual signs follow:

Shock.

Fear.

Intrigue.

Lust.

Sometimes, and more often than not, disgust.

No wide eyes. No stumbling over oneself at introductions. No fucking anything.

This is odd.

Claire, however, isn't in a hurry to introduce us. It's ignorant. I don't tolerate a lot, but bad manners are just a rite of passage for anyone who works for me or is in my presence.

I cock an eyebrow at Claire as my gaze shifts back to her. She stops mid-sentence and instinctively turns to her quiet companion with some surprise and apparent reluctance.

Before she can recover, I take over. "Would it be polite of a well-bred, smart, and successful woman who works for me to introduce me to her friend?" I say in a low voice. "Or is that beyond the realms of comprehension?"

Stupid bitch.

Claire flushes but recovers quickly. "My apologies, Mr. Medici, forgive me. This is my work colleague, Rayne Michaelson. She just started this week, and I'm showing her the ropes and training her on how you like things done."

Oh, I'll fucking show her how I like things done, tied to my bed.

My heart hammers in my chest at the thought. Then it hits me: *A fucking employee?*

Okay, so I don't ever stop at the gallery unless there's a new collection or an auction, like the one coming up, and I definitely don't keep tabs on who the current employees are; it's of no interest to me. I've got minions to take care of all that.

It looks like I may have to break my number one cardinal rule about fucking the help.

Her lips part as my eyes drop to her mouth.

Red lips. Fucking beautiful.

I imagine them wrapped around my cock, and I can't believe I'm getting a hard-on while I sit here enjoying my espresso.

"Angelo Medici," I drawl but stop short as she steps forward and does the unthinkable, holding her hand out toward me as if she intends to shake mine.

I don't miss Claire's shocked gasp as she does so.

I stare at her dainty hand, noting no wedding ring, with amusement on my lips, and it seems I'm in a good mood today, after all. Wonders never cease.

"Mr. Medici, I'm so pleased to meet you." Even her fucking voice is sweet.

Imagining my dirty hands on her body, makes me want to stalk her into the depths of hell.

Maybe Mondays are finally looking up.

I take her hand in mine, and before I can stop myself, I kiss her soft skin, my eyes never leaving hers.

"Miss Michaelson, welcome to the company," I reply as Claire stares at me with an open mouth. "I hope you're being instructed and trained to the high standard expected at Fortress Galleries. We thrive on excellence, reward loyalty, punctuality, and above all, expect obedience." *Take that how you will.*

The slight dig at Claire has her all but squirming back into the shadows.

I'm hardly known for my chivalry; this is comical even

to me, and I definitely don't greet any of my other employees in this manner.

If she knew the real me, she'd run a mile. Or maybe she already senses what lurks beneath, and she likes it.

Stranger things have happened.

"Oh yes, thank you," she says. "I've learned so much already, and everyone has been very accommodating."

I bet they have.

There are no doors that can't be opened by that degree of beauty.

Fortress Galleries is run by my tough-talking, ball-busting manager, Patricia, and she doesn't employ idiots, except Claire, who needs to pick her jaw up off the floor before she makes an even bigger fool of herself.

Rayne seems unfazed, which is odd and slightly disturbing.

Maybe I'm losing my magic touch?

I'm giving it all I've got, which usually doesn't take much, but she doesn't even spare a glance down my body. Thankfully, my open newspaper covers the missile I've got going on in my pants.

I'm a sexual man by nature, but this is fucking ridiculous. I didn't intend to nut one out before I got to the office.

Normally people know my reputation. Normally they're threatened by me, but that doesn't stop them from being drawn in. It never does. If anything, it's even more alluring.

The danger.

The power.

The peril.

The money and all the bullshit that immense wealth brings.

I've built my merciless kingdom up from ground zero,

and anyone and anything that gets in my way will suffer. They end up on their knees, begging for forgiveness.

Sometimes, I forgive.

Sometimes, I punish.

Sometimes, the devil smiles back and delivers as he sees fit.

I take what I want, and I want her. I'd love to tie her to my bed and take my time, keep those heels on her and kiss that red lipstick off until she's choking on my cock.

The femme fatale, that's what she is. A dangerous species that I am familiar with.

I don't need complications, and everything I know tells me to steer clear of her. But I'm also a man who enjoys a chase. Sometimes I prefer it when they play hard to get.

I also do not usually engage in conversation or meaningless banter unless it serves me, of course.

"You must let me show you around some time and give you the grand tour. I'll set it up with Patricia the next time I'm downtown." *You're not getting away, little fish. I want to know all about you.*

Her chest hitches just ever so slightly. "That would be lovely, thank you, Mr. Medici." The way my name rolls off her tongue sounds seductive, sensual, and forbidden coming from the lips of an angel. Like she's taunting me with every moment, and like she's completely unaware of the war inside me.

So, she is affected by me. That's no surprise, really, most women are, but it's just a face.

My eyes have a dusky blue-gray tinge, depending on my mood. I've been told they resemble bottomless pits.

Merciless and ruthless.

The eyes are indeed the windows to the soul, and mine are a never-ending guilt-less, brutal abyss.

I savor the moment because life's pleasures, like the one unfolding, come rarely. I'm going to fucking enjoy it.

What the fuck is in this coffee?

I let my fingers linger far too long on her skin, and I indulge in the thought of what it would be like to take her with my mouth… It's then I realize I'm still touching her. I also know what I do to women when I look at them like they're my next meal, but she keeps her guard well-fortified. It's even more impressive.

Shut this down, Angelo. She's trouble.

But I like trouble. I devour trouble. I enjoy chasing trouble until it can no longer haunt me.

"Well, Mr. Medici," Claire says, clearing her throat. "We best be going; we don't want to keep Trish waiting."

That irritates me because I despise how people shorten names, especially those whom you work for.

I tear my gaze away and reluctantly look back at Claire, giving her a curt nod.

She does not seem impressed by our little exchange, not one bit.

I stamp down my errant thoughts while also noting to text Gus, my driver and go-to guy for everything, to find out all we know about her.

If I interrogate Patricia, she'll only give me that look that tells me I'm playing with fire.

I also don't wish to sit here making small talk with Claire *what's-her-face,* either. I'd rather stab myself in the eye with a pencil.

She needs to go *now.*

"Until we meet again," I say towards Rayne, but it's more like a promise. I turn back to my paper, like the exchange never even occurred.

I haven't been laid in almost five days. That's what it is.

I glance at her retreating figure as they continue down the sidewalk.

I dial Gus.

"Boss?" he answers on the second ring.

"I need to know everything we have on a new employee by the name of Rayne Michaelson, as a matter of urgency. She just started at Fortress Galleries."

"I'll get you a full brief by the end of today."

I down the last of my, now cold, coffee and wince. "You sound chipper."

"Could say the same about you."

I snort. "Just get me the fucking file. You've got two hours."

I hang up and smile as I fold my paper back together.

I'll know all about you soon, pretty one, then I'll make my move.

I'll have all the ammunition I need, and then I'll do what I do best; take what I want without any mercy.

Just the thought of her...

No good can come of any of this, but when has that ever stopped me?

2

RAYNE

Angelo Medici.

The king of Boston himself.

The touch of his hand sent an electrical current through me, one I disguised well.

Of course, I know who he is. Everyone knows. Although in all of my wildest dreams, I never expected him to look like *that.* Or to be so utterly charming, in a cold, calculated kind of way, like an eagle eyeing its prey.

His name alone evokes danger.

He certainly demands attention, that much is apparent, but it's the weight of his glacial and unforgiving eyes that momentarily stun me.

Beautiful yet dangerous. It rolls off him in perilous waves.

He's the ruler of this town, the ruler of everything. I've been told he has no feelings, that he doesn't possess a sensitivity chip, and I can tell he's a man with secrets.

While I despise men like him, I don't let it show on the outside. I kept my composure, and I could tell from his body language how that may have irritated him.

I don't want to be on his bad side. Playing the game of chess takes precision and skill, and if I wish to be queen, I have to make my move wisely and keep one step ahead.

I've seen pictures of him on the internet, but in person…there is no comparison. How can a monster be so blessed with looks, charm, and charisma?

He's handsome beyond belief. Tanned with a sharp jawline and thick eyebrows framing a rugged, chiseled face. He has lips that could make you sit up and beg for buttermilk.

Angelo Medici is the god everyone makes him out to be and more, so much more, and it's slightly debilitating, like when you stare at the sun for too long and begin to see spots.

Claire turns to me as we make our way back to the office. Today, I'm stuck with her as my lunch buddy, which wouldn't be so bad if we had one thing in common. Instead, she treats me like an afterthought and an inter-loper, which I suppose I am, so I should give her some credit for being perceptive.

Plan A has already fallen into place quicker than I could have hoped for, and all it took was a reasonably tame Prada dress and showing a little skin.

I thank my mother for my looks. They sure as hell didn't come from my father, and I've been making sure I give extra attention to my appearance for when I eventu-ally ran into him. It was only a matter of time.

"You don't *really* know who Angelo Medici is, do you?" Claire exclaims.

I'm a little insulted by her incredulousness, like I'm some dumb blonde without a clue who just stepped out of college. But I need to act the part, so I play along.

"I've heard about him, of course," I say, biting my lip.

"It's not like you can move to Boston and not know who Angelo Medici is."

She rolls her eyes. "Yeah, he was acting weird, though. He isn't usually so… *hands-on.*"

Imagining that monster in bed does things to me that it shouldn't.

You hate him, remember. I tell myself. *You hate all of them.*

It's not personal, it's business, and I hope I managed to grab his attention enough that he wants to pursue me. It'll be so much easier and less complicated if he comes to me.

Angelo Medici meets a billion women a week, and he has the pick of the bunch. There is likely no woman in this entire universe that wouldn't be affected by him, which is a problem.

My stomach curdles at the thought of what I have to do.

While I have no choice in the matter, I have to get on his radar and make sure I stay there, exactly where I need to be, until my next move.

"Oh, how so?"

She pulls me to one side, then looks around her, as if we could be overheard. Clutching onto my trench coat, she whispers, "Angelo Medici is not someone you just latch onto, touching him like that. God, Rayne! You're lucky he likes you, or you'd probably get your head chopped off for even looking at him the wrong way, let alone shaking his hand!"

My eyes go wide as I pretend to be shocked. "I hope you mean that figuratively?"

She shakes her head. "Trust me when I say I'm not. He's bad news. Fucking gorgeous, of course, and a friend of a friend told me he goes all night and likes all kinds of kinky shit in bed." She practically swoons right there on the pavement. "Can you imagine him dominating you in the sack? I mean, it'd be too much. I'd never recover. God, I really need to get laid."

I bite my lip and smile, though envisioning him kinky in the sack shoots a pulse to my very core, not that it should. I've no interest in the enemy other than to do my job.

Claire isn't a bad person. She's a little clicky, but she seems harmless enough, and she might even give me some useful intel on the Medicis.

I frown at her comment. "Well, he is kind of cute, but I'd be way too nervous about being in his presence alone," I admit. "He has that whole dark and dangerous vibe going on."

She gapes at me. "Cute?" She actually slaps her forehead. "Oh my God, Rayne. Do you need glasses?"

I stare at her with wide eyes.

"No offense," she adds.

"What else do you know about him?" I press. It seems gossip girl may be able to give me something valuable after all.

"Well. It would not be cool to piss him off. I mean, if he really was serious and wants a one-on-one tour, then you do it. If he insists that you do *anything,* then do it. He isn't just called the king of Boston for no reason." She leans in to whisper. "I shouldn't say this, but you're best off hearing it from me. He's got links to the underworld…he's mafia. Some say he even owns the police."

Holy shit.

I think about the file on my desk in my apartment and what I already know so far.

He's the head of Boston; what else is there to know? This is *his* territory, and when he's not feuding with the Russians and other people of power, he's taking over every single thing in this city.

Angelo Medici.

Thirty-eight years old.

A self-made billionaire.

Former heir to the Medici Fortress fortune, now the ruler of the underworld and all the crime figures in it, good and bad but primarily treacherous.

I expected a snake.

I expected the devil incarnate.

Instead, I was met with a man who exudes effortless power, one where it would not be possible to pass him in the street without taking notice.

While I should follow the warning bells going off in my head, that isn't an option. The only choice is to step with open arms into the fire and welcome the flames.

"Jesus, Claire! I'm starting to wonder what I've gotten myself into here," I whisper-shout back. "The under-world?" I leave the word hanging, and we continue walking.

"It's best you know," she goes on, like it needs further explanation. "Angelo Medici is not a man to be trusted."

I stare at her strangely. "I don't intend on sleeping with my boss," I choke out. "I mean, he's attractive and all, but that is unethical, not to mention downright creepy."

She just shakes her head like I'm a lost cause.

Good, forget about me Claire Holdwright, that's exactly what I need you to do because you'll only get in my way, and getting in my way could be a mistake. I don't need her getting caught in the crossfire.

That burden is mine, and mine alone.

It's the next afternoon, and I'm sitting at my computer when a message pops up on my screen from Angelo

Medici.

I stare at the text as relief floods through me. *Finally.*

I did get his attention.

My heart thumps as I stare at the screen. How on earth is he instant messaging me on my work computer?

It reads:

Miss Michaelson. Patricia tells me that you're free this afternoon?

I just need to breathe and not read into this too much, though I doubt that he has anything but pattycake on his mind.

Hello Mr. Medici. Yes, I am free. Are you downtown?

I've decided that if I want to dabble in the devil's play-pen, I have to act like one of them.

Yes, and I'd like to give you that tour. Just like I promised. I'll be there at 4 pm.

I think about what Claire told me about his kinks. I can only imagine what that bastard likes to do, and it should not excite me. It should repulse me. He is the epitome of all the things I despise and –for lack of a better word –*hate.*

This is business, not pleasure.

Wonderful. I'll look forward to it.

I go to the bathroom to freshen up because I don't have very long.

Just as I leave the stall, my phone rings. I glance at the number. *Shit.* It's my attorney, and I have to take this, it's about my pending divorce and messy alimony situation.

"Hi, Ira, any news?" I say in a hushed tone as I walk back to my office.

"The bastard won't sign." My attorney is hard-hitting, that's why I hired her.

"What do you mean he won't sign?" I have an imme-diate headache just thinking about it.

The bastard tried to ruin my life, but now he won't

leave me alone, and unfortunately, I was the one with all the money.

The fact that I supported him during our marriage while he focused on his 'art' has left me in dire straits. If only I'd listened to sound advice and got a prenup. Young and in love, I didn't see the signs, not until it was too late.

"He's not exactly agreeing to our terms. He wants more," she goes on.

I pinch the bridge of my nose and whisper-shout down the phone. "What do you mean he wants more? I've given that fucking asshole of an ex-husband enough! If he wants a goddamn war, Ira, he's got one! I'm sick and tired of his lazy ass…"

I glance up as I enter my office, and my eyes widen.

Shit.

Fuck.

Double fuck.

Angelo Medici is sitting in my chair behind my desk. My eyes meet his, and an unexpected jolt of electricity shoots through me, like lightning striking twice.

"Listen, Rayne, it's all right. I'm still digging for information, this isn't over. Fuck them. You have to stay strong in all of this, just like we talked about. We've come this far, and we won't give up now," Ira affirms.

But it's all white noise.

I thought that seeing him for the first time was like swallowing razor blades, but this is sheer torture.

His mere presence is a force to be reckoned with.

Stay fucking focused!

I may have been a loyal woman in my marriage, but I'm not the sort of woman who is easily swayed by a man. Then again, Angelo Medici is in a whole world of his own.

I'm a little out of my depth, but I control my outward emotions as I clutch my phone with brute force.

"Thanks, Ira. I'm at work, and something's just come up, so I have to go. I'll call you later." I hang up on her quickly before she can respond.

My boss just heard more than I'd ever want him to know about me and witnessed me swearing like a sailor. If not for the slight twitch of his lips, I'd assume he was not one bit amused.

"Mr. Medici," I start, instinctively apologizing like any good employee. "I'm sorry about that…"

He holds up a hand to stop me. "There's no need."

I curse myself. This is not what I wanted. Letting my private life into any of this is a mistake I can't afford.

He definitely heard, and now I need to make a joke about my fuck wit ex.

"Ex-husband problems. They're like a cheap suit that you just can't get rid of no matter how hard you try."

He watches me closely, like he's some kind of serpent, assessing me before striking and devouring me whole. A slight brush of fear runs down my spine and I swallow hard.

Act the fucking part, Rayne, just like you know you can.

"That sounds troublesome. Need a better lawyer?" He lifts an eyebrow and then adds, "Or an undertaker?"

I think for a second that he may actually be serious. "Uh, no, thank you. My lawyer is amazing, really. My ex and I may be getting divorced, and I may want to staple things to his head, but I don't wish him dead."

He doesn't seem impressed, like taking out my ex, Dane, would be the least of his problems.

I wish I didn't notice that his scent fills the room, strong and spicy. His five o'clock shadow matches his dark mood. I wonder what it would look like if he ever smiled.

I know what he's here for, nonetheless I have to make Angelo Medici work for it.

"Pity." He glances at my computer, and it's then I realize he's probably looking at the spreadsheet I had up on the screen before I left for the bathroom. "You're good with numbers." It's not a question.

"I'm a mathematical nerd at heart." I shrug. "I earned my degree in finance but fell in love with art." Also, not a lie.

He motions toward the empty seat across from my desk. "Won't you take a seat?"

In my own fucking office? This jerk has some nerve.

I do as he says and fold my hands neatly in my lap. As I sit, I don't miss his eyes raking down my body. "I feel like I'm in the principal's office, and I'm in trouble," I muse, looking across at him as he sits back in my chair.

Though the office is small, with him in it, it feels claustrophobic.

"On the contrary. I like to make sure all my new employees are settled in. After all, we like to keep a close, tight-knit family here at Fortress." The lies that come out of his mouth should shock me, but nothing shocks me anymore. This is how far I've fallen.

Him and his fucking privileged life. Looking down from his throne at the rest of us while we beg for crumbs and grovel for scraps.

This is the last place I want to be.

I stare at him blankly for a moment, but he's waiting for me to respond. "That's very generous of you, Mr. Medici, considering how busy you must be."

"You come highly regarded," he goes on, like this is some job interview. "I can see why I pay Patricia so much when she finds such remarkable recruits."

It's like we're talking about the stock exchange.

"Have you been checking up on me?" I give him a playful smile.

His lips twitch again. "I always do my research, Miss Michaelson. I'm nothing if not thorough in all things, but especially in my vested interests."

Another lie, he didn't know I was an employee until Claire told him as much, but I simply roll with it.

"It's why I wanted to work for Fortress, Mr. Medici. The gallery here is one of the largest in the Northern hemisphere. I jumped at the chance."

"Well then, it seems we have an understanding."

How come it seems like the meaning of that sentence sounds precisely like the opposite?

That would be my first mistake; believing anything that comes out of his mouth.

I glance at my watch like I have somewhere to be, which prompts the response I'm after.

"Well, let me show you around." He stands and immediately buttons up his jacket.

His suit screams Hugo Boss and he fills it out to perfection.

"You're paying me by the hour." I shrug, not caring how that sounds. "Lead the way."

He glances at me as he rounds the desk, and I don't miss the way my heart thumps at his close proximity.

I'm glad the door is wide open. Being left alone with him, while exhilarating, could be overshadowed by palpable fear.

When all's said and done, Angelo Medici doesn't fuck around.

I can't help but wonder if he's not only about to lead me into the lion's den but enjoy every goddamn minute while doing it.

I guess there's only one way to find out as I steel myself for a bumpy ride.

3

ANGELO

I'VE NO FUCKING CLUE WHAT LED ME HERE, ASIDE FROM lust, of course. Which is just the right amount of stupid that you'd expect from a teenager, not a grown man who should know better.

What the fuck I'm doing giving anyone a grand tour of the gallery is anyone's guess, and it gets me a few sideways glances. I realize I'm singling Rayne out, but I stopped giving a shit what my employees thought a long time ago.

I feel my phone vibrate in my pocket, and without looking, I know it's Marco; one of my younger brothers. He keeps wanting an answer about tonight's extravagant bash, and if I'm going, it should be obvious since I'm the host. I do the dutiful thing and ignore the call.

Instead, I spend the next forty-five minutes of my valuable time pretending to be boss of the century instead of the horny bastard I am underneath it all. I don't know why this woman has me so captivated, then again, I'm a shallow son of a bitch.

I admire beauty and intelligence. And most of all, a

woman who can hold her own. There's something regal about her. Something that lures me in.

The life I lead gives me very little pleasure, so when something intrigues me and gets me this excited, I'd be a fool not to explore it in its entirety.

I watch her from my periphery as I show her around. From the loading zone to the high-tech safe where all the valuables and priceless art are kept.

I'm pleased to see everything is neat and orderly down here. That saves me from firing anybody today.

Rayne follows me around, asking questions in all the right places and politely nodding when I explain something. She's eager to please. I idly wonder if she's this submissive in the bedroom. A part of me hopes not, yet another part of me dares to imagine it, even if that would mean breaking my own rules.

The truth is, I wanted this distraction, I *needed* it. Everything in my life is complicated right now. Everyone wants a piece of me, but not her. Even if she is taking the tour with me out of obligation.

Maybe it was wrong to come here, I know that's possible, but I answer to no one.

And I admit, I want to fuck Rayne Michaelson so bad, but I know that can't happen.

For one, she's too sweet for me. Delicate like a rose. And I'm the thorn in her side, at least figuratively speaking.

I could slap myself for being so fucking weak, but my mother always told me that I had a way with women, just like my father before they got together.

"So, you hail from New York?" I venture, because clearly, she's not going to strike up a conversation.

"Born and bred," she replies. "Though I needed a change after the divorce and everything."

"Understandable."

She looks down at her hands. "Everyone told me not to marry him, guess I should've listened."

"We all make mistakes."

"Some worse than others, it seems."

"Tell me to mind my own business," I press. "But why the hell did he let you go?"

She turns to look at me, her green eyes bright as she assesses me. "Things got messy towards the end, and I ended things with him, which he didn't take too kindly to."

I barely know her, but I don't like the thought of anyone putting a frown on her face. It makes me want to hurt them.

"The guys a fucking idiot," I add. "Pardon my French."

She swallows hard. "Thank you for saying that. I tend to agree."

He hurt her. I can tell by the way she rubs her hands down both arms protectively. Now that has my interests piqued.

I shouldn't make it any of my business, but my gut tells me this guy is bad news. One thing I've never done is lay a hand on a woman with violence. I may get a little rough in the bedroom, but they're up for it and it's consensual. It burns the blood in my veins thinking about someone hurting her.

I make a mental note to find out more about this asshole cheap-suit ex.

My phone rings again, and I see it's Marco for the hundredth time. I really have to get going.

I silence him and glance at the beauty by my side. "I'm sorry, it seems I will have to cut the tour short. Perhaps we can reconvene sometime?"

Her eyes dart up from my throat, and I feel a surge of satisfaction that she seems affected by me.

Fuck. If I had a woman like her in my bed, even for a night, I'd make it a night she'd never forget.

"I'd like that," she says softly, reeling me in with every subtle gesture. "Thank you for showing me around."

I resist the urge to touch her, though a gentleman would kiss her on the cheek…if this were a date, which it's not. *She fucking works for me!* Added to that, I've never been a gentleman.

What I'd love to do is spin her around, pull up her skirt and plow into her from behind while biting down on her neck, one hand would snake into her hair, and the other would cover her mouth, so she didn't alert everyone upstairs to what we're doing. The thought excites me.

My hands ball into fists as I fight the urge. Going against my instincts never feels very good.

"Well, I hope you enjoy working for Fortress," I say as we ascend the stairs back to her office. "If there's anything you need, anything at all, just let me know."

She nods and smiles like a good little employee.

I leave the words hanging and I hope to God she needs something soon.

I grab a shot of whisky from the bar on the patio and walk into the double doors of my two-story townhouse in the middle of the city. It's lavish with marble and gleaming porcelain, and the vast ornate windows look out to the busy skyline.

It's not exactly a sanctuary, but usually, it's a place I can relax during the week. Especially when I'm not hashing out business arrangements at our family Fortress Compound twenty minutes out of the city. On the rare occasions, like tonight, I open up my house for a party, but I can't wait until it's over. The music is thumping and dance lights flash on and off, it's all good for show, but all I seem to want is quiet.

My head's been buzzing all day with the shit storm of work this week, we're acquiring more property, and in negotiations with the council, the casino plans are getting underway finally, and then there's the gallery auction that we will all be attending.

I crack my neck as I take in the surrounding chatter of people milling around, talking shit and sucking up to the governor, just one of my many influential guests tonight.

I glance over and see Tiffany at the makeshift bar, talking to some investment banker. Which has me seeing red almost immediately.

I don't care about being rude, and I need to fuck, although somehow, now I've got Rayne in my sights so it almost seems vulgar sticking it to another woman.

I try to shake off the feelings swirling inside me.

Tiffany and I have hooked up here and there, and we're not serious by any means, but everything tonight is irritating me. Not enough to grab her and shove her into the nearest hall closet as I have before. She notices me looking and a slow smile spreads across her face.

When did life get so complicated? However, I immediately know the answer to that, when I took over the Medici crime family.

Before she can intercept, an arm links through mine, and I turn to see Allegra looking up at me.

"Hello, stranger," she says, her bright blue eyes shining.

I smile warmly. "Hello, yourself. I thought you were out of town?" I kiss her on both cheeks.

She sips on a glass of champagne and screws up her nose as we work the room. "I was, but I came back early, duty calls and all of that."

It's been years since Roberto's death, and Allegra hasn't been one to move on quickly. We've grown close, however. I don't see her as often as I should, but we have lunch now and again and the occasional dinner.

"We'll have to catch up." At least it sounds like I mean it, even if my schedule allows for little downtime.

She places a hand on my forearm. "I'll hold you to that." She smiles as we head toward my brothers, who stand in a circle, looking like the ultimate bachelors of Boston.

I shake my head as I chuckle.

I place my hand on the small of her back as we move across the room.

"Don't the twins look handsome?"

I glance up at my brothers. Dante and Fynn are the youngest of the boys, with my sister, Valentina, being the baby of the family. Marco stands next to them, along with our cousins, Jonas and Santino, from my mother's side.

Every time we get together like this, I think about Roberto and how much trouble they'd all get up to. It's bittersweet because we were close. He would have made a much better Don than me.

Dante and Fynn are twins but look completely different. Dante is softer somehow, dark-haired with a tan. Fynn is the playboy of the two of them, blonde and blue-eyed and likes to party; he takes after my mother in terms of looks and personality.

Marco is tall like me, in fact, we often get mistaken for twins. He's typically Italian and speaks his mind, which is why we often clash. He's my right-hand man, along with my best friend Enzo, who isn't here tonight. He's probably off schmoozing some chick in his fancy sports car. He runs all the security at Fortress Industries and is the only one, other than my brothers, that I trust implicitly. He's like a brother to me.

"Don't tell them that," I muse. "Their heads will get so big they won't be able to fit through the door."

She laughs, and it's a terribly lovely sound, for I don't hear it often enough. I would have thought she may have moved on by now, but there's been no hint of anyone. Being she and Roberto were early on in their marriage, there were no kids from the union.

A part of me always wonders what could have been with them, what kind of father he would have made.

We settled the score with our rivals, for once not the Russians, and a turf war ensued. It's kill or be killed, and I've more than enough blood on my hands to last a lifetime.

I made Roberto's murderers suffer, letting Mario have the final blow.

I don't think he's ever gotten over it, and now he lies in a hospital bed waiting for treatment. Things have gotten progressively worse, but I update him every other day with the progress.

He, of all people, understands the hardships.

My brothers are arguing over football, and it seems like a good time to excuse myself.

"Excuse me," I say to Allegra as she turns to me. "I've got some business to attend to."

"So late at night?" she says, her eyes dancing with delight.

I kiss her on the cheek. "Get your mind out of the gutter," I say in her ear. "Gus will drive you home."

I slip away quietly, stopping to refill my drink from the bar before disappearing to my study. It's one of the few places where I can really find peace because it's soundproof.

As I turn, I see Allegra watching me in my periphery, yet when I meet her gaze, she turns away.

Not for the first time, an uneasy feeling settles in my stomach.

The way she was looking at me…I'm sure I only imagined it.

She's like a sister to me, and it's never going to happen again, not in this lifetime.

Or the next.

I'm restless most of the night, and I toss and turn like a wild cat. I'm sure it's Rayne Michaelson giving me nightmares.

I wake up extremely groggy and tired.

I roll over as the morning light blinds me through a crack in the velvet curtains. I rub my eyes and yawn. My thumping head is telling me I probably downed way too much whiskey last night. I spent the night reading the report on Rayne and now I've discovered some startling news.

Her ex-husband was up on assault charges, which were eventually dropped. The bastard probably talked his way out of it, and she likely spent far more time in that marriage than she should have.

My blood runs cold at the thought of anyone mistreating her. It makes me want to track them down and slice them, one by one.

I also have the other file Gus sent over, probably with the help of our in-house computer whiz, Vaughn, who handles all our IT and traces what we need in a rush.

I was too busy with Rayne's file to bother looking at any of it. She's consuming my every waking moment, and that is something I need to get a grip on.

It doesn't stop my hand from reaching down to my dick as I stroke myself. I imagine those

beguiling green eyes looking up at me under long lashes. Hearing her purr my name, *Mr. Medici.*

That tight skirt.

The way her blouse didn't give me any cleavage to devour only makes me wonder about what she looks like naked. I bet she has a tight sweet pussy, too; one I'd worship like it was a prize.

I need to know her, find out what her story is, wine her, dine her and fuck her senseless, over and over again. That'll cure this idiocy. That'll get her out of my system. Even though I already told myself I wouldn't.

I start to pump my hips at the thought, oh yeah that's what I want, *the chase.*

I need something different—someone who will challenge me. Bedding compliant women are getting kind of boring, not that I wouldn't love to see Rayne submit to me, kneel at my feet while I grasp her hair as she sucks me off. That'd be a sight I'd love to see.

I groan as I shoot my load hard and fast, like a fucking teenager, all over my stomach and onto my imported silk sheets that cost a fortune. And this is what I've resorted to, fucking my own goddamn hand.

Life couldn't get much worse if this is what I'm resorting to.

I need to see her again.

I need her right fucking now.

***

I know I dreamt about Lucia. My wife.

I should have gotten up the first time I woke, even though I felt like shit, but I fell back into a hazy sleep.

I hate the dreams I have about her, the nightmares. It rattles me every time.

I was married once, though it seems like a lifetime's gone by; I gave up counting years ago. We fell in love a few years after college. Back then, the business wasn't what it is today.

My father mainly had Italian restaurants scattered around the city, and he and Mario worked hard building and buying everything they could. Blood, sweat, and tears are my family's motto, and it paid off.

Lucia died in a car accident when I was only twenty-three, she was carrying our unborn child.

The horror of that day ultimately changed me, it altered my state of mind, and everything I thought was good in the world slowly faded. There really wasn't any good to be had if my beautiful Lucia could be gone. I spent a lot of time on a downward spiral, and Mario is the one who got me through it.

After my father passed away, Mario began training Roberto and me from an early age to take over the business one day. I've always been firm but after Lucia, everything changed. I changed.

When we lost Roberto, I knew that Mario saw me like another son, that he would pass the reins onto me, and I couldn't decline. There is no out in this business.

I never wanted it, that's the truth. I didn't need or want the power, ever. Then slowly, over time, I began to change.

Mario taught me everything. The good but chiefly the bad. How to bleed someone out without them passing out, how to inflict pain to make our enemies talk. How to not lose sight of yourself with all the power and the demands required of the Don.

I watched, and I learned how he controlled things.

He started off in the rougher parts of the city, gaining

power and trust from all demographics, creating loyalty amongst our people, alliances so thick that no one could possibly break the forcefield. People respect the Medici name, but not everyone toes the line, and our enemies lurk on every street corner. You never know where your next blow will come from, and that's how it is in a crime family.

Not only did Mario teach me about violence and vengeance, but he also taught me about finances and how to acquire property and then sell it for a profit.

It took a number of years, but I was able to secure the land to build what now houses the Fortress Compound and the security business that offers state-of-the-art security, including cameras, fences, guards, and twenty-four-hour patrols.

We supply security and surveillance to most high falutin' businesses like banks, high-end designer stores, resorts, and casinos. I'm proud of it. To achieve what I set out to in my thirties is a dream come true.

Each and every day, I think of Lucia and what path we would have gone down and, why she was taken from me, why I would never get to meet my unborn child. It's a hurt I never share, and I've never spoken of it to anyone except Mario and Enzo. Some pain just gets buried so deep, like with my father, I barely know it's there until my nightmares remind me. And they always come.

I loved her with every fiber of my being, with everything I had to give. That was when I was good.

There is nothing good about me now.

My only mission in life is to make Mario proud and keep my city and its citizens where I need them to be. I've lost too much and sacrificed many to get here. Now Mario is really sick and past the point of ever ruling again, so I must be the fearless leader everyone expects. The one I was taught to be.

My mask is firmly in place, and there is no one and nothing that will knock me off my throne. But like everything in life that constantly changes, life moves on. It either takes you along for the ride, if you're willing, or it chews you up and spits you out, leaving only part of your soul intact, the rest of you changed forever.

To protect myself, I've had to be soulless. I've had to develop a switch that I flip whenever I want. And I thought I had it under control. I thought I was untouchable.

But then, everything changed.

4

RAYNE

I THOUGHT THE LIKELIHOOD OF EVER SEEING ANGELO Medici in the gallery was highly improbable, so it was a surprise when he showed up to give me a tour.

I can't deny that he emanates everything you'd expect a mafia Don to exude.

He's immaculate. Calculating in every sense of the word, I cannot imagine anyone not being taken under his spell.

In-person, he's a force of nature.

I don't want to be nervous around him, that's not going to do me any good, and I'm not an anxious person by nature, but there's a first time for everything. With him, the waters are unchartered.

Being in a prior relationship where I've had to hide my feelings, I've become somewhat of an expert at it. However, it's all irrelevant because being seduced by him wasn't part of the plan.

It's not what I signed up for.

Under normal circumstances, would I be complaining,

even though I know he's trouble? Not at all. But these aren't normal circumstances.

They say he's not just difficult but that he's impossible to get close to. I guess that is until he sees something he likes… which is precisely what I've been counting on.

On the outside, I play the part of the new girl in a new city, starting afresh, looking for a new adventure. But looks can be deceiving. The reality is far from normal.

He'll kill me if he finds out I'm working against him, of that I'm certain.

In fact, I don't even want to think about the consequences, but I can't let my train of thought derail me from what needs to be done. After all, this is a game, and Angelo Medici does nothing half-asked.

He takes what he wants, and he's notorious for it.

Therefore, I'm counting on that at that charity auction tonight.

It's the night of nights for all the elite forces around Boston. Everyone will be here, and it's the perfect opportunity to get Angelo's attention.

All the kingpins will be lined up, ready to make their bids from politicians, billionaires, celebrities, models, rich housewives, and underworld figures posing as businessmen.

I stare at myself in the mirror as I smear on some red lipstick. It seems fitting for a date with the devil.

My eyes cloud over at the memory of the day my life changed.

I've been sent to muscle into Angelo Medici's life and get close to him to gain intel on his comings and goings.

They took my sister.

I've no idea who the person is or who I'm being bribed by, but they kidnapped my little sister, Mia, and are holding her ransom.

It all happened after I got the job at Fortress Galleries.

The details are pretty sketchy and I have no names. All I received was a file with a list of what they want, but it doesn't just stop there, they are also requiring information on his staff, his family, *everything*.

They won't even let me speak to her, but I have received a photo of her tied up to a chair, looking terrified.

I have to extract information in order to get her back. I've been told very little about where she's being held, just that they'll hurt her if I don't do what they say, and they'll send me the video showing all the damage they do.

I'm no Boston native, so I had no idea who Angelo was when I took the job at the gallery, only that he was a director.

I soon discovered that he was the head of the Medici mafia family and ran several illegal crime rings. I've been given the rundown on his extracurricular activities like controlling most of Boston, owning the Police, overthrowing politicians, and taking no mercy in business. He's the king of Boston, and he's well known for the crime syndicate that leaks through this city like a rotting sewer. The Medicis are even resurrecting an old building site and are turning it into their own extravagant Casino and hotel.

I'm no mastermind. I walked into this with a blindfold on and very minimal time to get my head wrapped around what was happening. I had no fucking choice. And the one thing they can count on is I'll do anything to get my sister back. *Anything*.

Where do these people come from? Scum of the earth who'll stop at nothing to get what they want. And they *want* Angelo Medici.

They threatened to sell her to an underground prostitution ring where she'll be smuggled out of the country and sold to the highest bidder. It turns my stomach, and I'm barely holding onto my sanity.

All because I'm the epitome of what Medici favors. And now I'm stuck in hell.

My own private hell, one where I'm supposed to let this stranger, the mafia boss of this city, do whatever he likes to me. Worse still, he's freaking gorgeous and nothing at all like I expected.

Not that I'm attracted to powerful and ruthless monsters, but he surely can't be any worse than the people who have Mia.

They won't let me talk to her. I've no idea what the hell they're doing to her day in, day out. I've got one way out of this now, and it's staring me in the face ……

I plan on hitting him where it hurts tonight, and if I can get closer, then maybe I'll be able to learn something new that they can use. I don't fucking care. I'm scared of failing, and even though I'm no goddamn spy, I have to do it. I have to try.

I put the final touches to curling my hair; it hangs down my back in long, Hollywood-style waves. Guilt riddles me as I think of Mia tied to a chair.

This has to go as planned…

He favors blondes. I hope he also likes figure-hugging black dresses.

I keep it conservative yet sexy, sliding into my sparkling high heels. The dress might be all work, but the shoes scream play.

I've been given a couple of auctions to sell tonight. Being I'm comfortable using a mic from my stint at Christies, it shouldn't be hard, and it's why I need to look my best, because he'll be watching.

The eyes of the man at the helm of the Boston underworld, how frightening.

I'm strong. I have to be strong. I can't involve the police. *Medici owns them.*

Getting under Angelo's skin has to be perfectly timed, so deliciously natural, as though our chance meeting was just that and our impending flirtations are all his idea. It wouldn't be any fun if I just fell over and into his lap like all the other women who get handed to him on a platter. Not that I will be doing that. I wasn't sent to seduce him, but rather to observe.

An hour later, the place is packed.

Security is tight, and the high rollers swish through the fancy room with designer suits and dresses, diamonds, and cufflinks. They've got enough money to feed an entire nation if they pooled all their funds together.

I know that he isn't here yet, as obtuse as that sounds. Angelo has the type of presence that when he enters a room, it's like Moses parting the Red Sea.

Not knowing where he is unnerves me. Each day, hour, and minute that goes by is another day my sister is bound and gagged. *No! Stop.* Thinking like that will only destroy me.

I spy Claire by Patricia's side, keeping close tabs on things behind the scenes. It's a big night for everyone, and I need to impress Patricia and Angelo in one sitting.

I avoid taking one of the glasses of champagne to my office and downing it. Now isn't the time for nerves or to get sloshed, but I need guts made of steel to get through this.

It's just like any other auction. I tell myself. *You've done hundreds of them.*

That I have, but not with most of Boston's elite sitting there staring. It's always nerve-racking at the best of times, but I stand up straighter and don't allow the pressure get to me.

As long as I have sight of Angelo, all will be well…

When the guests begin to be seated in the embellished chairs in front of the podium, a string of waiters appear in black and white, handing out overpriced champagne in long flutes.

That's the trick; get the punters smashed so they don't realize how much they're actually spending on the artwork they don't actually need.

I notice an empty chair at the very front and I wonder if he's coming.

I absolutely hate how wired he has me.

Steel yourself, Rayne. Just breathe. This is just like any other auction…

The lights dim, and I'm momentarily distracted by the emcee for the night, a rather loud and obnoxious man with a three-piece suit and top hat on. A little over the top, but the crowd seems to like it.

He begins by introducing himself and then makes a big speech about how important it is to support those in need. He pulls out a couple of jokes, mainly poking fun at the high-flyers, and introduces the first auctioneer of the night.

My colleague, Melody, takes the microphone. She works in my department, and I've had lunch with her a few times, although it's clear from her approach and delivery that she's been in the spotlight more than once.

A beautiful gold trolley is wheeled in, and on it stands a Chinese glazed porcelain blue and white Qing Dynasty vase. Kindly donated by a congressman I've never heard of.

Melody begins the bidding at eight hundred dollars, and it quickly escalates back and forth through the room to over two thousand. She's good, playing the bidders off between themselves as she hikes the price up.

I stand in awe of her, a true professional, she's certainly

good at what she does and commands the floor with precision and grace.

She bangs the gavel down with an elegant tap, and everybody claps to the winning bidder in the middle row.

I clap, too, smiling into the crowd. In my few moments of watching Melody call the auction, I realize the spare seat in the front row is now occupied.

I stare into the icy blue depths of Angelo Medici, and a shock travels through my body. My heart accelerates as I stare back at him, my unaffected face mask is well in place, however. His eyes show no emotion either, and it's dangerously seductive.

I watch as his eyes then dip down the length of my body, his jaw ticks as he takes me in, and I think my dress just got the green light.

By the time the Arthur Clifton Goodwin painting is sold, courtesy of the Ritz Carlton Hotel, Angelo's lips turn into an arrogant smirk and I look away. He's too much.

I suddenly realize why some asshole's making me do this... because nobody in their right minds would be dumb enough to go up against him, in any way, shape, or form.

I didn't come into this without doing my homework. I know who he is. His ruthlessness is legendary.

Am I a professional spy, willing to put my life on the line for an underworld boss who cares about nobody but himself? No, but I have to get what I need from him and get it as fast as possible, and I'm dangerously realizing that I may be in even deeper than I thought.

Will I sleep with him to get my sister back? A lump forms in my throat at how sick that is, yet I can't bring myself to say no.

What I've got to lose is worth far more than any Qing Vase or ridiculously priced piece of art. What I've got to lose can't be replaced. I'm dead either way and so is Mia if I fail.

In my periphery, I feel him still watching me.

One thing Angelo Medici isn't counting on is a woman who can match his own ruthlessness. I may not be a merciless barbarian with links to organized crime, but I will get information in any way possible to help free my sister.

Angelo is well known for his loyalty to his family, it's why he's unbreakable, and he has the respect of most Bostonians and his men. It's why he's at the top of his game.

I try not to let my hands shake as I take the podium when my auctions come around. My first piece for the night is a lovely pair of James II silver candlesticks. The detail is stunning, the vine pattern swirling down each stem is magical, and added to that, they're in mint condition. I commence the bidding at five-thousand dollars.

It fazes nobody. The bids rise quickly. Six thousand. Seven. Eight.

"Ten thousand dollars."

My lips part, but no words come out, my eyes darting to the front row.

Angelo sits calmly as my eyes fall on him. His bid is overpriced for two candlesticks that seem very doubtful he even wants or needs. Or maybe he likes burning the midnight oil?

Of course, Mr. Medici has to win. This is what he's good at.

"Gentleman's bid," I say, giving him a smile of approval.

His look is predatory as he sits there like a fucking king, one knee crossed over the other, his hand resting idly over the back of the chair. Like he's almost bored with it all.

I don't know if it's because everyone is scared of him,

but nobody outbids him, and I slam the gavel down with force as our eyes meet. "Sold to Mr. Medici for ten thousand dollars."

The next item rolls out—a pair of stunning Harry Winston diamond earrings.

"Lot number seven for the evening is a pair of white gold, pear-shaped Harry Winston diamond and sapphire earrings, encased with nine hundred and fifty platinum. They measure at approximately one point three centimeters by one point two centimeters, weigh seven grams, and have a carat value of one point nine six. Can we open the bids at fifteen thousand dollars?" They're worth more, but it's always nice to see people outbidding one another, it makes the game all the more fun, and these are exquisite.

Angelo Medici raises his paddle. Shocker.

He immediately gets outbid, the price going up by two thousand. Oh this should be good.

He doesn't look rattled as I flick my eyes around the room as more bids erupt around us. Good old Harry.

"Nineteen thousand, ladies bid, twenty-two thousand in the back, can I see twenty-five?"

"Thirty thousand," Angelo Medici calls out as gasps ring through the crowd, even I stutter as I flick my eyes down to him. Son of a bitch.

For the first time since I have met him, he gives me a slow smile. He likes the game, and he knows how to play it.

"Mr. Medici has expensive taste, ladies and gentlemen," I quip as muffled laughter rings through the room. "Do I have any further interest on thirty thousand dollars for the exquisite Harry Winston earrings? Going once, twice.… Sold!" I make a big show of banging the gavel down as I return his smile.

He buys my next lot; a Boston landscape painting by

Gertrude Fiske, for five thousand dollars. Never mind that she was the first woman to be appointed to the Massachusetts state art commission in nineteen twenty-nine, my big selling point.

I don't think Angelo Medici cares because next, he gets into a battle of wills with another wine collector over two cases of rare Chateau Margot Cabernet-sauvignon merlot, aged over twenty years.

It's eye-watering, even to me.

Everyone is excited as a buzz goes around the room while the two gentlemen battle it out.

I know who will win.

Angelo Medici doesn't own this town because he is weak, he owns it because it's in his blood.

The hunt. The thrill. The chase.

I feel my skin flush at how he looks at me, sitting there sexy in his polished suit, unrelenting as I act unaffected by him.

"First call at one hundred and fifty thousand dollars," I call, lingering, avoiding his penetrating stare that's daring me to hurry it up. I won't, I'll drag this out. "Second call, are we all done at one hundred and fifty thousand…this is the final call…"

I flick my eyes back to him as he rubs his chin with infuriating arrogance. He knows he's got this. And I'm happy to say he's paid more than we thought it would fetch.

"Sold, once again, to Mr. Medici, the big bidder for the night, congratulations." I bang the gavel and raise my eyebrows ever so slightly at his exasperating run of bids.

This one went for a while.

Everyone claps, and I can see people whispering and shaking their heads, probably at the exorbitant amount he just paid for two cases of wine in his own gallery. All in the name of charity, of course.

He acts like he just bought a newspaper, not spent my entire salary, and then some.

He's bought every fucking thing on my list tonight. Halfway through the last auction, I wondered if he wasn't just raising his paddle so I'd look at him.

Conceited asshole that he is, I wouldn't put it past him.

The emcee comes back to the microphone to announce a refreshment break, congratulates the winning bidders and ushers us off the stage. Patricia gives me a nod of approval as I step down.

"That was crazy!" Melody says, linking my arm as we both swipe a glass of champagne when nobody's looking. She pulls me with her toward the staff room.

"Tell me about it," I reply, glad to finally be off stage.

Mr. Arrogance personified had to buy up big. It's just another way for Angelo to reinstate his authority as if it were under any doubt.

"I'm just going to freshen up," I tell Melody as she nods, sipping her champagne.

I escape down to my office to pull myself together. *Just breathe.*

I do just that, steeling myself as I guzzle half the champagne down like I've been stuck in the desert.

I halt in my tracks, my back to the door.

I feel him before I see him.

His scent permeates my small space, and nothing could distinguish Angelo Medici more than the dark and musky cologne that sends fire to my belly.

I take a deep, silent breath as I count to five.

"Mr. Medici," I say as I turn to face him. "We meet again."

5

RAYNE

"Miss Michaelson." He looms in the doorway of my office, looking ever the handsome, devilish bachelor in his expensive suit and tie. He could have stepped off the front of G.Q. magazine.

I walk toward the front of my desk and lean my ass against it as he watches me. He towers in the doorway, taking up all the space. There's tension between us, as much as I don't want to admit it or believe it. And I don't like it one bit.

Instead, I sip my champagne and smile up at him. "That was a lot of money for a few bottles of wine…" The lavish display did not go unnoticed by anybody in that room.

"Twenty-four bottles," he corrects. "And it was worth it. I like my wine a lot like my women; smooth, uncomplicated, and a little spicy."

His words roll off his tongue like silk.

"It's a pity I'm complicated." I shrug like it's too bad.

He smirks. His face is so much more pleasant when he's not frowning. "You make up for it in other ways."

"Oh? How so?" This should be interesting.

He moves toward me like a panther, and I swallow hard. My hands grip the desk behind me, as if it can save me from his onslaught. He's like a dark cloud about to throw down a thunderstorm.

I'm not here to be affected by him but fuck me, he's making it very, very difficult. The situation I'm in makes this really sick, *I need to get my sister back.*

His voice has a hard edge when he says, "The way you bang that gavel down, the way you commanded the audience out there…I like a woman who can take control of a mob with poise and grace, it's quite becoming."

Mob being the operative word.

I laugh. "Well, I've been doing it for a while. I worked at Christie's for several years, and you're probably not wrong about the mob, but that's just a fancy name for most of the hierarchy in Boston, isn't it?"

His lips twitch as he stands in front of me, blocking my exit, blocking any chance of escape.

"Are you seeing anybody?" His voice is deep and masculine, and it's not hard to figure out he's got sex on his mind.

I'm sure to shake my head, but at the same time, I say, "That's a very personal question to ask your employee."

"Technically, I'm not your boss, Patricia is."

I bite my lip as his eyes shift down. "Any more questions?"

"You didn't answer the first one."

"Well, it wasn't a noteworthy question."

His eyebrows quirk. His jaw clenches. I doubt he's used to a woman speaking to him this way. It almost makes me laugh.

Being a woman with so much to lose, I sure am acting cavalier.

He stares at me. "Are you fucking anybody?"

I roll my lips inwards as he assesses my reaction. "Wow. Direct."

He waits, his striking blue eyes not letting me get out of it. He's completely serious.

"Well, are you? Answer me," he demands, his nostrils flaring.

Fucking demanding prick.

"I am single right at this very minute, Mr. Medici." I pause as I meet his gaze. I won't tell him how long it's actually been. "With no fuck buddy, if that answers your question."

There's a tug at the corner of his mouth.

Two can play at this game, asshat.

"I'd like to buy you dinner after the auction," he tells me, swooping right in.

This is splendid news. "Do you think that's wise, being that my boss is probably two seconds away from firing me?"

He frowns. "Why on earth would she do that?"

"I think we caused a little bit of a spectacle out there."

"Do you think I give a fuck?"

I don't believe he does. "Clearly not."

He tilts my chin up, so I meet his gaze. Even though only one finger is touching me, it feels like I've been burned by fire. "I rule this town, Miss. Michaelson. I can buy anything."

"Anything?" I quirk.

"Yes."

I lick my bottom lip and then bite down on it. "What about people?"

My heart lurches at the very notion, at what I've been told about him, about his underworld businesses that make my stomach crawl...my mind spins to my sister,... *don't.*

"People who want to be bought can be bought, it's quite a simple equation, nothing complicated."

"What about me?" I counter. "Do you think you can buy me with fancy dinners and pretty things?"

His jaw tenses again. If I didn't know any better, I'd say he's enjoying this. "I would definitely say not. You're a woman with substance, a woman who had the whole room under her command tonight. Everyone was bewitched by you."

I flash him a smile. "Everyone? Even you?"

"Especially me."

"So, you want to fuck me, Mr. Medici, is that it?"

I wish he didn't smell so freaking good.

He still hasn't removed his hand from my chin, it's like he thinks he needs it to keep me in place, that's his whole modus operandi, but I'm not running.

"I'd be lying if I said it hasn't crossed my mind."

"But you'd like to wine and dine me first."

"Not necessarily in that order."

I know my eyes are dancing, and I know he knows.

"I can't sleep with you, Mr. Medici."

"Call me Angelo."

"That seems very informal for around the office."

"There's nobody here but us." His eyes drop to my lips. "I could kick this door shut and persuade you to call me by my first name."

I smirk. "Of that, I have no doubt."

I swallow hard, my attraction to him startling even me. His words hit my core like a freight train as I start to imagine all the ways he'd get me to call him Angelo.

He moves the finger from my chin up to my lips, it moves slowly, circling, then he cups my face with his hand. "Have dinner with me, *Carina?*" he asks again in a low voice. "Unless you're one of those girls who doesn't like to eat?"

Now he's talking to me in Italian? "I can't tonight. I have to wrap this up until the bitter end, I'm afraid, perks of the job," I say with a small, regretful smile.

His lips twitch. I'm all too aware that women probably very rarely say no to him, if ever, but this is where I want him.

"You like to be wooed, Rayne Michaelson, is that it?" He grows more intense with each passing second, blowing my thoughts to a million pieces.

"I think you'll find I'm not like most women." The minute the words leave my mouth, I want to retract them. I don't know what game I'm playing here…

However, he chuckles, and I glance up in surprise. "Glad to hear it. I'll book a table tomorrow night. I'll text you the details." It sounds more like an order than an invite.

"I've heard you're not a man to be messed with." I still clutch the desk behind me tight, like that will save me.

He grins. "Is that what you've heard?"

I nod, biting my lip.

"I'm sure you can indulge me at dinner with all about what you've heard." He reaches a finger to my chin again and tilts it up, so I'm looking directly at him. I notice he has cufflinks with his initials on them, and his scent, *this close,* takes me to a whole other level of consciousness.

I'm shocked at my arousal to him. He should make my skin crawl, he should make me do many things, which is why I need to keep one step ahead and not fall down the rabbit hole.

"Tomorrow," I confirm with a nod. "I look forward to it."

He knows he holds the power here; he could take what

he wants at any moment. I'm not a fool to disbelieve that, he knows what he's doing.

"And don't look so worried. You might actually enjoy it," he adds, his eyes crinkling in the corners like he wants to laugh.

"Admittedly, with moving and getting my life back on track, it has been a while since I've had much enjoyment, Mr. Medi –" I trail off as his eyes narrow. "Angelo," I quickly correct.

I know I sound like a loser, but that is precisely the point.

My heart jolts when he says, "That's better." Then he leans down closer to my ear, his scent washing over me, tantalizing everything I thought I could so easily avoid, things I never thought would be an issue. "I don't bite, Miss Michaelson, but sometimes they like it better when I do."

My eyes go wide. "You can call me Rayne," I manage to splutter.

He straightens and pulls on the lapels of his suit jacket, walking to the door. His ass looks perfect in those tailored pants. "Tomorrow," he hollers behind him without a backward glance.

I stare at the door as he leaves.

Panic and turmoil quickly run through me as soon as he's gone.

What the fuck?

I don't want to feel anything for this sadistic asshole. I *have* to be here, it isn't like I have a choice. Furthermore, its aesthetics are plain and simple, and I refuse to be blinded by a pretty face, penetrating eyes and – from what I can tell – a body made for sin.

My head needs to be in the game now more than ever. I have to stick to the plan even though I know it is becoming more dangerous with each passing minute. Now Angelo Medici has me in his sights.

It may cost me everything, but it's the price I'm willing to pay.

We're wrapping it up for the night, and the arches of my feet are screaming at me to get out of my heels. A hot bath and a glass of wine are looking extremely promising, and I can't wait to get back to my apartment and relax.

Melody has other plans, though, since she saw Angelo go into my office.

"What the hell is cooking between you two?" she whisper-shouts as we fold the tablecloths and put them back in their perspective boxes. "He bought the entire collection of Chateau Margot."

"Nothing's cooking." I shrug. "He came to say thank you. I guess he just likes expensive wine."

She spares me a look. "He wasn't in your office long enough to say *thank you* properly. Does he have a brother?" she muses.

"Three, actually." I almost slap myself for knowing that.

"Hey!" Melody cries out, as I feel a hand tug on my elbow from out of nowhere.

I spin and see the inconceivable sight of Dane, my ex, standing right behind me.

What the fuck is he doing here?

This isn't part of the plan. He can't be here...

I stare at him and try to wriggle free at the same time.

"What the hell?" I snatch my arm back and step away when the realization finally hits.

"Rayne, I just need a minute to talk," he pleads.

The mere sight of him makes my hackles rise. How I

could have stayed with him as long as I did now seems obtuse.

Melody quickly catches on and stands protectively beside me, her hands on her hips.

This is not what I want, not here, not anywhere. He's supposed to be in New York with no idea where I am! *Double fuck.*

"Dane," I whisper-shout angrily. "If you want to speak to me, you have to do it through the lawyers, you know that."

"You heard her." Melody steps in and yanks on my other arm, but people are starting to glance over at us, and I shake my head and decide to not make this bigger than it needs to be.

"It's okay, Mel, he's my ex," I say to her, keeping my eyes on him. I nod toward the entrance; I need to get him outside. "You've got one minute."

He looks like hell, like he just got over a bad flu or something.

"Rayne, you don't have to do anything. I can call security." Melody does not seem impressed by his sudden intrusion. In fact, she appears like she might tackle him.

"It'll only take a moment," I assure her, and I stalk towards the entrance as he quickly follows behind. I step out into the cold and wrap my arms around myself. I walk up the street a door or two away, so we're not directly outside the gallery.

I spin to face him. "What the hell are you doing here?"

He stares at me, towering over me. He has dark circles under his eyes that tell me he's still drinking heavily.

"I just want to talk, you won't take any of my calls," he says, low but insistent.

I scoff. "You know, you have some nerve showing up here like this, after the hell you've put me through this last year. I've got nothing to say to you that I haven't said already."

He reaches for me but I step back. "Please, Rayne, I miss you…"

He misses my money, more like.

"Don't touch me, please just leave. I'll remind you that you're in violation of your restraining order, I don't want this to get ugly, so just go."

He stares at me. "You weren't serious about that, were you?"

"Surely you can't be serious about that ridiculous extortion attempt at alimony, the one that's going to make me broke. You can't just show up like this!"

"I'm ready to reach a settlement, Rayney. I didn't want it to be this way."

I shudder at him calling me that nickname. "Great, you can talk to your lawyer, who will talk to my lawyer about it, and that's that." I'm about to really lose my shit with him.

He steps forward, and this time, he catches me on the upper arm, the force shocking me.

"Dane! Stop it, you're hurting me!"

His face is angry in a split second; this is how he is, volatile. "You're my wife, Rayne, and I want to come back." His hand grabs me tighter, squeezing hard. "You can't just cut me out of your life. We could've worked it out…"

"Ex-wife," I seethe through gritted teeth. "You're not coming back. You need to wake up, the time for talking was a year ago, but you didn't want to do that. I'm done, now let go of me!"

His eyes narrow. "That's fucking unfair and you know it!" he growls back.

My eyes dart over his shoulder at the very large man

coming up behind him, it's then that I see Angelo right beside him. Oh no.

"What the fuck is going on?" Angelo spits when he reaches us, glaring at Dane, then he sees his hand on my arm and he looks like he might explode.

"He was just leaving," I say, pulling away once his grip loosens.

"Get your fucking hands off her!" Angelo barks in his face, grabbing him by the shirt as he yelps in surprise. Angelo's bodyguard is dark and mean-looking and about twice the size. He stands there looking just as menacing as Angelo, who hasn't let go of Dane's shirt.

"Who the fuck are you?" Dane cries out, trying to get away.

The scene unfolds before me rapidly as I put a hand over my mouth, seeing but not believing it.

"Dane, please don't," I begin, knowing it's fruitless.

I don't know everything about Angelo, but I do know enough to know that picking a fight with him is not a good position to be in.

"What the fuck did you just say to me?" Angelo snarls, pushing Dane back, so he stumbles.

"Is this the new guy?" Dane sneers, his eyes darting to mine.

Angelo doesn't wait for an answer, his eyes flick to mine. "Are you all right?" he asks.

I nod, stepping further away from Dane and closer to Angelo and the burly guy who looks like he's about a few seconds away from slugging him one. It's strange to feel safer with them right now than with this person I used to love.

"Go over to the limo," Angelo tells me in no uncertain terms, nodding to the awaiting car in front of a startled-looking Melody, who has come out onto the street to look for me.

"Angelo, I –"

"Move!" he barks at me as I jump in fright.

"She's my fucking wife!" Dane spits. "You can't tell me what to do!"

"She said ex-wife, fuckface. Is this what you do for kicks? Is it, big shot? Intimidate women on the street? Assault them when they say no?"

"Who the hell are you?" Dane repeats.

I stare between the two of them, wishing the ground would swallow me whole, this definitely is not part of the plan.

"Your worst fucking nightmare," Angelo sneers.

"She always was a fucking little slut!" Dane calls after me as I retreat backwards.

I turn as I see Angelo punch him in the face, then uppercut him in the ribs. He then twists his arm around when he tries to swing. Dane drops halfway to his knees, crying out in pain as I hear a loud snap.

"I'll say this only once. Don't talk to her. Don't contact her. Don't even fucking look at her. You hear me, asshole?" Angelo growls menacingly.

I back further away towards the limo, watching what's unfolding right before us.

"You broke my fucking arm!" Dane wails as he collapses to the ground.

"That's not all I'll break if you come near her again," he snarls and turns on his heel toward me. He shakes his head at the big dude leering behind him, who looks disappointed he doesn't get to join in on the action.

Angelo comes towards me as I step back. His eyes are dark and cloudy, and frankly, he looks downright furious.

He puts his hand on the small of my back and pushes me gently forward into the open car door.

"Get in," he says close to my ear.

"Melody!" I call, but he turns to his burly bodyguard.

"Make sure she gets home," he says, nodding towards her.

I've no idea where we're going, but we leave Dane rolling around on the ground as the limo swiftly drives away, and I do not dare look back.

6

ANGELO

When I slide in beside her, she's pretty shaken up with eyes like a deer caught in headlights. She looks distraught and highly vulnerable.

"Oh my God, Angelo ...." she splutters, clutching her hand to her chest.

"Rayne, you need to calm down," I say in as level a tone as I can muster. Freaking the poor girl out more than she already is probably isn't the best idea, though I want to go back out there and put a bullet in his brain. I've killed for less.

".... What the hell just happened?"

"With what?" I reply nonchalantly as I sink back into the luxurious seat, unbuttoning my suit jacket like nothing happened. "Rayne?" I prompt when she doesn't answer.

"Back there ..." She thumbs back to the curb where I've left her ex lying on the ground in a crumpled mess, probably not a good look so close to the gallery doors, but my guys will move him on.

I don't answer the question. "Is that motherfucker really your ex-husband?" I retort. It seems hard to believe from where I'm sitting. I dust imaginary lint off my pants while I wait for her answer.

"Unfortunately, yes. I don't even know what he was doing here..."

"I don't like a man putting his hands on a woman like that." I straighten out my tie and glance at her. "Where to?"

She looks back at me with wide eyes like she's surprised by my admission. I'm not a total fuckface. My father and Mario may have raised a tyrant, but my mother taught me how to treat and respect a woman.

"I can only assume you don't want to just ride around in the limo all night," I drawl.

She looks a little frantic for a moment, "Wait, I left my jacket back at the gallery–"

"I'm sure it will still be there in the morning." I glance at her and raise an eyebrow. "I think it's best we get you home, don't you?"

"Let me just text Melody, she'll be worried."

"I've made sure she will get home safe," I say, crossing one leg over the other.

I wait anyway as she fishes her phone out of her bag and quickly sends a message. She sits back and stares ahead of her.

"So?" I ask her carefully.

"Oh... umm."

I smirk at her sudden internal struggle on whether to give me her address or not. Little does she know I already know where she lives.

"Back Beacon Hill." She reels off the address, which I bark through to Gus, then I put the partition up. Dom, my bodyguard, sits in the front with him and we roll away from the curb.

"Nice area," I comment as I reach forwards and open one of the decanters built into the limo.

"Right in the heartland." She nods. I'm sure she's just filling in space, and I have the urge to smile.

I pull out the Dom Perignon instead, pop the bottle, and pour a glass for her without asking if she wants a drink. I think she could do with something a little stronger, but she doesn't seem like the whisky-slinging type to me.

"This Plentitude Rose is exquisite," I say, leaning over to pass her the glass, then pour myself a whisky neat.

"Did you just have that chilling?" I can see she's calming down a little bit as she takes a sip.

"You never know when the occasion is going to strike," I tell her simply.

"Do you always ride around in a limo?"

I smirk. "Only for occasions like tonight. Patricia was beside herself, by the way."

"I think that's mainly because of you," she quips.

I may have dropped some serious cash tonight, especially on the wine, but I deem it both purposeful and necessary.

"You were amazing," I tell her.

"Maybe not after what just happened out in the front of the gallery."

"My guys will take care of it, don't worry."

"What does that mean?" she says, alarmed. "What are you going to do?"

"It means you have nothing to worry about. Now, tell me, what was a woman like you doing married to a guy like that?" I'm still dumbfounded.

She looks like she may not want to tell me, but then, "We met in college," she obliges me. "We got married right after of graduation. He was my first love, I didn't know any better. People change over the years, and he's not the man I thought he was."

I find her honesty quite refreshing, "What did that asshole want?"

She sighs and rests back while taking another sip of champagne. "I've no idea what he was doing or what he wanted, some lame-ass attempt to grovel for forgiveness, I suspect."

I watch her pretty little mouth move and realize she's nervous, she bites her lip and looks at me.

"You sure about that?"

"I haven't seen the idiot in over a year. I thought I was rid of him, aside from speaking through lawyers."

My mind flicks back, I heard her in the office only a few days ago declaring war on an extortion attempt at paying him more alimony. I suppose I am a stranger to her and the owner of her workplace, maybe she wants to keep it close to her chest about what's truly going on.

I would consider that fair under normal circumstances, but for some reason, this whole thing has me rattled and I'm going to dig up every fucking thing imaginable on this asshole.

I feel like killing something in her honor.

It disgusts me at the very thought of someone like her paying for his fucking upkeep, and I feel a protective surge for her rear its ugly head from absolutely nowhere.

She isn't yours. I tell myself. *Not yet.*

"I could mess that fucker up. You do know that, don't you?" I throw my shot down in one swig and circle the rim of my glass with my index finger. She watches the movement and flicks her eyes to my lips, seemingly nervous, and she ought to be. "If I thought you were in danger or anything untoward, I wouldn't be happy, little *Carina.*"

She thinks she has a clue, but she really doesn't know shit about what I can do.

"Why? You barely know me."

I raise my eyebrows at her boldness. "That doesn't matter."

"Angelo–" She laughs nervously. I think she's trying to gauge if I'm serious. "There's surely no need for that, he's an idiot, yes, but I don't want him harmed."

"Why not? He hurt you, didn't he?"

"Only a few times."

"Physically?" I seethe out. So the fucker was violent in their marriage, another reason I get to cut him.

"He didn't beat me up." She defends him quickly, "Nothing like that, but he shoved me a few times, like tonight grabbing me when things got messy. He never hit me, not with a fist."

Oh, how fucking wonderful, my anger just grows and grows. "So, he slapped you then?"

I'm not letting her wriggle away from this.

"Just once." She nods, and I want to kill every motherfucker who's ever done her wrong, not just this asshole. He's already dead.

"Fucking perfect, so he liked to be the big man, did he?" I can't wait to get my hands on him again. This time, I won't give any mercy.

"It really wasn't as bad as that," she maintains, but I'm already seeing red.

I can't imagine some fuckface laying their filthy paws on her in that way. A slap is the same as a punch, it's still fucking assault.

"I should have broken his fucking face," I mutter to myself.

"It doesn't matter, I'm sure that will be the end of it."

"Well, it better be." I continue, "I can tell you one thing, *Carina*, he's just messed with the wrong fucking guy. Trust me when I say some of the unsavory rumors I'm sure you may have heard about me could very well be true."

She gulps, my eyes flick to her throat. I want to bite her neck and mark her with my mouth all over her beautiful creamy skin. I want to suck on those tits and fuck her into oblivion; it takes all my strength to not pull her closer to me along the seat and feast away.

I take what I want, when I want. But I don't want to scare her. I'm a powerful man, but I've still got principles.

And anyway, this is foreplay to me. I fucking love the chase.

I shift uncomfortably at the thought of doing what I like to her, my dick kicking, alive and well, and pour myself another drink.

"And *you* don't hurt women?" she blurts out from nowhere. Clearly the champagne is going straight to her head, so I let the tone slide.

I laugh without humor. Of course, she thinks this about me, how little does she really know. "These hands have done a lot of things in their time, sweetheart, but beating up on a woman isn't one of them." I pull out the Dom Perignon again and top her glass up, I kind of like it's making her a little brazen.

Her eyes are on mine when I glance at her, she's trying to gauge if what I've said is true. She's heard all sorts about me, I know it. There's no way in hell she's ever going to be able to size me up, but it turns me on big time at the attempt.

"Thank you, though... for getting me out of that situation," she says softly after a moment of silence. "It was quite an unpleasant way to end such a great evening."

"It's no problem. I'm glad I was there, ex-husbands are my specialty." I flash her a grin in the dim light.

"What does Carina mean?" she asks me after a moment, almost a little shyly, like she's been thinking about it.

I grin, not expecting the question. "It's a term of

endearment, it means cute or nice. I've never said it to anyone, but I think it suits you."

"You think I'm cute?"

"Very much so, I also think you're very stunning Rayne, among other things."

I know I have an effect on her. I know that even in this darkness, she wants this as badly as I do, even if she won't admit it. I want her to feel her effect on me too, and with my raging libido around her, my dick is as hard as a rock every time we meet.

I have to stop thinking about sinking it into her sweetness, hard but slow. I could do things to her that would make her head spin and have her begging me for more. I'm not a selfish lover, I like to give pleasure as well as receive it. It turns me on the way she's a little conservative, a little reserved, and it only drives me further to want to know what lies beneath the surface.

I want her in my fucking bed.

Patience, hotshot.

I glance at her beautiful eyes; she has long, full lashes and perfectly arched eyebrows. Her makeup isn't heavy, and she's blessed with clear, creamy skin that gives off a glow about her. I can see freckles on her nose—a natural beauty.

She's way too pure for me, which makes me like it even more. Even if I can control the darkness within me, she could never understand the life I lead. She'd never believe the half of it. I don't profess to be a saint, but I don't look at myself as a complete devil either. I've killed people, yes, but it wasn't like they didn't deserve it. Trust me, they all did. Every last one of them.

Am I a vigilante with a heart of gold? *Nope.* But I take no prisoners in business or in my personal life. If people get too close to my affairs, my family, or something I care about, there will be consequences.

"Why do you want to have dinner with me?" she asks suddenly. I know we can't be far from her place now, only strangely, I don't want her to go.

"I find you interesting, Rayne, intelligent, and obviously attractive. Aren't those good enough reasons for a man to be smitten? When someone piques my interest, I owe it to myself to find out more about them, to see if we're compatible."

Her eyes go slightly wide at my confession.

Maybe I should just fuck her and be done with it.

I feel like she's just reeling me in, and I never let women reel me anywhere. Her naturalness is beguiling. Without sounding like a total asshole, I'm not used to being around women who have to think about being taken out to dinner.

I'm not short of female attention, although that's not always a good thing. I made a pact years ago not to get too involved with any one woman, especially after my situation, they make men messy, and in my line of work, it's not smart to have a permanent woman you care about who can be used against you.

I'm certainly not thinking about anything permanent, but it does get a bit old year after year. A little mystery and intrigue never hurt anyone, maybe that's why I like her so much.

A small smile plays on her lips. "You make a very valid point."

If she keeps up the coy flirting, I'll have to slide her onto my lap and have her ride my cock. When I'm done with her, she won't be able to walk for the rest of the week. Then I'll move onto her mouth.

"I always speak my mind; I find there's less bullshit that

way. No point beating around the bush." I tilt my head to the side, enjoying her reaction.

"That's not a bad trait to have, it could be worse when you think about it."

Oh, you have no idea, sweetheart.

"It could." I grin, because the fucker in me is enjoying this a little bit too much. If only she knew the inner workings of my devious mind. She will soon.

We reach her place far too soon, and I somehow manage to keep my hands to myself, though after socking her ex, I'm ready to fuck. I've never needed or wanted a woman so bad.

"I'll walk you out." I place my glass to the side as she hands me hers.

"That was delicious."

I smile, loving the slightly warmed pink hue on her cheeks.

Gus opens the passenger door, and she steps out first. I'm impressed with the tree-lined streets and the neighborhood she lives in.

"Nice digs," I say as she opens the iron gate to the elegant Brownstone. I follow her right up the path toward the door.

She fishes her keys out of her purse. "Thank you, it was kind of you to..." She trails off, motioning toward the limo.

I rub my chin. There's nothing kind about me.

She looks like she wants to ask me something. "What is it?" I give her a chin lift as her eyes lift to mine.

"You're not really going to do anything else to Dane, are you?"

I lean toward her slightly, digging my hands into my pockets, and shrug. *Ah, so that's his name.* "I don't like assholes, Rayne, so that leaves me wondering what I *should* do with him. He's a problem, and it doesn't seem like he's getting the hint."

Little does she know I'll have a field day with him when I feel like it. I don't like how he manhandled her, and I don't like his track record of battery or trying to extort her for money, either. I plan to enjoy taking him down very soon.

"He's all bark, honestly," she tries to tell me.

I motion to her arm; I can still see the red mark where he grabbed her. "Doesn't look like it."

She swallows hard, and I step toward her. "Don't you worry your pretty little head about any of that."

"I don't want him.... permanently hurt," she maintains. "It's genuinely not worth it."

She can't say the words, how sweet.

I choke back a laugh; she has no idea what is worth it for me and what isn't. "Lawyers can only do so much," I say. "And they don't protect you from restraining orders."

"How do you know about that?"

I hold her gaze. "I heard you yell it at him."

That she did, but I already know everything I need to know about that cocksucker.

She looks down again. Fuck she looks like an angel. "Well, it's been an eventful evening, and thank you for making me look good in front of my boss."

I smirk, "You did that all on your own, *Carina.*"

We step into the architrave, and I hold her elbow gently, turning her towards me.

"You're a beautiful woman, Rayne. I know you know that." Her scent wafts around me and it turns me on so bad.

"I, I don't know anything," she stammers, backing up a little, her eyes dropping to my lips.

I cage her in, resting my hands on either side of her head.

"I think you do." Everything about her teases my cock. It thumps between my legs, begging to be let out.

"Angelo-" she breathes, her lips parting. I want to lift her up and push my cock between her thighs so she can feel what she does to me, give her some friction I know she will enjoy even through clothes. The urge to get off overwhelms me, but it's her pleasure I want to own, not mine.

I tilt her chin up and kiss her gently, her lips soft as they meet mine and my heart beats in my chest so fucking hard, I'm sure she can hear it.

I grip her cheek and push her back into the door. She whimpers when I deepen the kiss, my tongue seeking entry, and this time I press my body against hers. My aching cock presses against her stomach. She makes the most delicious sound as I let her feel all of me.

I don't know how long we kiss for, but I pull back first when I've had my fill. When I do, she's panting and breathless, her cheeks flushed, eyes shocked.

All I can picture is her on her knees, naked, sucking my cock into that pretty little mouth.

"You're a fucking vision," I tell her in her ear, moving my mouth to her pulse point and gently biting down on her tender flesh. "This is how I want you; breathy, flushed, so fucking turned on that you can't take it anymore. You might think you can run from me, Rayne, but we both know you can't hide. I won't ask for more until you beg me to take you, and when you do, I'll be waiting." And beg, she will.

I reach into my coat pocket and retrieve the small velvet box. pressing it into her hand. "Wear these for me the next time we meet." I hope it's with nothing else on.

"Angelo…"

"Goodnight, *Carina,*" I say, pushing off the door. It takes all my might not to turn around and go back and ravage her, I know she wants to, but she's holding back. I know she'd probably let me slide my cock into her right here, right now, if I wanted to, up against her door.

Nonetheless, this is about me seducing her and getting her ready for me, and I wasn't kidding; I want her to beg me.

Make no mistake. She's *mine.*

7

RAYNE

I CLOSE THE DOOR BEHIND ME, AND AS SOON AS THE LOCK clicks, I turn and press my back against the wood and sink to the floor.

I press my fingers against my lips and touch the bruised skin from our illicit kiss, wondering why I feel that thrill running through me like this when I shouldn't. I should hate the fucking prick, he's just like the rest of the criminals and low lives in this Godforsaken place. But worse, he's the ringleader. Diablo.

I need to calm myself, but it seems that whenever I'm around him, the lines get blurred.

I stare at the box in my fist and dare myself to open it. He didn't….

I flip the lid of the box, and the Harry Winston studs I sold to him earlier tonight for thirty grand stare back at me.

He gave me the fucking Harry Winston earrings?

They're beautiful, small, and dainty, the diamond and sapphire stones gleam back at me. They are absolutely stunning.

I swallow hard.

I need to lock them in the safe until it's time to wear them for him. Obviously, I've never worn jewelry worth this amount in my entire life. Once this is all over, I can pawn them and get the cash, fuck knows, I'm going to need it if I have to run.

It occurs to me that there is no corner of the globe where I could hide from someone like Angelo, but it's best not to think about that right at this moment.

Heat rolls through my body in waves as I sit on the floor and close my eyes.

Breathe, Goddamn it.

I don't get like this.

I don't ever get like this.

I've been strong up until this point, but maybe deep inside my soul, there's a dark part of me that wants to be taken and owned by a man like Angelo Medici, even if for the night.

Maybe I need him to take control.

Losing myself with him would be like sweet surrender, something that I may never come back from, but it's not like I'm going to lose my head. I'm aware he's hypnotizing and intense, that's all part of the Medici charm, and I'm not here to be charmed by him, as much as my body's telling me otherwise.

He has a presence that not only spells danger but also calls to me on another level, one that almost sickens me because I know I should run. Except I can't.

I'm in this game, and the clock is ticking.

If only I could just breathe….

In my lust-filled haze, I try to remember that this is all just a fantasy. I can never have him that way, and I wouldn't want to. He has no soul; cold-blooded killers never do.

The things he does, how he thinks he can buy people, what he stands for. When it's all said and done, he's the enemy. He's the head of the mafia crime family for a reason.

Nobody can be trusted, least of all me.

And it's not why I'm here.

My purpose in all of this far outweighs my ridiculous, lust-filled thoughts. Thoughts that I shouldn't even be having since he's not only the enemy but also the solution to all my problems. A means to an end.

I don't know what's come over me. I'm obviously having some kind of out-of-body experience because this feeling washing over me isn't normal.

I should get as far away from Angelo Medici as possible, but I know I can't, even as the thought enters my head. I hate that I can't help Mia any other way, that these cowards stay hidden and out of sight, yet they watch my every move.

I hate going along with this charade when all I want to do is run.

I glance at the clock and wince. The call will come in soon to check on my progress. I take one long last breath as I think about Angelo's mouth assaulting mine. How I wanted him to push his way inside my apartment and take me with force. Make me forget every wretched thing going on in my life. Ravage me because that's all I deserve.

I imagine what he would be like in bed, how big he is, what he would do to me, and then I realize I wouldn't stop him from doing whatever he wanted. I not only wanted him to, but I also *needed* him.

When I'm with Angelo, as ironic as it sounds, I forget all about what I'm really doing here. It's like my memory lapses, and I forget I'm here to spy on him and, ultimately, betray him. I know deep down they want intel because they intend to bring him down, and I knowingly will help them.

Even though he's a criminal and not a good person, it still makes me sick to think I could do that to another person. It doesn't sit well with me, but I remind myself that his history shows he's just as bad, if not worse, not that it makes me feel any better.

Each time I see him, the lines become more blurred.

He has this ability that just for a second, I let myself get carried away and forget who he is. I forget who *I* am, and most of all, what the hell I'm supposed to be doing, not fantasizing about Angelo and how he'd leave me satisfied and sated and ruined for any other man. That isn't part of the deal.

I tingle from the tips of my fingers down to my toes. Lightning seems to strike through my body every time he's anywhere near me. His scent alone, his touch… it's all too much.

He's too much.

I know who and what he is, yet I ache for him to touch me. *What does that make me?*

He's part of the problem in this city, like many of the elite, and I would still willingly let him take me. Not only that, I'm sure I recall a strangled moan that left my lips as his tongue slid into my mouth. I felt his hard cock press into me and I wanted more, so much more.

I could have dragged him in here by the lapels of his jacket and let him have his way with me right here on the hallway floor. Rough and dirty, just how I bet he likes it. I must be fucking crazy, but the sorrow I feel for my sister is turning me into a lunatic, and for some reason, I'm directing it at all the wrong channels, including him.

The feeling of weakness and helplessness overwhelms

me and threatens the illusion I have created of this all turning out okay. It's far from okay, it's catastrophic.

Would I honestly turn a man like Angelo down if I weren't in this predicament? I want to say yes, I would, but I know the truth.

While heat and lust fill me, so does disgust. This criminal mastermind and the people he surrounds himself with belong in jail, still why do I find myself reaching into my panties to touch myself to soothe the ache.

This isn't normal.

You're right, Rayne, this isn't normal. So fucking pull it together!

I don't give myself the satisfaction of relieving my tension. I don't deserve it. I'm already sick to my stomach with all of this charade.

I go to the fridge and pour myself a glass of wine. I know I've had enough already with the champagne in the limo, but I have to take the edge off. Of course, it's not Dom fucking Perignon, but it'll do the job.

I kick my heels off and put the television on for background noise.

I sit at the island bench and take a considerable gulp, steeling myself for what's to come.

I try and will myself to not lose it. My survival ability has always been strong. The fact I've come this far and lived to tell the tale is a miracle in itself. I can be going through absolute chaos and can keep it all contained, like nothing is happening. It's a mask I know how to wear well, but it's all just an illusion.

It's not how I was raised, but how things turned out as I grew up. I learned to not show any emotion or let my guard down. Little did I know back then how valuable that would all be, especially getting involved with the mafia.

Then the call comes, making me jump as I gather my thoughts.

I take a few deep breaths before answering. "Hello," I say tentatively.

The voice always sounds robotic. "I see you had a successful evening."

I close my eyes. "Yes. Everything went as planned." *You asshole.* "I have him right where I want him, and he wants to see me again." I was told not to say any names over the phone. We both know whom we're talking about.

"That's very good news, but I need to know his next move. What do you have?"

I pinch the bridge of my nose. "It's been a little difficult getting any information without making it seem suspicious," I say, then quickly add, "But we're having dinner tomorrow night, he's picking me up. I'll be able to get something more then." At least, I fucking hope so.

"Things have changed since we last spoke."

Fear grips me as I steel myself. "What do you mean?"

I need to talk to Mia. I need to talk to her now!

The garbled voice laughs. "Come now. I saw how friendly you were with him. All over each other, it made me reconsider things. You wanted him to fuck you then and there, didn't you?"

What in the ever-living hell?

My anger soars. "Need I remind you that I'm being *bribed* into doing this, so it doesn't necessarily matter what I do or don't want him to do, I'm merely a puppet."

"Yes, and *my* puppet will do exactly as *I* say, no questions asked."

"I'm doing everything," I remind him. "I promise you. Please, let me speak to Mia."

The line goes quiet for a moment, and I think he's hung up.

Realistically I don't know it is a *he,* it could be freaking anybody.

"Need I remind you that you don't get to bark orders at me, just remember what I can do to you with just a snap of my fingers."

Panic runs through me. He's right. I have to play the game. While I want to demand that I won't do anything more until I speak to Mia, the deep-rooted fear that she will be harmed is more prevalent.

I grit my teeth. "I'm sorry, it's… it's been a long day."

He tuts. "I chose well. I can see that. Anyone would think you'd do this regardless of what you had to lose."

My toes curl at those words.

I swallow hard. "That isn't true," I lie. "Angelo Medici is a despicable monster, and nothing will give me greater pleasure than to see him brought to justice."

There's laughter. "That's poetic."

"It's the truth." I'm getting so good at lying that it almost scares me. "The man's a snake, he's everything you said he'd be, and he's taking the bait." The bait being me. I have to stall for time, and this is the only way.

"You know what you have to do next. I'm sure I don't need to explain how important it is that you do exactly what I say."

I close my eyes and pray. "I need to speak to her, that was the deal," I plead.

"Well, you can't. If you're a good girl and get me what I want, then perhaps I'll let you speak to her when you actually have something I can use."

I bang my fist down on the counter, I want to wail but I keep it in check. "That's going to take time."

He laughs again. It sounds so cold and menacing. "I'm sure you can use your powers of persuasion. After all, being a whore is really no different to being in business; we all get screwed one way or another."

I try to disregard the comment. "What do you want me to do?"

"Seduce him," the voice says simply.

Holy fucking crap.

"I…I don't know if…."

"Remember, Mia can be given back to you unharmed or in a body bag, the choice is yours."

Shit. Fuck.

"How is seducing him going to get me information?" I plead.

"He'll begin to open up, to trust you. Pillow talk is highly underrated."

"But I…"

"Your sister won't look so pretty if I cut her eyes out."

I swallow hard. "Please. I'm begging you," a sob leaves my throat as I try to contain it. Every inch of hate and fury boils up and threatens to spill over the sides. "She's all I've got."

"What a pity. Better make sure you hang onto those memories then, Miss Michaelson. It may be all you have left of her other than ashes and dust."

The line goes dead before I can say anything else.

I stare at the phone in disbelief.

Fucking bastard!

Anger boils up in me so fast and furious that I drop to my knees and scream. I don't care if the fucking neighbors hear me. They can all go to hell, because that's exactly where I'm going.

But the one thing I vow to myself is that I'll take as many of these bastards down with me—every last one of them.

If I'm going down, they're all going down too. That's my promise to Mia.

I can't sleep.

I wake several times during the night, not knowing where I am, and it takes a few moments to calm myself and slow my ragged breathing. I'm not used to this apartment yet or anywhere near feeling settled. After Mia was taken, everything else went on hold, including unpacking some of my boxes. Inanimate objects just feel obscure now. Including the earrings Angelo gave me. I placed the box on my nightstand and I haven't been able to look at them since.

Everything about them represents everything I *never* wanted to be. It's as if they're poison and I don't want to touch them, even though I know I have to for our dinner date.

Seduce him? I honestly don't know if I can when all is said and done, but I know for sure that Angelo will have no problem or qualm seducing me. Maybe it's for the best that I let him lead. He's going to anyway. It's who he is.

The nightmares won't go away, then I wake, and the real-life nightmare begins all over again, except this time it's in color.

Mia is the most important thing to me in the world. We lost our parents when I was a teenager in a horrific car accident. An oncoming car crossed the road, a drunk driver.

Mia was in the backseat but survived. I'd chosen to go to a friend's house that night rather than watch my little sister sing in a choir. She walked away with minor scratches and bruises. Our parents died on impact.

It's been Mia and me ever since. We went to our aunts to live, but that was neither a loving nor very warm household. We both learned to confide in one another and be each other's support. We left when I was old enough to be Mia's guardian and we fled. I worked two jobs to make ends meet and got my degree through a scholarship. I never wanted Mia to go without, she'd already lost so much and she was such a sweet, endearing child; she never asked for anything.

I can't even imagine what she's going through right now…

I flip the duvet off and pad to the kitchen for a glass of water, it's not like I can forget it, but I don't want to be reliving any of that right now.

My heart feels like it may beat out of my chest cavity, it's always the nights that are hardest. Sometimes I take a sleeping tablet, but I always wake up groggy, and it's worse than a hangover.

I only wanted to speak to her, just to hear her voice, and that rat bastard had to just dig the knife in a little further.

She could be dead for all I know, and I could be doing all of this for nothing.

I close my eyes and clutch the kitchen bench with both hands, I don't know what the fuck I'm going to do. I know thinking like this won't get me anywhere.

Nothing will make me lose power or momentum faster than thinking I've already failed.

But here, in this apartment that I get to call home, here I get to be me.

Here I don't have to pretend. I don't have to wish everybody dead and that they all go to hell.

Here I get to lower my mask for a while.

I open my eyes and down two Tylenol, then saunter

back to bed. I wander over to the enormous, ornate windows, looking out onto the sparkling street below, the city stretched beyond as far as the eye can see.

It's pretty this time of night. There's not much traffic and barely anyone in sight on the pavement below.

I wonder what Angelo's doing at this very moment.

He has quite a few properties around the city, he could be at any one of them.

A townhouse he holds for parties and super social events.

A compound, where I suspect he does most of his plotting and dirty work, and a place out in the country that is so private that I don't even know where it is.

He rarely ever goes there, so they say.

The only thing that interests me next is getting into his apartment.

It's time to let Angelo get me alone, when he does that, his guard may slip a little. Each second that ticks by is another I won't get back. And I won't let my sister down, I won't let them have her.

I need to take back control.

I know that if I get caught or if Angelo even gets wind that I'm trying to extract information, it'll be met with a swift hand.

I can't let that happen.

I need to put my game face on now more than ever.

And that means I have to let Angelo seduce me.

My pulse quickens, and I no longer fear the dread now I just fear failure.

I need to make it a good show, and make him believe every second of it. He likes the chase…. and in this game of cat and mouse, I will surrender.

If Angelo Medici wants me, he's going to have to fucking work for it.

8

ANGELO

The dalliance on the steps of her apartment has me reeling and hard as a rock.

When I relax back in the limo, I can still taste her sweetness on my lips, wondering all the while why I didn't tell her to let me inside so I could peel her clothes off and bury myself inside her for the rest of the evening.

The fact that she has this whole almost innocent act going on is what gets me the most, it excites me like I'm a teenager again, and I have no self-control. Around her, I don't want to have any.

I momentarily close my eyes and enjoy my own fantasy, which lasts for about ten luscious seconds before my phone rings loudly inside my pocket. When I pull it out and glance at the screen, I see it's Marco.

I sigh, enjoying what was, because he wouldn't be ringing me this time of night for nothing. "Brother." I pinch the bridge of my nose and contemplate throwing another whisky back.

"Angelo, where the fuck are you?"

"Nice to talk to you too, bro."

"Very funny. I sent you a text fucking hours ago."

"I was at the Gallery Fundraiser." I sigh, realizing now I have a few missed messages from him I didn't bother replying to. "Would have been nice for some of the Medicis to have also been there to show some solidarity."

"Been up to my elbows in it, actually."

"Pussy?" I scoff. That's nothing new.

"Yeah, I wish. I've been back and forth with the council permits all day. Fucking Fynn is nowhere to be seen, and fuck knows where Dante's whereabouts are. Feels like I'm running this whole show here by myself."

Big fucking baby.

Both the twins are equally haphazard but in their own separate ways.

Fynn is the oldest of my two younger twin brothers, he's slightly unpredictable and the typical playboy. His twin Dante is much calmer and level-headed, but both are equally a pain in the ass.

Marco, being next in charge when I'm not around, worries a lot. I keep telling him it'll turn him gray, but it doesn't seem to do any good.

We're waiting on council approval and a work permit for some new land we've purchased, and we're also building a bunch of boutique apartments. That's project one and then there's the casino which has been years in the making, since Roberto's funeral. And that's almost complete, thank fuck.

Marco is the brains of the property development world, so he has full reign over all of it and my unwavering support. He loves it; he's chomping at the bit for the hotel and casino to open. He's impatient, though.

I've told him repeatedly that councils won't be hurried up just because he wants them to be, bribery included. I have already slipped a sizable 'donation' to the mayor's upcoming campaign and an under-the-table handshake for the homeless city appeal, a portion will come from the charity event tonight.

So, I'm not without morals.

"What's so urgent at midnight?" I glance at my silver Rolex, I feel wired.

"We got shit to clean up downtown."

I hear the strain in his voice, which I didn't detect earlier, and sit up a little straighter.

"At the warehouse?"

"Yes, at the warehouse, we have a screamer; the Rombaldi shipment has gone completely haywire, we have one of their own under guard."

"Has he talked?"

"Nope."

"Good, wait till I get there." I hang up.

There's no rest for the wicked, but the distraction might be good. All I can think about is telling Gus to turn around so I can go pound Rayne's door down and fuck her senseless. Instead, I tell him to take me to the compound, what I lovingly call *the fortress*. I need to pick up my truck and drive to the warehouse alone.

The warehouse is where we take prisoners, who are usually held at the Fortress, so we can question them and get any information we need. It's also less messy, being concrete walls with no furniture to spill blood on.

Marco's outside smoking when I arrive.

He's a whisker shorter than me, meticulous with his appearance, there's not even one jet black hair out of place.

Between Dante and him, I can't tell you which one is more hung up on appearances. Pity that didn't extend to Fynn, who flies by the seat of his pants with his looks but still reigns in all the women with ease. He has a boyish charm that none of us ever got.

"I thought the auction ended hours ago?" Is the first thing that comes out of his mouth when I walk over to him. He eyes me dubiously. "You get some tail, bro?"

I narrow my eyes at him. "Why the fuck do you care?"

He shrugs. "I don't know, you seem a little more …. relaxed than usual."

I nod towards the door and ignore his statement. "Who've we got in there?"

"Oh, you're gonna love this one, an employee of Rombaldi. Rocco snagged him, shooting his mouth off about the human cargo shipment that's docking at the end of the week, he couldn't keep his gums from flapping."

"Human cargo?"

"So he says."

"Where's Rocco?"

"Inside with him now, he and Enzo picked him up."

Enzo runs a tight ship with Fortress security. His main man Rocco is the brawn in most, if not all of our situations, along with Darko, my head soldier and a few other ex-military guys we call our army.

I try not to get too excited at this prospect, but I live for this shit, this is what I do.

I crack my neck side to side as I enter through the side door. It's a large, industrial warehouse that looks like any other with no windows and a security system so advanced that it took Enzo six months to perfect.

This is where we conduct the illegal side of the business. We have a safe house basement right underneath as well, just in case. It's bomb and fireproof and could probably withstand nuclear fallout.

There's not much to it outside or in; an office off to the side, a bathroom, and one large open area that we use for interrogation. A table sits in the middle, and extra chairs are stacked up in one corner, depending on who or how many people we're torturing, or as I like to call it, gathering information.

There's two-way glass from a storage area where we get changed before the meets and greets begin. Some of these tough motherfuckers aren't so tough when they're tied up.

The man through the glass has been running an illegal underage prostitution ring.

My stomach fucking lurches at the thought, not just because I have a little sister, Valentina, who's early in her early twenties. Still, she's quite innocent, and a niece from my mother's side, Bria, who's twelve, and if anything ever happened to them in this kind of regard, I would find and cut the perpetrators so severely there would be nowhere on this planet they could hide.

Some of the girls I hear about are barely older than Bria. While we may have dealings in other illegal extra-circular activities, things like human smuggling, child abduction, and underage prostitution aren't any of them. That's where I draw the line.

We've cleaned up Boston as a whole, and gotten the riffraff out of our neighborhood. I can't say it's been easy or a quick process. These lowlife scumbags are like weeds; you rip one out, then another pops up.

Some of the low-lives we've dealt with have been as widespread as petty thieves and rapists to corrupt politicians and media moguls. Some of the sickest human beings pose as everyday businessmen in suits or men with a badge.

The dark side of humanity runs deep, and sometimes it even shocks me at the names that are involved. They make me fucking sick, and they keep the good people down, something I'm trying to rectify personally.

I'm far from a saint, but Fortress security doesn't just provide twenty-four-hour surveillance, the best security cameras that money can buy, round-the-clock armored guards, fencing, security alarms - you name it - we also offer paid security services. The illegal kind.

The kind that makes bad people disappear. People far worse than us, and make no mistake, there are worse than us.

Rombaldi is a known Brazilian arms dealer, and the word on the street is that he's been wheeling and dealing in human trafficking for some time. We've been wanting to get him for years and he's slowly grown more and more powerful, that's never good for business, and biding our time may well have just paid off.

Rumor has it he's working with some other high-profile accomplices we haven't yet been able to pinpoint, but we're closing in. His days are numbered.

This is my fucking town, and I say what goes.

Boston had the lowest crime rate in history last year. The Police are well and truly in our pockets because we'll hand this sting over straight to them, and the Commissioner will get a standing ovation, probably a medal of honor, and I'll get his assured loyalty. It works both ways.

That's the thing about corrupt cops, they'll sell out to the highest bidder, but at least the crooked cops I associate with do want the greater good: that and a fat paycheck. Nobody wants pedos and traffickers living in their city. This way, everybody wins.

Enzo comes out of the office. He's more tanned than what the current Boston climate can account for, his sandy locks and brown eyes have most women on their knees at first glance. Fucking pretty boy. He grins at me.

"You good?" I nod as we shoulder bump.

"Yeah, Rocco and I picked up the douche. He was

willing to squeal for a price, pity he didn't know who we were at the time."

Now we have him strung up and tied to a chair. Perfect.

"Christ, how good an informant can he actually be?" I mutter.

Enzo shrugs, clearly bored with the situation at hand, I guess they've been here a while and want to get the execution over with.

"How long's Rocco been at it?" I nod over to the mirrors where he looms over our captive.

Rocco does all the dirty work. He knows how to keep hurting a man without making him pass out. He's good with his fists, never uses weapons, he finds he doesn't need to. I can't say I share the same sentiment.

The guy sits naked and bleeding, his nose broken and dripping with blood.

"Almost three hours."

"Fuck, and he hasn't squealed yet?"

"Keeps slipping in and out of consciousness. He's given up other pimps, denies he's pimped underage girls, yadda-yadda."

"Is that so?"

He eyes me again. "What's your next move?"

I give him a look. "Well, I'm not fucking around with this all night, I need to sleep. If only Rocco enjoyed knife play." I grin.

"Yeah, is that why you seem happy?"

"Not you too," I mutter as I undo my cufflinks and roll up my sleeves.

I should change, this is a nice suit after all and I have clothes here I can change into. The thing is, I don't plan on being here that long.

He slaps me on the back. "Go get 'em, tiger."

I shake my head. "You've been using that expression since we were ten years old, it's time to get a new line."

Fucking Enzo. He would grin at the devil before he struck him down.

I edge toward the door and flip Enzo the bird over my shoulder.

Rocco glances up from his squatting position in the front of the man oozing blood from his nose with sweat all over him. Fucker pissed himself at some stage.

I light up a smoke, something I indulge in from time to time. "Roc."

He stands and raises his eyebrows. "Boss."

"You get what we need?"

"Almost."

I snort a laugh. "You just like playing with him, don't you?"

He's about to answer when the dude, I don't even care to know his name, begins to rouse. He's gagged, of course, no need for them to speak until necessary.

"Ahh," Rocco says, giving him a few slaps to his face to help him come round. "Here he is."

The guy's eyes widen with alarm when he sees me. He knows who I am, at least.

I crouch down, staying far enough away, so I don't have to touch his slimy ass. Filth like this, you can never entirely scrub from your skin. My anger and blood boil at what he's been doing.

I think of the sweet young women in my family, and I know tonight he will die.

"My friend here tells me you've been doing some bad shit," I say. "What's worse is you did it on my turf."

He tries to struggle, I don't know why, especially since Rocco was in the military when he was younger so he knows how to tie a knot.

"So, this is a dilemma. My buddy says you've given me another name, a pimp like you, except that's not who we want. We want a fucking *real* name. So, I'll make this really simple. Other than Rombaldi, who's recruiting these girls? Where else are they being sold to? Tell me now, and I might let you keep your dick."

I reach behind me and pull out my leather gloves and peel them on. Then I flick the small but lethal blade on the side table near me out from its cover. It looks anything but ruthless.

I nod to Rocco, and he pulls the gag down to let him speak.

Instead, he spits, it lands a little damn too close to my three-thousand-dollar pair of shoes.

"Gotta be someone worth protecting," I say, my eyes meeting his. "Well, I can't say I didn't warn you. Do you know there are ways to make a man bleed out for days before he truly dies?" I should know I learned from the best, my own father.

"I told you..." he gasps, still trying to struggle free. "I'm independent. I don't know where they're being snatched from or where they go. The girls I had working for me were all of legal age."

I laugh coldly. "Right. Aren't you just pimp of the year?"

I look up to Rocco. "Board."

He flashes me a curt smile and walks toward the table of devices I sometimes like to use.

"I was hoping it wouldn't come to this," I say sagely. "But I've entertained a hot piece of ass tonight and frankly I'm beat. Hence, why I need to speed this up a bit and get out of here."

Rocco brings the small wooden table over with the strap and proceeds to release fuckface's hands, keeping one tied behind him to the chair.

"I gave you a name…" he cries as Rocco spreads his hand flat and straps his wrist down.

"The name of another rival pimp ain't shit," I reply. "And, like I said, I've got more important shit to do tonight, so…" I stand. "It's a pity, they are such pretty fingers…"

Before he can blink, I bring the knife down on his pinkie finger and slice it off, well, part of it.

There's no fun just leaving him a stump.

He howls and spits and squirms as blood flies everywhere. Lucky for me, I step to the side so I don't get coated by it.

"You pricks think you're so fucking smart, don't you?" I sneer as I walk behind him. "I despise cunts like you, it makes me fucking sick. I saw the pictures of what you sick bastards make those girls do. Let me tell you, fuckface, I'll take every single fucking finger off your hand, piece by piece, bit by bit, until I get what I want. Got me? I can draw this out, or you can piss yourself all night until I've got a collection of your fingers. The choice is yours."

He trembles and stutters and shakes as I move back around, and, fuck it, I slice the rest of his finger off below the knuckle as he howls in agony.

I'm not in a good mood anymore. I'm also extremely frustrated.

"Sen…Senator…fuck….Senator Mendes…" he screams as I dodge his spit.

Rocco and I look at one another. Well, I'll be fucking damned.

"You sure about that?" Squeaky clean-cut Mendes, eh, there's a turnout for the books. Nothing shocks me anymore, however. "Didn't he recently run a campaign to fight for women's rights in the workplace?" I ask, scratching the back of my head at the irony.

Rocco shrugs. "I don't fucking know, man, but this ain't good."

I turn back to fuckface. "You messing with me? Keep in mind you have seven fingers left, two thumbs, and then we move on to toes."

"I'm not..fucking...lying!" he cries, then curses some more as he snivels away like a little girl.

A knot forms in my stomach. This bastard deserves to die, and die he will, but I need to make sure he's not just stitching up the first name he can think of to try and dig himself out of a hole. Not that it'll matter, the hole's too deep, and he's already buried. Although it's not like I can dig him up and question him again should this information not be accurate.

I've done this enough times to know that pricks like this are slippery, though I do think he's telling the truth. That cocksucker Mendes has always been a little too clean-cut for my liking. It's always the quiet ones. The ones who kiss newborn babies before election day and visit old people's homes. He won't be doing that for too much longer.

"You better not be, because I know all about you, you low-life piece of shit. Birdie told me you like them young yourself, that shit doesn't fly on my streets." I twirl my blade around. I want him to suffer, but I don't want to touch his stinking dick, lucky for him.

"Mendes has been ordering girls for years... he likes them young...nothing above fifteen...but I was just the middleman...I didn't have anything to do with...giving him the girls. I was just the messenger."

It sickens me how he's trying to worm his way out of this. "Just the messenger? You pimped the girls out to him, sold them... innocent, underage girls who were easy pick-ings because they were poor or from broken homes or on the streets....you think that makes you some kind of fucking hero?"

The rage boils again, and I know I don't want to hear any more.

"It makes you scum, you motherfucker. And I clean up the scum in this town."

"I never…"

"Shut the fuck up!" I yell. I can't take anymore, and his smell is starting to seep into my pores. I turn to Rocco. "Gonna bag him up for me?"

"With pleasure." He grins.

"Wait...what? *No!* You can't do this...you can't...I gave you the na…" He doesn't even get to finish. I'm done with this; we've wasted enough time.

I slice the blade up his throat and straight into the jugular, his blood splays all over the place as he gags and chokes on his own liquid. I stand back and watch as Rocco waves his fingers in a farewell gesture. It takes less than thirty seconds for him to stop flailing around, bleeding out, and only then does he slump back in the chair, his head falling back.

"Took your time about it," Rocco complains.

I turn to him. "Fuck you. Now clean this shit up, and text me when it's done. Call Santino to help if you need to." He's another one of my cousins who's good at disposing of bodies.

"Got it, boss."

I feel better. One less scumbag on the streets.

Next will be the raid on his turf, more accolades for the police when they bust the underage prostitution ring. It's swings and roundabouts. They'll owe me, and when I need to call on them, they won't refuse. This is how my world works.

And it is *my* world. I direct everyone in it.

If there are any chinks in the armor around me, I fix them.

This is why I'm the fucking king.

I point to the two-way mirror, knowing Enzo is still watching the show. "Find out everything you can on Senator Mendes. I want a full report."

I should have changed my fucking suit.

9

RAYNE

I GET A MESSAGE FROM ANGELO THE NEXT DAY ABOUT OUR dinner date. He's going to pick me up at eight from my apartment. I don't know where we're going, and since he doesn't tell me, I don't ask. I'm sure it will be somewhere swish, but I hope it's somewhere private.

Angelo is a man who gets photographed pretty much wherever he goes.

He has it all.

Flash cars. Multiple houses. Women on his arm and at his beck and call.

There is nothing a man like him can't get. Which is why I plan to offer him a little resistance, playing a little coy. It's clear he enjoys the thrill of the chase, so why not play a little hard to get.

My instructions are to seduce him, but that isn't how Angelo works, oh no. He's all alpha. *He's* the one who will be doing the seducing, he is the one in complete control, let's make no mistake. We both know it. He can get anything he wants.

I may be doing this because I have no choice, and I have

to save my sister, but one thing Angelo is not going to do is buy me. He can give me flashy earrings equivalent to three months of my paycheck, but that's all it is. A commodity. And he's a means to an end.

I hold it together as best I can, thankful that I have my wits about me, but that doesn't mean my mind isn't reeling with the danger and complexity of what I'm about to do.

I knew going into this it was risky. But that isn't solely it.

It's what he does to me that shouldn't have me feeling like this.

I should detest this man, he's the epitome of everything I hate.

A powerful man who takes what he wants, when he wants, and picks and chooses who lives or dies. A man who has soldiers working for him, not ordinary men, one who owns the police and politicians. A man who lives in a literal fortress with security everywhere he goes. A man who can buy anything he wants.

And yet here I am.

I question his conscience, but then again, I have no right to, for what about my own? I can't deny that my soul is tainted. Even if sleeping with him makes me feel like one of his whores, another part of me craves him to do it. To take control. To make me forget.

The lines are not just blurred, they're impenetrable, and I can't let that happen. I'm here to get intel and I need to get something on him at dinner. If I don't have something to give Mia's captors on him soon, I know things will go from bad to worse.

I also can't stop thinking about Dane's little stunt at the gallery and how embarrassing that was. I just hope Angelo hasn't caused me more problems. I heard the snap; I know he broke his arm and probably cracked some ribs. The last thing I need is another lawsuit on my hands.

As if I would ever go back to a loveless marriage with a drunk. Dane will never change, and there's no reason to think otherwise. What I do want is my divorce to finally be settled and now I'm rattled he'll retaliate after being beaten up by Angelo. He could press charges against him. If he's smart, he'll leave well alone; then again, I could press charges for him grabbing me first and prove self-defense since there would be footage on the surveillance cameras as well as Melody as my eye-witness.

The next morning, I'm waiting in line at the local Starbucks while contemplating my divorce, what to do about Dane, and Angelo's panty-melting kiss, when someone taps me on the shoulder.

I turn around and a stunning dark-haired woman with piercing green eyes and beautiful, flawless skin looks back at me.

"Can I help you?" I say, wondering who she is.

"I'm so sorry," she replies. "Are you by any chance the woman that was at the gallery auction last night?"

I nod. "Yes, I work there."

She smiles kindly. "I thought I recognized you. Hi, I'm Allegra, I'm a close friend of Angelo's."

She holds out her hand, and I, in turn, shake her hand.

"Nice to meet you." I smile back.

"I didn't get a chance to introduce myself. It seems Angelo was rather smitten keeping you all to himself." She giggles a little as the surprise shows on my face.

I wonder how many other people noticed?

"Oh, well, no, it's nothing like that…"

She nods knowingly and then taps her nose. "It'll be our little secret, don't worry."

Shit.

"Really, there's nothing to tell." Except I'm having dinner with him and I've got to seduce him, or my sister – who's been kidnapped– will be harmed. "But he does seem like an amazing man. He's accomplished a lot for someone so young in his field."

His field being mayhem, corruption, crime, and murder.

She studies me for a moment, but her smile stays in place. I can't tell if she's friend or foe, yet she seems friendly enough, even if there is a slight edge to her nosiness. Suddenly, she laughs. "A woman not affected by Angelo? That's a first."

"I work for him," I reply awkwardly. "So, it's strictly professional." *I am so going to hell for lying.*

Her lips twitch as she leans toward me and whispers, "Well, if you get to spend some time in the sack with him, it really is worth crossing those boundaries because that man can move, and he's very gifted with his mouth if you get my drift, between us girls that is."

Ah. *So, she's slept with Angelo.* My stomach knots ever so slightly.

"Thanks for the tip."

"Not that I'd know, of course." She laughs and pats her chest as I force a smile. "Typical of Angelo to seek out the most beautiful woman in the room."

"I'm sure that he has a long line of admirers, though I just sell art." I hope that sounds believable.

She gives me a cheeky smirk and nods, and I know she thinks we're fucking; it's written all over her. At least she's not a jealous ex.

Thankfully, the line moves up and I place my order at the counter and move out of the line.

She places hers, too, and I pretend to look at something on my phone.

"It was nice meeting you," she says, passing me by towards a table. "I'm sure I'll see you again sometime."

"Likewise," I reply, nevertheless I've no intention of doing any such thing.

I wonder if Angelo is friends with all the women he's slept with. If so, he's probably besties with most of Boston's elite.

I shake it off. I don't give a shit about what he did before me, it's what he's going to do now that matters. *Stay focused!*

I clean my apartment when I get back and get ready for my date, soaking in the jet tub before wearing a tight camel-colored body con dress and nude patent heels. It is slightly revealing but hopefully doesn't scream *come and take me.*

Leaving my hair down, I curl the ends and take extra special time with my makeup. I want to look nothing like myself. I want to look like someone completely unrecognizable, because that's how I feel at the moment; like a zombie who's going through the motions. Maybe it's better this way, maybe the sins of my mistakes will not be so blemished if I hide who I really am. And I have to. Angelo doesn't get the real me. Nobody does.

The vulnerable, loving, kind-natured girl I used to be, she's gone. He gets the person I have become. And all the bitterness and anger I feel will bottle up inside me until this is done.

When I'm satisfied with my appearance, it's almost time. I head downstairs and see a shiny BMW waiting at the front of my apartment.

The same driver from the other night steps toward me and opens the door.

"Good evening, Miss Michaelson."

"Hello," I reply, feeling awkward. "Sorry, I didn't get

your name last time, it feels a little impersonal not to know what to call you."

He gives me a nod but stays stoic. "It's Gus."

See, that wasn't so hard, was it? "You can call me Rayne," I tell him.

"Very well."

I expect to see Angelo there when I climb in, but the seat is vacant.

I frown as the door closes, and when Gus climbs in the driver's seat, I say, "Um, Gus, where's Angelo?"

He glances at me in the rearview mirror. "There's been a change of plans," he says. "My instructions are to drop you off at Casa De Roma for the evening."

Casa De what?

"Um, where is that, please?"

He pulls out into the evening traffic. "His townhouse, miss."

I swallow hard but smile in thanks as I sit back in the chair and stare out the window.

Like a fucking call girl, I've primmed myself up like meat in a raffle. And instead of going out to a restaurant, he's going to seduce me at his house, where nobody can see. I guess this way it is easier with nosy prying eyes like that girl Allegra who seemed to notice an awful lot.

I chew on my lip and ponder what I'm going to do. A million things run through my mind.

What if we have a one-night stand, and that's it? He seems like a one-time kinda guy.

And that won't do because I need to get close to him. If I'm no good to him, it means the job is over.

I close my eyes.

Steel yourself, Rayne. You can do this. He's just a man, flesh and blood.

Yes, a very dangerous man, and now I'm caught in his lair with nowhere left to run.

I've been acting the part for so long now, it almost feels like it's natural to ignore my feelings or anything negative that screams at me to get the hell out of the car, and that's the most dangerous thing of all.

I stare up at the sand-colored bricks and try not to gape.

I've seen his house on a Google search, but the photos don't do this place justice.

It's magnificent.

It's three stories, with black wrought iron detailing around a high wall. The brick has ivy growing up and around the building, making it look ethereal, like it doesn't belong in the city.

I never thought he'd live in a place so pretty and almost feminine-looking.

A set of huge black front doors with gold handles stand proudly. The facade is so elegant and sophisticated that I'm almost sure I'm underdressed to set foot inside.

Gus opens my door for me, and I thank him as I get out.

When I reach the front door, I ring the bell. A few moments later, a woman answers the door.

She's dressed in a neat black dress with small heels and an apron.

"Miss Michaelson," she says before I even get a chance to answer. "Please come this way."

I follow her inside and try not to roll my eyes. Of course, this is a great display of his wealth thrown in my face. Like a lion stalking its prey, Mr. Medici just has to show off all of his grandeur.

Diamonds. Champagne. Fancy cars. Drivers. Multiple houses. Staff at his beck and call.

I don't quite know how people live like this.

I glance up and I'm met with a huge chandelier dangling from the ceiling, at least three stories up. It glitters and sparkles like diamonds in the sky.

There's a grand staircase with dark mahogany wood to my right, and the entire foyer is donned with soft, white speckled marble floors.

It probably cost more money than I'll see in this lifetime.

I follow behind as the woman leads me through the foyer, passing by a massive wine cellar with clear doors and a huge study with a large desk and a whole wall full of books. I can see a laptop and a pair of glasses laid on top of some papers. *His workspace. Excellent.*

We pass by too fast to see any more.

She leads me through a set of double doors and into a vast, commercial-looking kitchen with shiny metal appliances and a huge marble wrap-around countertop.

I open my mouth and then close it again as I see Angelo, Mafia King himself, standing at the stove. To say I'm shocked is an understatement. There's an open bottle of red wine and a half-empty glass to his left, and some kind of metal contraption – that looks suspiciously like a pasta maker – to the right.

Angelo is cooking dinner? Well, I'll be damned.

I turn to the woman staring at me, I realize she's asking me something and I didn't even hear a word of it.

I see her lips twitch, but she doesn't smile. "Your coat, miss," she repeats, motioning to my wool parka.

I smile, unloop my belt and slide it off my shoulders. She takes it and leaves without another word.

I can feel Angelo staring at me. I turn to look at him

and his eyes follow down my body and slowly trail back up again. I hope he likes what he sees, because I'm not getting any better than this.

"Good evening, Rayne," he says, his voice dark and sultry. "You look beautiful."

I smile at him. "Good evening, Angelo, this is a surprise. You have a lovely home." I glance around the vast space appreciatively.

His eyes gleam mischievously, and I can't help but like the fact he hasn't shaved. I also think about how bristly that would feel between my….

"The jewelry looks fetching on you." He glances from my earrings down to my neck. I wore them, of course – just like he told me – and judging by the way he's looking at me, I think I've hit the spot.

"Thank you, Angelo, you really didn't have to –"

He cuts me off. "I wanted to, they were clearly made for you. Would you like a glass of wine?"

I detest red. "I'd love one, thank you."

He pours a glass and I admire him for a moment.

He's wearing charcoal pants and a white shirt, loose at the nape and the sleeves rolled up. He's the ultimate bad boy.

A slight shiver goes through me at being alone with him, in his house.

He hands me the glass.

"You never told me you're a chef," I muse, taking a sip, trying not to spit it back out.

He watches me, a smirk playing on his lips. "There's probably a lot of things about me that may surprise you," he says. Our eyes lock, and he tilts his head to the side. "Being a chef probably isn't one of them."

I nod to the contraption on the bench. "You're making pasta from scratch?"

"My Nona taught me when I was a boy. She was the best cook in the family. Everything was in her head, she never had a recipe book, so you had to watch very closely."

It's the first time he's mentioned anyone in his family besides his brothers.

"What are you making us?" I ask. "It smells delicious."

"Traditional carbonara, I didn't hold back on the gravy, it's the best part."

I watch as he pads barefoot to the stove and dips a large wooden spoon into the pot and has a taste. Then he brings the spoon over to me. "Taste test?"

He smirks as I part my lips, and he holds the spoon to my mouth, my eyes flick to his as I take a small mouthful. "Delicious," I say, as my tongue dips out to lick my lips, and before I can blink, he leans over and kisses me, his mouth open as I gasp in surprise, it's quick and full of promise. My core pulses with a need I didn't know existed.

Why does this dangerous man bring out such a reaction each and every time?

"It certainly is," he muses, pulling back as he moves back to the stove and turns the pan down to a simmer. His bristly facial hair is so damn sexy…

"It shouldn't be too long," he says, gesturing for me to take a seat. I comply and slide onto the stool in front of me.

"Do you usually cook for all your dates?" I ask, a smile playing on my lips.

He takes a sip of his wine. "Never."

"That's a shame, it's a beautiful kitchen."

"I didn't feel like going out. I didn't feel like sharing you with the world."

I'm about to take another sip of wine but hold the glass just short of my lips. "Yes, it seems that perhaps we're not being as discreet as we could be."

He frowns. "How so?"

I wasn't going to bring it up, but a devilish part of me wants to see his reaction. "I ran into a friend of yours, Allegra, at the coffee shop this morning." I make sure to keep my tone light and playful.

"Allegra?" He frowns a whole lot more.

"Yes, she was giving me some tips on bagging you."

His eyebrows rise in surprise. "She, what?"

I laugh into my wine as I take a sip. "It's all right, really, I know you're a man about town and have slept with probably hundreds of women; I think she was just trying to give me the skinny."

He looks very annoyed. "The last time I slept with her was in college," he states firmly.

I look up at him. "It's fine, you don't have to –"

"It was brief and before my cousin Roberto. She married him many years later."

I gulp my wine down, wishing I'd never brought it up, as his eyes turn thunderous.

"She was just being funny, I don't think she meant any harm by it," I go on.

"Let's make one thing very clear," he states, accentuating every word. "It's ancient history. She's a family friend, nothing more, and she never will be. Allegra would do well to keep her fucking nose out of other people's business."

Oh well, I guess it's her problem now that she's on the wrong side of Angelo.

His temper flares as I try not to feel a little satisfaction that she'll be in trouble for her comments.

I lean across and put my hand over his. "I'm sorry, I shouldn't have said anything, it was just girl talk."

His eyes soften. "I'll deal with her later. It's time to eat." His words have a double meaning as he turns back to the stove and turns the pot and the pan off simultaneously.

Like a well-choreographed orchestra.

No matter what, Angelo Medici in gray slacks, barefoot, and cooking for me is about as delicious as you can get. His ass is tight and delectable and I can't tear my eyes away from him. It's so fucking hot.

"A little bit hungry or a lot?" he asks over his shoulder.

"A lot," I call back, then add, "I'm not one of those girls who doesn't like to eat."

"That's my girl," I'm sure I hear him mutter.

I can't help the smile that spreads across my face.

ANGELO

A SMILE TUGS AT MY LIPS AS I STARE AT THE WOMAN before me.

Those earrings and the necklace she wore for me turn me the fuck on. It's hard to tell if she's affected by me, she doesn't show the usual signs, which could be one of the reasons I seem to be falling hard for her.

Something's up with me lately. I don't bring women around here like this, to my home, to cook for them. Only I find myself wanting to know more about her. I want to find the reason she has my full and undivided attention that very few women ever receive.

I drain the pasta and place some into each bowl, then pour the carbonara gravy over the top and mix it, this is a full-proof dish and I know she will love it. I bring the bowls around to the other side of the wide island and place them down. I've already put out the parmesan and cutlery. I top up our wine before sitting down.

"Angelo, this looks amazing," she says with a big smile.

I encourage her to dig in. I'm interested to see if she is, in fact, a woman with a healthy appetite, she's going to need all the energy she can get tonight… My dick aches with the thought of fucking her on this very benchtop, bunching that skintight dress up to her armpits while I suck on her plentiful tits. *Jesus fuck.*

I take a forkful of pasta to distract myself as she smiles across at me.

"So, tell me about yourself, Rayne. I don't know much about you, other than your auctioneering skills."

She glances up, swallowing and reaching for her wine, she seems a little nervous about talking about herself, but I am curious and want to know more.

"There's not much to tell, really. I grew up in New York, I've been there up until recently because I wanted to get away from my soon-to-be ex-husband. I got into the art world early on, I've always loved fine things. Though I have been told from an early age by my parents that I had champagne taste on a beer budget."

I smile back, noticing how timid she seems on this subject. "What about your parents? Family?" I probe.

Her eyes flick down then, she instantly looks uncomfortable, and I think I've asked her the wrong thing. She takes another mouthful of food, and I wait.

"I can't really talk about that," she says quietly after a few moments.

"I'm sorry. I don't mean to be pushy." I do, but this is the first date.

She takes a long, deep breath. "It's a long story."

"I'm sure I can keep up." Yes, I'm being a nosy prick.

"Ummm…" Those big green eyes flick up to mine under her long lashes. "I don't want to get into the details, but I lost them a long time ago."

Fuck. I know just how to put my foot in it.

I observe her as she eats some more pasta, I put my fork and spoon down and tilt her chin up when she's finished chewing. "Rayne, I'm so sorry. Is it just you then, do you have any other family?"

"It's just me," she sighs, "my parents and my, um, my sister were killed in a car crash."

I close my eyes momentarily, and for a few seconds, I'm at a complete loss for words. "I'm so fucking sorry, that must've been devastating." I can see now why she doesn't want to talk about it.

"It was. I guess that's why I'm a bit of a loner and have been ever since." She downs some wine and keeps eating slowly.

I take a sip and we eat in silence for a while.

"I too lost my wife in a car crash," I say. The minute the words leave my lips I could curse myself. There's no turning back now. "She was carrying our unborn child."

She looks up at me suddenly. "Angelo, I'm so sorry."

"I've rarely spoken of it, but it's safe to say I know a little bit about loss."

"How long ago was the accident?" she asks.

I circle the rim of my glass with one finger. My skin prickles. "Fifteen years ago."

"It never gets any easier," she whispers.

I squeeze her hand gently. "That's something I know to be true."

I get up once I'm finished and walk over to the other side of the room to the bar. I pick up the stereo remote and start some light soft classical music; I have inbuilt speakers all over the house.

I want her to forget her sadness, even if it's just for tonight. Her confession has thrown me, frankly so has mine. And after all these years of seeing and doing everything, it sometimes still amazes me about people, as much as you think you know what's going on with a person based on their exterior persona, you just don't know what's going on inside them at all. She hides it well. I've been an expert at it for a while now.

I walk back over and reach my hand out to her. She looks up momentarily alarmed, I'm not sure what she thinks I'm going to do to her or what preconceived notions she has, but right now, I just want her company.

I sit back down.

My mind flicks to Lucia. Losing her is something I've never gotten over. Maybe that's why I don't believe in relationships, maybe that's why I can be such a cold fucker with no feelings most of the time, someone without a soul.

Tonight though, I'm not going to be that monster. I want to show her that I'm not always a sadistic bastard.

I've never cared if a woman wanted me back; it's always just sex, an exchange, nothing more. With her, I want to seduce her fully and intentionally. I want her to know how desirable I find her. Ever since she shot me down on the first dinner date at the auction, I've been smitten. Nobody has ever turned me down.

I know I want to do things to her that will make her forget everything bad, even if for a few hours.

I tilt her chin up to look at me, her eyes look momentarily lost and I can't help myself; I reach down to kiss her. I softly brush my lips over hers, testing the waters, and I'm delighted when she kisses me back. Gently, my tongue seeks entry and her cutlery clatters to her plate as she lets go, giving in to my demands, which is something she'll get used to when enough time has passed.

I know right at this moment; I'm going to have a hard time staying away from her.

Her hand reaches out and clutches my sleeve and a small mewl leaves her throat. It gives me all the ammunition I need, and I feel my cock swell at her reciprocation.

I actually can't control my cock around her anymore, I

pull back slightly as she bites her lip, and I slide off the stool, moving between her legs. I brush up against her so she can feel my erection and she gasps. Her sensuality and this sweet, innocent act are so fucking hot.

"Do you like that?" I whisper.

"Yes, Angelo…" The breathy way she says my name as I caress her flushed cheek has me grinding into her. I want her so badly; my dick is begging to be let out.

"You're a very sexy woman," I murmur, reaching down to her neck and breathing in her beautiful scent, which smells faintly of roses. I can't help it anymore. I slide her from the stool and lift her, placing her ass on the counter, shoving her plate away as she pulls me to her by the lapels of my shirt.

Fuck, that's hot.

We kiss more urgently; her hands roam down my back as her legs wrap around my waist and she grips my ass. Fuck yeah. I could take her right here, right now, but she's no whore. I want to fuck her properly and take my time.

I lift her up, and she wraps around me like we've always fit perfectly and I plant her against the wall, grinding my cock into her stomach.

"Feel that, *Carina?*"

She nods.

"You've got my cock so fucking hard ever since the day I met you."

I fucking need her.

Her eyelids blink rapidly as I grin at her swollen lips. She's gonna be sore everywhere pretty soon…

She wraps her arms around my neck and I plunge my tongue back in her mouth urgently, my hands roaming up the side of her body and up to grasp her succulent breasts.

I can see her nipples are already pebbled through that tight material, and I want my mouth on her tits so bad. I want to make her scream like this before I go anywhere near her pussy.

I thumb both her nipples as she groans at my touch. I know if I reach between her legs, she'll be sopping wet, but I can't go there just yet. If I do, I know I'll ravage her.

She doesn't make things better for my control when she runs her hand down my stomach, feeling the ripple effect as she goes and grips my cock through my pants.

I moan like a dying man as she squeezes me, knowing there's no way I can keep this under control.

"Fuck, Rayne." I squeeze one breast a little harder and push it with my palm as I grasp the side of her face.

"You like that?" she whispers, using my words back at me, and it turns me the fuck on.

"You're a fucking bad girl, Rayne," I growl. "So fucking bad, look what you've done to me."

"I've got you very hard, Mr. Medici," she teases me. "If that's what you mean."

I lean to her ear as my hand moves to her throat and I squeeze it gently. "You want my hard cock inside you, *Carina?*"

She whimpers and I chuckle into her neck. "I'll take that as a yes." I feel her thighs and push her dress up to her hips. I don't dare to glance down and see if she's wearing underwear; I fucking hope not.

I push my cock against her pussy and she gasps. "Angelo…"

I rub up and down as she cries out, gripping her hands into my hair as she pulls.

I reach down and roll her dress higher, up to her armpits. Her large, beautiful breasts are bared to me, and a lacy pink sheer bra stares back at me, but I can see her dark nipples through the material.

I suck one nipple into my mouth, grinding into her further as she calls out.

"I can't fucking wait to taste your pussy," I whisper, moving to the other nipple as she tilts back and moans up to the heavens. It's divine and so sensual.

I yank the bra down and try to fit as much of her breast into my mouth as my tongue swirls over her hard peak. My hand pulls on the other nipple as I, in turn, pay the same attention to it with my mouth.

I feel her reach down between us, brushing my cock again as she hastily tries to undo my buckle. I've got to give it to the girl, she's multi-skilled. She has my zipper down in seconds, squeezing me through my boxer shorts, feeling her way inside as she grips my cock and pulls on it with her hot little hand.

"Fuck!" I groan. "Fuck yeah, touch it, *Carina*, touch my cock." I shove my pants and boxers down to my knees as my dick bobs free. She looks down at it and swallows hard.

"Jesus, Angelo."

"He won't help you, baby."

I pull back from her tits to look down and watch her hand squeezing and jerking me off. I love seeing her against the wall, her dress off, and her tits out on display. I'm gonna fucking ravage her like there's no tomorrow and come all over her, marking her as mine.

She *is* fucking mine. And so is this sweet little pussy and anything else I want from her.

I reach a hand between us all the while and find her clit through the lace panties, feeling how soaked she is through the material. I pull the lace aside and swirl my finger over her clit repeatedly. She begins to rub against me, needing friction. I shove a finger inside as she cries out, then another. I fuck her like that and swirl my thumb over her nub as she starts to come.

Her face flushed, her tits heaving, and her eyes closed, she calls my name like it's a prayer from the heavens above. Hearing her come like that only makes my dick swell even more, and she's still playing with it, pulling it hard as my precum leaks out the tip.

I'm not done yet. Oh, I'm far from ever being done.

"Yeah, that's it, baby, give in to me."

It takes several moments for her to come down from her high. I'd love her to suck me off, but I won't last five seconds. Thank fuck I asked Sophia, my housekeeper, to leave for the evening because you could hear Rayne calling my name at the other end of town.

"I'm delighted to hear you're a screamer," I muse.

She pants as she stares at me. It makes me wonder how long it's been since she had an orgasm that extreme, and I don't want to think about another man inside her. I'd kill them.

"That was intense."

"You want my cock, up against the wall like this?"

She nods. She can't even speak, but her look says it all. I reach down to my pants pocket and pull out a foil packet, ripping it open with my teeth, rolling it on within seconds.

I grab my dick by the base and rub the tip through her wet folds up to her clit as she moans.

When she squeezes me around the middle with her thighs, I can't hold back anymore.

I line up and push into her entrance with force. She's so fucking tight. I still for a moment, letting her get used to me, and then I hold her by the hips as I begin to slide her up and down on my cock. She feels so fucking good, so slick and ready for me.

"You're so big," she whispers, and it's like music to my ears. It is true though hearing her say it makes me grow ten feet tall.

My vision blurs at the sensation of my cock easing in and out of her tight hole.

"Fucking hell," I say, as I crash my mouth to hers again and pump her harder, moving my hips faster. She begins to climax as I slow it down, dragging her orgasm out until her hands scratch at my scalp and I need to change positions.

I move her off the wall, still buried inside as I walk toward the couch, then I pull out for a moment as I lay her down.

"Spread your legs, let me see your pussy," I growl. She complies and I stare down at her beautiful body. I reach over and peel her dress and her bra off, then rip her G-string off and fling it, only keeping her heels on. She's so fucking beautiful.

I want to eat her out, but I need to come. I line myself up again and plow back into her as she groans at the intrusion. Her tits bounce as I rest my knees on the end of the couch and she wraps her legs around me. I told her I'd fuck her hard and I wasn't kidding.

I shift so I can see my dick disappearing into her pussy, it's the sexiest thing I've ever seen.

I close my eyes and revel in the feeling, I'm definitely not going to last watching her pussy take me. I lift her hips slightly as she rests back on her elbows, her eyes devouring me as I reach down and rub my palm over her swollen clit. Her hands trail south over my hard stomach as she looks down and watches me take her.

"Touch your tits," I manage to choke out. I need to see her touch herself.

She complies and pushes them together, plucking her nipples as she groans. I dip my head down and suck on one of the peaks in my mouth, laving it with my tongue, then I pinch her clit and suck harder. She gasps, and I move my hips faster at a maddening pace until I know she can't hold on anymore, and I don't want her to; I can feel her pussy clenching.

"Oh God, Angelo, oh God… fuck me, fuck me…"

Her pussy strangles my cock as she comes all over my dick and it's so fucking hot.

I can't hold on myself. My dick pulses deep inside her, and I'm no longer in control when I groan loudly as I still and ride through my glorious orgasm.

"Your tight little pussy just milked every drop," I choke out as we both gasp for breath.

"That was so fucking good," she whispers, her arm covering her eyes. I don't like it when she hides from me.

We lay unmoving as we catch our breaths.

There's not a fucking chance she's leaving tonight; no way have I had my fill of her yet. I plan to draw this out and the next stop is my bed. I need room to move. I need time to explore every single crevice of her body and leave her spent and sated, and ready for me whenever I want. Because that's what I need.

I need her to be mine.

Her smooth, creamy skin, soft touch, and tight little hole. I'm like a man who's been in the desert and is in dire need of water. She's my fucking well.

And I plan on draining her for all she's got.

11

RAYNE

I DON'T KNOW HOW I'M FEELING, BUT TOO MANY EMOTIONS run through me all at once.

This man who's many things, a criminal, a mobster, someone who kills for pleasure, for revenge, for whatever the hell he pleases.

He's the reason I'm in this fucking mess in the first place, and here I am, willingly sleeping with him... or should I say, willingly letting him fuck me. That's more appropriate for what just happened.

Raw. Carnal. And so very fucking hot.

Instead of recoiling and feeling disgust run through my very being, all I want to do is reach for him. Beg him for more, beg him to do it again. Because even though what I'm feeling is sending me into some sort of tailspin I can't decipher, I still want *more* of it.

Here, I feel alive. Here, I feel in control. Here, I feel like a queen, even if it is all make-believe.

His vicious, beautiful, sinful eyes stare down at me.

I know that I'll never grow tired of seeing him look at me like this. Not ever. No matter what occurs between us.

In the darkened light, his eyes resemble blue sapphires, sharp and strong. They could cut through glass, and they're cutting me, piece by piece, little by little, and I'm powerless to stop it.

I want to, believe me, I fucking want to, but he's like a magnet that drags me toward him. And I'd go freely, reveling in this twisted, toxic thing I've created. And it is *my* doing.

I agreed to this.

That dark place inside me doesn't care who he is, what he does. There are worse people out there than Angelo Medici. If this makes me a whore and a traitor, then so be it. All rationale left the building when he scorched me with his touch.

"You're a very beautiful woman, Rayne," he tells me, his voice gruff. He's still inside me, and by the look in his eyes, I realize this is just the beginning of our night of debauchery.

I just want him to make me feel. Make me his for tonight.

I stare back at him, unable to form words.

"I want to take you every which way. That tight little pussy is mine, understand?"

My eyes go wide, but I nod.

He snorts. "Not going to fight me?"

I pull myself together and smile coyly. "Do you want me to?"

He kisses me chastely, then lifts off, sliding himself out. He pulls the rubber off right in front of me and ties it in a knot, dropping it into the trash can next to the couch. His dick is still at half-mast and it's a beast, just like him.

I'm a little sore, but that all goes out the window as I stare at his perfectly chiseled body. He's like something out of a mythical fantasy.

How can one man look so perfect? So dark and dangerous and deadly all at the same time, while doing it effortlessly.

Perhaps I never stood a chance.

He smirks when he catches me staring. "Like what you see, Rayne?"

I nod. "That was so hot."

His eyes drop down to my body as I lie there, naked, on display for him.

He smirks again, his eyes dark with desire. "Feeling brave?" he whispers.

My heartrate kicks up about a thousand notches as my brain tries to scramble to what he has going on in his head.

"What did you have in mind?" I reply.

He reaches out his hand to me, and I take it. He pulls me up off the chair and his eyes look darker than ever.

He tugs me and I follow him silently as we both pad through his mansion, naked, toward the large, winding staircase so grand it belongs in a museum.

We climb higher and higher, and his grip on my hand tightens as we ascend.

We walk down a dimly lit hallway, the cool marble floors gleaming like they've never been walked on, until we get to a double set of doors. *His bedroom.*

My heart rate beats so loud I'm sure he can hear it. He pushes the doors open, and the first thing I see is a massive bedroom fit for a king.

It's minimal, masculine, and all Medici.

The gray walls surround a four-poster bed with giant, soft-looking cushions and a large black and gold Versace duvet. It looks like the comfiest bed I've ever seen.

He pulls me towards him as he slams the door closed with his foot. He reaches down and cups my face with both hands and kisses me passionately. I freeze on the spot.

I've done my part in making him want me, but I didn't expect him to kiss me like this. To want me like this. I thought he'd just be a big, overbearing brute. It never occurred to me he'd be so sensual.

He's so composed, so in control that it makes me want to submit, like I have no choice but to bend to his will. I know that makes me weak, however everyone has a breaking point, and I'm newly discovering that Angelo Medici is mine.

What's even stranger is the reaction I have to him at this moment; I want him to do whatever he wants.

He pulls back to look at me, and my belly flips at the primal gaze he gives me.

Why is he making me feel like this?

It isn't fair. I'm stronger than this. I've had to be. Only when he looks at me like he is now, I couldn't care less about anything else going on outside this room.

Tonight, he's mine.

The tension between us is palpable. He wants me. And I never thought I wanted a man to look at me with total possession like he is, until now.

His hands move down from my face to grip my hips, he pulls me to him, and that's when I feel he's hard again, really fucking hard.

"Look what you've gone and done," he growls in my ear.

I reach down and grasp him in my hand, he's throbbing in my palm. His cock is just as perfect as everything else about him.

To be a rich, powerful, intelligent, sexy mafia boss and have a perfect cock that can actually render a woman powerless, is truly a gift. And doesn't he know it.

I don't wait to be asked; I drop to my knees and sheath him again as I suck on his tip.

He watches me with hunger as I take him further into my mouth, his eyes closing momentarily and his hands moving into my hair.

I slide my tongue down his length and he hisses. His cock tastes just as good as the rest of him, if not better. Gripping his base, I tug on his dick harder as he swears out loud, his eyes opening as I work my mouth up and down slowly, reveling in every second.

His eyes stare at me with wild abandon, so much so that a thrill of fear runs through me.

I realize I like turning Angelo into this wild creature, it gives me a sense of power, a sense of bravery that I can withstand him, whether the storm while I devour him.

He groans, and when our eyes meet again, I squeeze him, feeling his length, getting my fill of him as I swirl my tongue, licking the precum that leaks from his tip. His hands get tighter in my hair, guiding me, not quite at the point of pain, but I sense he's holding back.

He rocks his hips subtly, and the next groan he makes has my pussy weeping for him. I'm so turned on, it's so delicious. So raw and damned perfect.

Before I can blink, he's yanking me off the floor by my upper arms and picking me up as I wrap my legs around him. He claims my mouth, our tongues clashing as his hot hard cock presses into me, his taste still on my tongue as I hold onto him for dear life.

He walks us to the bed. "So wanna fucking tie you up," he mutters. "Then you'd be at my complete mercy."

I pull him closer, biting down gently on his bottom lip as he groans. "Then why don't you?" I've never, ever, been tied up before, but this is the rabbit hole I fell into, and I'm all in.

He grins. "I'm too fucking eager to be inside you again," he whispers dangerously. "But first, I think it's only fair I return the favor where oral skills are concerned."

He must see the trepidation in my eyes as he asks, "What's wrong?"

I never thought I'd be truly honest with him, but before I can stop, I blurt out, "My ex didn't like doing that."

He frowns. "Knew I should've slit that fuckers throat when I had the chance." Something in his tone tells me he's not joking.

I slide down his body as he sets me down on the soft, plush comforter and spreads my legs wide.

"Lean back on your elbows, I want you to watch me."

My heart races with excitement as I spread for him.

I made sure I was primed and ready for him long before this moment. The fleeting thought that I am no longer on my own terms flies out the window.

I'm on Angelo Medici's terms now, and we both know it. What's more, I can lie to myself all I want, but the devil inside me knows that I'm doing this part readily.

He drops to his knees on the floor beneath me, and that action alone has me biting my lip as I squeeze my core. I need friction. I need him to take the ache away.

His eyes drop to my wet center as he devours me, his hands circling my inner thighs softly.

Never in a million years did I think Angelo would have a soft touch, but he does. It's sensual and sexy and very unexpected.

His cock hangs heavy between his legs and it looks angry and thick, ready to burst, but he somehow holds off from shoving it in me. I want his mouth on me so bad, but I also want him deep inside me. I need him to make me forget.

He moves his thumbs to part me, and he whispers something in Italian I don't understand as he bends and swipes his tongue through my folds. I just about leap off the bed as he chuckles.

"Eyes on me," he says suddenly.

My eyes pop open and he begins again. Licking me, swirling over my clit with the tip of his tongue. It's been so long that I forgot what the sensation felt like, and it's fucking amazing. I feel like I'm a puppet dangling on the end of a string, *his* string—a puppet for his amusement.

Guilt floods through me, but I push it down. I'll deal with the guilt and self-loathing later…

"Angelo," I gasp. I'm so fucking close.

He latches onto my clit, sucking it into his mouth as I cry out. Then I feel him insert a finger, it slides right in because I'm so fucking wet from need. Hearing my shuddering moan, he laps his tongue harder, faster, as I come undone, crying out his name, as he pushes my knees back to the mattress when I try to close them. He rides me through it as I collapse back on the bed. Seeing his head between my legs and how he's watching me like that, is too much.

He's too much.

This sweet, beautiful, forbidden creature that has me squirming under his touch.

I feel him shift as his hands and mouth leave my body. I sit back up on my elbows and I get to witness him in fine form, standing before me, his hard cock ready to punish me as he rolls on a rubber.

His abs and pecs are like a sculpture, glistening in the dark as he commands all my attention. And he has all of it. My eyes hungrily take all of him in.

He climbs onto the bed between my legs as I scoot backwards, his face predatory, like a lion stalking its prey, and I'm completely beguiled by it, like a deer cornered with nowhere to go. *And where would I go?*

Settling over the top of me, he plunges his cock into me so deep that I cry out from the intrusion. He moves in and out of me faster than before, mercilessly as he holds his weight off my body, then he shifts to lift my legs up to his shoulders and tilts my hips. He hits me at such a deep angle that I close my eyes as I see stars. As my orgasm begins to build, it feels like my insides may explode.

I cry out, my orgasm dragging on and on as he milks me.

"That's it, baby, you scream all you like. Nobody but me can hear you," he growls.

He sets my legs down and flips us over so he's on the bottom, and I straddle over his lap. My hair wraps wildly around my face as he holds my hips and immediately impales me on him. I press down on his chest as I ride his cock. His hands reach up to pluck my nipples, pulling at them as I moan, throwing my head back as I grind down on him.

Angelo Medici is a fucking God.

"Touch yourself again, *Carina*," he hisses, his dark eyes flicking to mine.

I replace his hands with mine and cup my breasts as he watches me play with myself, pushing my breasts together as his hands wander down my torso, appreciating every inch of my body.

He looks like a forbidden angel, his eyes alight with a fire I've never seen before.

"It feels so good," I whisper. "So, so good, please don't ever stop…"

He grips my hips so hard; I know there'll be marks there tomorrow.

"Ride me, ride my hard cock, Rayne, show me what I do to you, *Carina*."

His dirty words are my undoing as I come again. Just as

I do, he thrusts up into me with a pace that's so maddening that I almost feel my soul leave my body.

I cry out as my body shakes from the pure pleasure ripping through me like a freight train. My body sags forward as I clutch onto his shoulders, then he shudders and calls my name violently.

Three mind-blowing orgasms in one night, how much more can a woman take?

We breathe heavily together for a few moments before he rolls me over onto the soft mattress.

The man is a devil in the bedroom.

I lift my arm to cover my eyes as I struggle to breathe.

"Your body's made for me," he says, panting hard. I feel a slight shiver of satisfaction knowing that he's so exerted.

"Your cock's made for me," I reply.

My skin is flushed, and I feel it burning. Burning because I'm so hot for him.

It's so dirty and delicious, and I almost forget that I'm here under dire circumstances. I'm here under a guise. And if Angelo ever finds out what I'm doing, I know I'm a dead woman.

He won't have mercy on me.

This is a business transaction, nothing more.

I have a major fault, and trying to keep my feelings separate from my mission is proving to be even more complicated than I ever expected.

1 2

ANGELO

I wake up in a cold sweat. It takes me a few seconds to register that there is another person in my bed.

I run a hand over my face. I never do this. I never let a woman sleepover.

I glance at the clock next to me on the bedside table and blink to ensure I'm not seeing things.

5:00 am?

I've never slept for longer than three or four hours at a time in as long as I can remember.

How could I let this happen?

I glance at the petite, warm body next to me, her hair strewn across the silk pillow like some kind of fallen fucking angel, and then I know why. She's the reason.

I can't explain why, but she makes me calm. She chases the demons away, and I've no fucking clue how. I've not shared sleep with a woman since Lucia, and that was years ago…

I get up quietly and pad across the room to the bathroom to take a leak. When I come back, she hasn't moved.

I climb back into bed and turn on my side to face her.

Aside from being a gorgeous woman, she's also very smart and I find myself itching to know more about her, wanting her to open up more to me. It's like she isn't afraid of me. She doesn't have that trepidation in her eyes that most women do when they meet me or when they find out who I am. There is a man behind the mask.

I also can't remember the last time I essentially spent the whole evening with a woman and didn't talk business…it's been years. There's always something going on with the family business, or my brothers calling me, or my cousins, Allegra needing help with something, or Mario… I have to go check in with Mario. It's been almost a week, and I know he'll want a full report on everything going on. Even on his fucking death bed, he's still got half his ear to the ground.

I brush my fingers over Rayne's shoulder and caress the ends of her hair. It's soft and silky, and though it was impeccably styled earlier, she looks like she's been fucked into next week.

I contemplate waking her up so I can take her again, so I can really punish that little pussy that's been teasing me for far too long. She takes my cock so fucking well. The sight of her on her knees before me was something I'll never be able to erase from my memory, and why would I want to. It was utter perfection.

Imagining her lips around any other man makes me want to slice his throat.

She's mine.

I know for a fact I want to see her again and that doesn't scare me as much as it probably should.

Rayne's body moves with mine, in tune, like we're two pieces of a puzzle. She enjoyed pleasing me as much as she did receiving. She wasn't afraid to completely let go in the moment and show her body to me. I fucking dig that.

I love a woman who is confident with her body and isn't afraid to show it off.

I settle back into sleep and the next thing I know, I wake up again, and her side of the bed is empty. Then I hear the shower turn on.

I listen to her move around the bathroom and I know I want to go in there and bend her over and take her from behind. I'll never be done with her sweet body.

I gave her a mild version of the beast last night, but now I feel like just taking what I want.

My cock agrees with me, tenting under the sheet as I fling the covers back and swing my legs out of bed.

I saunter into the bathroom and see her silhouette through the glass, the steam billowing as she sighs. I love that fucking sound.

Never have I contemplated tying myself to a woman, not since Lucia, yet I can't help that my mind wanders to what it would be like with her.

She's a lot like me in many ways. Guarded. Fierce. Very capable and intelligent. I bet she's good with money, careful with it, puts some away for a rainy day.

The thought is fleeting, even if I had the time to indulge in a relationship, I doubt she'd want this kind of life. One that's meant for a Stepford wife who asks no questions and looks flawless on your arm, one who's also good at spending your money. Fuck that.

Sure, in my line of work, you need a woman who looks the other way, but you also need one who can keep your secrets and comfort you when nobody else can. Who knows what you need without words. That's not indulgent, that's fucking impossible.

I've never found my equal, my other half, even in my marriage. Lucia didn't want the life; she'd made that apparent time and time again.

I stare at Rayne through the glass as I touch myself, walking toward her as I slide the door open.

Her eyes dart to mine, and I gaze down her voluptuous body. She's using my shower gel, soaping up her hands as she runs them over her slippery, full breasts and torso. It's fucking hot. My desire piques as she flicks her eyes down to my cock, it's not like she can miss the thing.

"Sleep well?" I muse, as I continue to watch her assault her body with dainty little hands.

"Yes, thank you." She smiles softly. "That has to be the comfiest bed I've ever slept in."

I stare at her hungrily. "It suits you."

She swallows hard.

"I want you," I say simply.

Her eyes dart south again. "I can see that."

I reach for the shower gel and take over washing her body, kneading her breasts and running my hands down her back and her ass as I pull her closer to me.

"Around you, it never comes down," I growl, kissing her again, my cock pressing against her stomach as she lets out a tiny mewl.

She presses her hand against my chest, and I feel one hand run down past my abs and then she plays with the hair south of my belly button before palming my cock with her hot little hand.

I liked waking up with her.

I push the thought away because it's ridiculous.

"Put your hands on the glass and stick that pretty little ass out," I growl.

I'm pleased when she does as I say, and I move around behind her. I pull her hips back as I run my hand between her legs, feeling her heat, making her gasp. I can feel her arousal mixed with the water. Fucking dirty little thing.

"You feel so fucking good," I whisper in her ear.

I rub my hands all the way down her back and then move around to cup her tits. I pull on her nipples as she jolts forward and I grunt a laugh as she almost hits her head on the glass. I love how fucking responsive she is.

I move my hands back around to her lower back, then her ass, and I give it a smack. I can't wait to fuck her here too, but that's gonna need some time.

Instead, I rub through her folds, brushing her clit with my thumb, but I can't ignore my cock begging for release. I line up and push into her hard, she gasps and I plunge out and back in again, her breath comes out in a huff as I move in and out with vigor gripping her hip with one hand and holding the back of her neck tightly with the other. Her pussy grips my cock like a vice, and I get completely lost in the moment.

I know I don't have a rubber on, and so does she, yet she isn't stopping me. It feels so good bareback, so goddamn good I could pound her into next week. I tighten my grip on her hips as I caress the mark I left on her ass. Good, I want to mark her all over, so everybody knows she's mine.

I reach around and brush her clit with my fingers. She convulses as soon as I touch it and pushes back against me, moaning as she sinks her head onto her bent arms.

My cock gets swallowed up with each and every roll of my hips. I move faster, knowing I'm on the edge, but I want her to come one more time. Lucky for me, she explodes as our skin slaps together and I pull out, holding my cock with one hand and squirt my release all over her back. I've never heard myself moan like a fucking bitch but moan I do.

This woman is going to give me a heart attack.

I should make her clean me up with her tongue, nevertheless I've probably done enough damage for one date.

Instead, I pull her backwards and wash my cum off her, and then she leans back into my chest as I kiss the top of her head.

"So, how does this rate as a first date?" I quip.

I feel her laugh beneath me, it's such a sweet sound. "I'd rate you eleven out of ten, Mr. Medici."

It's music to my ears as the warm water cascades over us, and I feel my chest jolt with satisfaction.

***

Hours later, after Rayne has left, the phone in my office at Fortress rings.

Dante's calling me.

"The prodigal son finally returns," I say, sitting back in my chair.

"Speak for yourself," he retorts with a laugh.

"Thought you'd emigrated, or did you finally find a piece of pussy that wanted you for more than one night?"

"Very funny, fucker. Marco told me about the latest update at the warehouse," he goes on. "And what needs taking care of."

He's talking about the human cargo shipment take-down and looking into this Senator Mendes piece of shit.

Although the phone lines are secure, we never discuss business. I've also got my house completely swept for bugs, and it gets checked regularly.

"We need to take care of it pronto."

"The Gala Ball is coming up, it seems like a good enough time. Lots of people and activity. Nobody will be expecting it. Sometimes you gotta hide things in plain view."

Not a half-bad idea from my little brother, but I don't tell him that. "Get Fynn on it with you. He's been MIA of late, and it's about time he pulled his weight around here, I'm sick of doing all the heavy lifting." I absently wonder if Rayne would be up for a night on the town with me, it would undoubtedly get some tongues wagging, but I barely give a fuck about that.

The question is do I want to share her with the rest of the world just yet.

"We need to talk about our fellow friends from the Soviet."

I don't ever say Petrov or the Russians over the phone.

"What about them? Aside from the usual?"

The Petrovs have always been trying to get their hands on our turf, and for the most part, we've weeded them out.

Boston is mine, long before Mario handed it to me, and I will go down in flames before letting any of the Petrovs take what's mine.

It's Medici territory, always has been, always will be. Threats come and go almost daily, but I've heard from one too many sources that the Russians are going underground.

For one, they're trying to flush us out of the casino by orchestrating illegal gambling and betting on fights all across the city. It's absolute bullshit and fucking disrespectful to think they can get away with it. I have no idea what they believe they are doing unless they want a war. Maybe they think they have nothing to lose, or perhaps they just have a death wish.

I grin at that thought. I'm afraid of no one, not these fucking Russians, and definitely not Rombaldi and his merry band of human trafficking smugglers. The plot is to get them all and take them out one by one. Trust me, they wouldn't offer us the same courtesy.

Being ruthless is part of the job, it's second nature.

"There are some pretty loud whispers of them turning tricks. This new gambling ring is getting outta control."

"I think setting up a meeting might be the next best idea." There are ways for me to spread a message, but meeting with the fucker is the starting point before we charge in with guns blazing. I'm not an unreasonable man. Even when our own livelihoods are called in question, they're lucky I'm being this lenient. "Let's have dinner tonight to discuss, message Marco and Fynn."

"On it, Angelo." There's a pause down the other end. "So, where were you last night?" He sounds amused.

I know they all went to our club Bijou drinking last night and had a round of poker in one of our private rooms. Enzo messaged me when I was halfway bringing the delectable Rayne to her knees in my bedroom; I was much too busy to reply until later.

The corner of my mouth turns up, remembering it, and us in the shower this morning and how well she takes my cock. How good her pink ass looks after being spanked.

"I was home," I say simply. "Did you miss me?"

"Not Tiffany again?" he groans.

Ah, Tiffany, yeah, I've been ignoring her messages. As well as Allegra's. She tried calling, too, and I'll definitely be returning the favor to find out what the fuck she did by telling Rayne all that shit. I know she's just playing with her, but still. Not cool.

"No, I'm done with her."

He chuckles. "Well, you know it's Marco talking shit about it. You know what he's like, jealous prick."

Out of all of us, Dante is the most selective of the women he chooses to be with, maybe even more selective than I am, and utterly opposite to Fynn or the equally vivacious fuck buddy cousin, Jonas, who will screw anything that moves.

I know all too well what he's like.

"But, man, that rack." He whistles down the phone.

I laugh, knowing full well I paid for that rack of Tiffany's but say nothing of the sort. I'm also not at the stage to be telling any of my brothers I banged Rayne all night or that she works for the gallery. I don't need their judgment or their catcalling.

"It gets old pretty fast," I mutter. "You should try staying in some time, you party way too much."

He snorts. "What the hell would I wanna do that for?"

Touché, really, it's easy come, easy go in our world, yet one thing I've learned is getting too carried away with the gambling, the booze, and the women means you get easily burnt out.

You can't do it forever, I keep telling them all this, but none of them listen.

Maybe that's why I've got little Rayne Michaelson on the brain.

I don't know exactly what's different about her because I can't pinpoint it to one thing alone, but I know it's more than just attraction.

I've been around long enough to know that much and how I feel when my heart almost stops when I'm buried deep inside her. She's so tight it's like the first time all over again.

"You're right. Keep doing what you're doing. You'll burn out soon enough, and you'll end up screwing anything that moves, but eventually, you'll end up sad, twisted, and alone."

"Like you?" He laughs.

Fucking pretty boy.

"Very funny, asshole. I've gotta go, unless you've got anything else newsworthy to say that I don't know already?"

"I know I'm your favorite brother, you don't have to admit it."

"Stop wasting my time," I growl. "Find out when this next gambling run is going down. I want to be prepared."

"On it."

When I click off, I call Marco to find out how the permits are going so we can start building the apartments. Time is money. I can tell by his earlier texts that he's not in the best of moods. When things don't go Marco's way, he sees only red.

Later, I head to Fortress and sweat it out in the gym. We have every known state-of-the-art piece of equipment known to mankind in there with mirrors surrounding the whole goddamned place that's the size of a six-car garage.

We're not often all there at the same time; sometimes, Enzo and I sweat it out or have a few rounds in the ring. I like coming here to work out, it's one of the only times I'm ever really alone without Gus or security hanging around me or my phone ringing off the hook.

While I'm punching the bag, I work out some of my frustrations in life, and I always feel better afterward when I've got it all out.

I start thinking about my beach house in West Falmouth because I haven't been there in so long. It's a massive property out on an elevated peninsula reaching out from the Saconesset Hills between the Great and Little Sippewissett marshes. It's a summer house, more like a safe house, registered under a fake name under a hidden company of mine, so no one except my immediate family knows about it.

It's my paradise. Set entirely on the beachfront with twenty-three acres. A place I use as refuge once or twice a year to forget my cares of the world for a while and totally switch off.

Something stirs in me about taking Rayne there, I've no fucking clue why I would do that, but it's on so many acres of land we could hide away for a few days and nobody would know about it, no prying eyes.

When I've pounded it out enough in the gym, I rip my boxing gloves off and pull out my cell. The other thing I've been meaning to do, other than calling Rayne to take her out again, is sort out that piece of shit ex-husband of hers. I don't think he'll bother her again after I broke his arm, but you never know, some fuckers just need to learn the hard way. If he reaches out to her again or sends her anything through her lawyer, I'll slit his throat myself. It isn't like he's dropped the ridiculous alimony claim in her divorce settlement, I know that for a fact.

The guy is a complete scum bag, and it'd be my pleasure to send him to the bottom of the Charles.

However, I've got business to attend to, and they may or may not include doing away with her ex-husband; I'm in that kind of mood.

I dial Gus, who, as usual, answers on the second ring. "Have the car ready in an hour at Fortress."

"Sure thing, boss."

I hang up. One thing's for sure, I can't wait to be back inside Rayne again. I'm calmer whenever she's near, like all the storms in my life pale by comparison to her beauty.

I know she sees straight through me; she looks at the devil inside me and doesn't care that he's corrupt and has no soul. And that's the part I like the most.

13

RAYNE

I've been struggling to take my mind off Angelo Medici and our dirty rendezvous. It's all I've been thinking about all day. The man's insatiable, his appetite in the bedroom is as formidable as his reputation in business.

I'm on tenterhooks since we haven't made any further plans to see each other again, and my one slip about the car crash with my parents, even mentioning my sister, has me reeling.

I told Angelo nobody survived the crash because I didn't want him prying into my life. It's best if he thinks I'm an only child that way, I can keep my secret about Mia safe. I deleted my social media accounts when this whole thing went down, so there's no way he can find out anything there.

There is no denying our chemistry, as much as I try to pretend it isn't there. It stares back at me and dares me to dance with the devil, disturbing me in more ways than one.

I swallow hard when I think about what I did while Angelo slept....

I slip out of bed first to use the bathroom, then, seeing he's still fast asleep, I tiptoe down the hallway quietly and head downstairs. I saw his office on the way in here and I know exactly where I'm heading. The house is still and quiet in the dead of night. How fitting. Dead being the optimum word, because while I should feel dead inside, I've never felt more alive doing what we just did. What does that make me? I brush it off, not wanting to go there. Like I do every second of every day, I think about Mia and how kind and sweet she is. How she'd never hurt anyone, how unfair all of this is; that she has been dragged into all of this. If I could take her place, I gladly would.

It sickens me to think I've been cavorting with this monster while she's been held hostage, but

I'm here now, in his house, about to pry through his things.

My only job is to get information.

Angelo and his brothers are hard to pin down. I tiptoe down the stairs, glad they don't creak or groan and head down to the kitchen to grab a glass of water and make sure I haven't woken him before venturing into his office.

When the coast is clear, I sneak on in. The first thing I see is that huge dark, mahogany desk, which draws my eye in the dim light, it has a high-backed luxurious looking leather chair. The floor-to-ceiling bookshelves surround the entire walls, in fact, I've never seen so many books. It does not surprise me that he's a Tom Clancy fan and has many other books ranging from philosophy to artworks.

It's evident to me there hasn't been a woman's touch around there in some time, some stupid part of me wonders why. With the bevy of women at his beck and call, why settle on just one? My fingers brush the ancient spines of some of the older books, first editions that are probably worth a fortune. I stop at his desk, checking behind me again just to make sure I'm alone; my heart races with every second I spend in here.

I see an open diary sitting on the desk amongst the other

paperwork stacked in one pile, it's got to contain something that I can use.

I pull out my phone from the robe I slipped on and snap some photos of his upcoming schedule, amazed he even has a paper diary but glad all the same. It fills me with dread that I'm doing this. Tonight, I've questioned everything I know.

If Angelo is such a monster, why does he treat me like a queen? His queen. None of it makes any sense.

When I'm satisfied, I have at least something worthwhile to show I've been in his house, maybe that will earn me some talk time with Mia. There's no way I can go snooping around in his drawers and around his desk, I'm too afraid of getting caught.

I take my glass of water back upstairs, slide under the covers and immediately snuggle back into his huge bed. He seems to sleep so soundly; I watch the slow and steady rise of his chest as I drift off back to sleep....

It was so fucking dangerous doing that, if he caught me snooping— I don't even want to think about it.

I don't think sleepwalking would be a good excuse to keep him from questioning me and potentially slitting my throat when he found the photos I'd taken on my phone.

I hate that we have this connection and that, if I'm honest, I've let myself feel something for him, even if it is fleeting. We fit together. *But it's just sex,* I tell myself. *Nothing more.*

No matter what I try to tell myself, I *wanted* him to touch me. I wanted him all along.

Angelo Medici has me all mixed up, there is no denying it.

I'm in utter turmoil.

I've been given a no-reply email address to send the photos to, then I delete them from my phone. I've given them weeks of appointments, dinners, and places Angelo will be, namely the Gala Ball.

Later that night, when I'm alone with my thoughts, I get the call that I've been dreading.

"Finally, some progress," the voice says with amusement. "I take it you had an enjoyable night."

"Did you get the photos?" I say quickly. "I emailed them earlier. I need to speak to my sister."

"We'll get to that."

I want to scream and jump up and down. I'm that highly strung and angry, but I know that this may be enough, it might keep them satisfied so they can do what they want with him, and I get Mia back.

"Please," I beg them. "I can't go on like this."

"You've earned a reward," they say as I hear scuffling for a few moments. I run a hand through my hair, gripping tightly at the roots.

"Wait!" I call, thinking that they're going to hang up.

"Rayne?" comes the voice down the phone after a second.

I almost drop my cell on the ground as my heart thrums in my chest.

"Mia!" Relief and adrenaline rush through me at the same time —she's alive, thank God. "Are you all right?"

She sobs into the phone, and I want to break something. Seriously, if I had a baseball bat, I'd take it to their heads right now. I've never been capable of violence, even when Dane started to shove me around, I never fought back, but this is different.

This is nuclear. I'll find them, and fucking kill them all.

"I'm okay..." she cries. "Please come get me, Rayne...*please...*"

"Have they hurt you?" I pace the room, pulling at my hair as I hear her crying.

"I'm okay ... sort of...." There's a commotion, and then I don't hear her anymore.

Sort of?

"Mia!" I call. "Mia!"

I swallow hard, my throat thickening like I've swallowed cement and I think I'm going to pass out.

"She's alive, there's the proof you need," that bastard says, coming back on the line.

"You won't get away with this," I whisper.

"Oh, but I am. And don't go getting any fancy ideas. Remember, I have eyes everywhere."

"She didn't even get to speak to me!" I screech, losing all self-control.

"You'll attend the Gala. We'll send the details through, and that will be that."

"That will be what?"

The line goes dead and I feel like I'm going to faint.

What fucking details? I try to calm down. *Mia is alive,* I remind myself. *To hear her voice....that's all that matters.*

Tears well up in my eyes as I sob. They'll probably be happy if I end up blowing my cover. What's one more dead body to them anyway?

I have to be strong even though my mind runs rampant.

Whenever I think about just giving in and going to the police, I'm reminded that the man I'm currently sleeping with owns the police.

My phone rings again, making me jolt.

The devil himself is calling me, how fitting.

I clear my throat before answering and dab the tears from my eyes with my sleeve.

"To what do I owe this pleasure?" I say, biting my lip, hoping my voice doesn't sound awful and shaky.

"Just thought I'd see how you are, *Carina.*"

Oh lord, if only he could see me now. I straighten myself and take a sip of my wine.

"I'm doing very well, thank you for asking."

"So, did I pass the first date dinner challenge?" he asks.

What the ever-living fuck?

I laugh softly, trying not to grit my teeth. "You make a mean carbonara if that's what you mean."

I can hear the flirtation in his voice. "What about the rest?"

"If you're referring to how you made me see God several times, then I'd say you're very, very talented in the bedroom."

He chuckles. The sounds goes straight between my legs. It seems now I've had Angelo; the mere mention of his name sends me into a flurry. It's a mixture of all the pent-up rage I'm feeling. I don't know which emotion will carry me through any of this, and I don't rightly care.

"It's not that hard when the woman you're trying to seduce is the most beautiful woman you've ever laid eyes on."

I somehow find the will to laugh softly. "On the contrary, I can argue that it *was* very hard, several inches of it that I can still feel every time I move," I whisper the last part, like I'm somewhere where I could be overheard instead of in the safety of my own apartment.

"Good. I like you sore and sated, *Carina*, until I'm inside your pussy again, which will be soon."

You need an invite to that exclusive fucking Gala....

"When can I see you again?" I ask. I can almost see his lazy smile stretch across his terrifyingly handsome face.

"I'm coming to arrange the pickup of the wine tomorrow evening, will you still be there at six?"

Damn, tomorrow?

The sooner I get to see him, the sooner I can get closer, and hopefully, he'll start to trust me and invite me to be his date for next weekend.

"I'll be there." I bite my lip, my heart buzzing again in

my chest, I squeeze my knees together, but that will never relieve the pressure of what he can do.

He pauses. "I can't stop thinking about you," he says quietly.

I swallow hard. "Me either," I whisper back.

"I'd come over right now if I could, but I've got a pressing matter that needs my urgent attention."

I think about him with another woman and pain hits my chest. *Stop it!*

"Duty calls, I understand," I say, when the reality is my insides are clawing at me. "But I can relieve the ache until then."

I hear a low growl and it makes me smile.

"Touch yourself," he demands. "Reach into your little panties and rub yourself for me."

I take another sip of the wine and comply, slipping my hand down my panties and feeling my wet center.

I need him so bad...

I walk over to the couch, resting my wine on the coffee table as I lie back against the cushions.

"Did you like my mouth on you, *Carina*? Sucking your sweet pussy?"

"Oh God..." I cry, circling my sensitive and swollen clit, wishing he was here to do it all again. "*Yes*, oh, Angelo, *yes.*"

He chuckles again. "Stick your fingers in your hole, baby. Finger yourself for me."

I slide my middle finger inside and then add another, all the while imagining it's his cock annihilating me. "That feels so good."

I can hear the need in his voice. "Fuck yourself till you come," he breathes darkly, and it makes me wonder if he's not jerking off himself.

I move my fingers in and out faster, my thumb brushing my clit as I buck my hips, moving them at a maddening pace. I set the phone down on speaker and pull my tank down and pinch one of my nipples. *God, I wish it were his mouth.*

He makes me come undone so fucking easy that it makes me sick. Hearing his dark, sexy voice only spurs me on and wounds me even tighter.

"Angelo!" I call out.

"That's it, *Carina*, come all over yourself, give it to me, imagine my tongue fucking your tight little hole as you ride my face."

"Oh…oh…"

"I'm going to fuck that tight little ass next time. You won't be able to get enough of it," he goes on as I feel my face reddening and my tits bouncing as I work my hand faster. "You're so fucking beautiful."

"I'm going to…I'm going to come…"

"Fuck," he calls out. "Fuck, Rayne, oh fuck…"

So he is jerking off?

The thought he's doing to himself what I'm doing to myself sends a shiver through me, and I climax hard, so hard I see stars. I wish it were his tongue or his cock inside me; I need it like I need air.

"You made me come all over myself," he says, his voice husky and raw.

"Same," I breathe heavy. I am still circling my clit as I lie there, utterly exhausted. "Why can't I see you now?"

"I wish I could, trust me." At least he sounds like he means it.

"Until then," I sigh, waiting for him to hang up.

"Goodnight, *Carina*."

"Goodnight, Angelo."

He clicks off without another word.

I stare at the wall for almost an eternity.

Do you know what you're doing?

I can't say I genuinely know the answer to that.

The next day at work I find it a little hard to concentrate, the past few days are definitely catching up with me. I've just been recapping my conversation with Mia over and over again, hence why a light knock at my door has me jumping like a cat on hot bricks, Melody pops her head in.

"Hey, have you got time for a coffee?" She's all smiles and comes wafting over, then halts mid-step. "Shit, Rayne, are you okay? You look like you've seen a ghost."

I want to facepalm myself. The last thing I need is people noticing my strange demeanor, especially at work. I wish I could confess to someone what's going on, and I half want to, I really do, but I don't want to put Mia at any more risk than she already is. I refuse to do that.

Instead, I smile.

"I'm okay, just day dreaming." I wave it off. "Ex-husband dramas and I'm just a bit stressed about this new exhibit, it makes me a bit nervous with Claire breathing down our necks. Being the new kid on the block, I want to get it right." If only that were my biggest problem.

She smiles sympathetically. "I'm sorry, sweetie, exes can be such dick wads. Don't worry about Claire, she's got an agenda to get in Trish's good books, that's all. You'd think neither of us had a degree, for fucks sakes."

I laugh now, and it's nice to feel real, even if it's only for a moment. I already smoothed over the other night at the gallery with my ex so I'm glad that kind of took care of itself, and she hasn't asked too many questions, just for the skinny on Angelo and if we got up to anything that night in the limo.

I've come to truly like Melody in the short time I've

been here. "Tell me about it. You know, I'd love a coffee. Maybe we can chat about it all down at Starbucks, I haven't had lunch yet."

She nods enthusiastically. "Great, I'm dying to hear all about what's cooking with you and the king of Boston," she whispers with a chuckle.

Shit. I wish he hadn't made it so freaking obvious that night. I guess there really was no hiding the electricity between us, and I'm not sure how I will answer questions about him and me.

"Nothing's going on. He was trying to outbid a rival that night, I just so happened to get caught in the crossfire, and then Dane happened..." God, I feel like such a bitch lying to everyone. This is what my life has become.

She gives me a skeptical look. Yes, one big pack of lies, Melody, I'm sorry.

We've arranged to see each other later tonight. Lord only knows how I'm going to get through the rest of the day thinking about what I need to do next, it's a wonder I can even concentrate on work. A coffee break is just what's in order, despite knowing I'll have to give her something on Angelo and me, she isn't going to buy that rubbish that nothing is going on.

God, I wish I had someone to talk to in all of this.

My soul agrees, not that there's anything much left to salvage there. I sold it the minute Angelo let me into his bed.

"Shall we go?" Melody says, jerking me out of my reverie once more.

I nod and grab my bag, and we make for the elevators.

14

ANGELO

I DIDN'T INTEND ON GOING INTO THE GALLERY AT ALL, BUT the temptation was all too much. I can't go another day without seeing her.

Just as I'm leaving, I get a call from Allegra.

"Hello, stranger," she says when I answer.

"Allegra." I still haven't forgotten what Rayne told me about their conversation in the coffee shop.

"Have I caught you at a bad time?"

"I'm about to go into a meeting."

"I was wondering if we could have dinner this week before I have to fly to London."

Allegra is always traveling. She runs a textile business that Roberto founded, and she took over when he passed away.

"I'll have to see if I can fit it in."

"I barely got to see you at the auction. Mario said you met somebody."

I stiffen my jaw. "Seems you've met her already."

She laughs softly. "If you're referring to the little chat in the cafe, it was just girl talk. I'm protective of you, so I wanted to make sure she's good enough."

"I'm a big boy, I don't need you looking out for me." I know I sound harsh, but she has to learn to stay out of my affairs. I have one annoying little sister already; I don't need another.

"Don't be so mean, I simply want what's best for you."

"Did you tell her we slept together?" I already know the answer to that.

"No," she says. "I was just trying to get information, and I'll admit, I was being a little bit nosy. Don't be a spoilsport."

I pinch the bridge of my nose. I know she's just trying to help, but I don't need her prying into my love life. "Well, stay out of it from now on. You know my life is crazy, things are always changing and I don't need you meddling. You're as bad as Valentina." I try to take the sting out of my tone, but annoyance is my number one virtue.

"Fine. Sorry for caring."

"You can care, just don't meddle."

A few moments of silence ensues before she asks, "So it's serious, then?"

I don't know why she's prying and poking her fucking nose in all of a sudden. I've enough drama with my sister and ma on my hands without her adding to my stress.

"I didn't say that."

"Are you sleeping together?"

"Allegra."

"What? I'm not meddling, I just want to know how serious it is. We should get together and have a double date if she's going to be part of the family..."

The words 'double date' have no meaning at all in my vocabulary. None whatsoever.

"I'll have my assistant text you my schedule, if I can fit you in for dinner then it'll have to be before the Gala."

There's another long pause, and I know she won't be happy about the 'fitting her in' comment. Allegra has always been a very strong, very capable woman who knows what she wants. And I know she's interrogating me. For what reason, I don't know, but I doubt it is out of genuine concern for my welfare and more like good old nosiness.

"I'll be leaving right after it, so that's perfect timing, actually."

"Fine. I'll work something out."

"Sounds good. Well, have a good day, and say hello to Rayne for me."

I don't know why but the hackles on my neck stand up. "I have to go, Allegra."

"Ciao, Angelo."

"Ciao," I say, hanging up. I don't have time for this shit.

I don't mind talking to her if she has something interesting to say, but I'm not here to be her cabana boy and answer her fucking questions.

I may have a million things to do tonight as I'm needed at Fortress. Marco has the permits finally approved for the apartment block and we need to lock the builders in asap.

I head straight to the Gallery, annoyed I have to skip out on dinner and make this quick but at least I get to see her pretty face again.

I meet her down in the cellar where I'm collecting the wine from the auction. I smirk to myself as I hold a bottle of the Chateau Margot in my hand. It'll be an excellent addition to my private collection. Perhaps I'll get to have her in there too.

I can't understand why she seems more timid tonight when I kiss her on both cheeks and ask her how her day has been. I know we fucked, and I've seen every inch of her, but now isn't the time to play hard to get.

"Hello, Angelo. I'm fine, how are you?"

Fuck she's beautiful. She looks like a naughty secretary dressed in a creamy white skirt suit with a floaty gray blouse. Her hair is pushed up into a neatly packaged bun, one I want to reach up and undo so her blonde tresses cascade down her back.

"I'm fine. It's been a long week already."

She nods, then bites her lip.

"Is there something wrong?"

She looks worried for the first time since I've met her. This should be good.

"Did you have something to do with my ex-husband accepting the divorce settlement?"

Oh. That.

Not what I was expecting, but I guess she's figured out what I've been up to the last twenty-four hours.

"It's probable," I say airily. "Or maybe he wants to keep his other arm from being broken before I move onto his neck."

I can't help the smile that creeps across my face when I think about breaking his arm and how fucking good that felt. He was hanging upside down in the warehouse a fair while. Nothing like a little scare from a bunch of hooligans to get him to stay away from my girl.

The fucker deserves it. Gus found out he's been taken in for battery just a few short months ago; assaulted a young woman in a nightclub. He will be put out of his misery if he's not careful.

I might be a bastard, but I'm no fucking woman beater.

Rocco let him go eventually; we just wanted to scare him a bit. There's nothing quite like the simple act of coercion to get people to comply with what you want them to do.

She turns on me, with fire in her eyes, and my cock springs to attention. *Oh, give me some of that fire, Rayne Michaelson, I fucking dare you...*

"Angelo, what did you do?"

I ponder for a moment. I mean, how much do I want to reveal? Given the fact she's on *my* turf, in *my* building, on *my* time, and really, who gives a fuck? The guy had it coming. If anything, I've simply sped up her settlement process.

"That's a question tinged with possibilities."

She stares at me. "Is he…is he…still breathing?" Alarm taints her pretty features.

I chuckle. "What kind of man do you think I am?"

She swallows hard as I pinch her chin. "Answer me," I demand.

Her eyes pop open. "I don't know who you are, I don't know you that well."

"Try me."

She sighs. Oh she knows all about me, and if she's honest with herself, she doesn't fucking care.

"Well, I think you take the men much weaker than you, and you leave your mark on them."

I laugh. "Is that what I do?"

"Don't you?"

I tighten my grip. "What if I did, does that make me a monster? What if the men deserved it? Men like your ex-husband."

"I don't wish him dead!"

I scoff. "I didn't do away with him. I just gave him an indefinite warning. When you mess with me, you better have a good excuse. He touched you. He touched what's now mine. I can't allow that." I move my hand down to cup her throat. She doesn't struggle.

"I'm not *yours…*"

I can feel her pulse racing under my fingertips and I'm so fucking hard.

"You are until I say you are."

She swallows hard. "Is that all I am? A plaything until you get sick of me. Disposable? Like all the other women you seduce?"

I smirk slightly. "You've never been a plaything, *Carina*. The minute I laid my eyes on you, I knew we'd be a match. We have similarities that you might not see, but I *see* that fire in your eyes. You want to be afraid of me, but you won't allow yourself to be. You're stronger than you think, so much stronger, and that spirit is what has me coming back for more."

I caress her lips softly with mine as she submits to me.

"You're a monster, is that it?" she whispers when I let her have some air.

"I'm whatever you want me to be."

"I don't want you to kill him. No bloodshed, Angelo, please."

I don't like it. He obviously doesn't respect her or women in general, so why should I respect him? Not that she can tell me what I can or can't do, but if hurting him is going to make her hate me, then I have to rethink things.

"I bet that deep, dark part of you thinks about what it would be like to find out your ex is at the bottom of the Charles. Am I wrong?"

She groans. "Please…please don't, Angelo."

"I'd never hurt you. If that's what you're afraid of. I've never hurt a woman in my life. I like it rough and so do you, and I bet if I reached into your panties right now, I'd find you wet and ready for me, wouldn't I?"

The flush on her cheeks tells me everything. The truth is, after her ex, I don't know where her hard limit is and I want to know, I'm not a total brute.

Her lips press together, and she shakes her head. *Liar.*

I kiss her again, our tongues meet, and I snake a hand down the front of her skirt, brushing over her lace panties. "You want me to fuck you now, don't you, Rayne?"

She surprises me by running a hand up my stomach, across my chest and she grips my bicep, the one that's still holding her in place. Her lip's part, but no sound comes out.

"Answer me, *Carina.*"

"You know I lose all sense of reality when I'm with you," she says, surprising me. "I want you so bad that it scares me. I want to resist you, but I can't find the will to do it."

I'm like the fucking devil as I devour her with my eyes. "I don't want a fucking submissive, I want fucking fire."

Her eyes widen. "You want me to fight you?"

My cock twitches as I grin. I'm fucking sick in some ways. "I want you to tell me you don't want it."

"I don't want it," she says quickly.

"Fucking liar." I kiss her again. This time I grind my cock into her, and she gasps. I reach down and grip her skirt, pushing it all the way up to her hips, she tries to pull it back down, but I'm too strong. My hand reaches into her lace panties and I feel the heat. "This is telling me something different."

Her breath is coming in hard and fast as she looks down at my hand; I cup her harder.

"Whose is this sweet little pussy?"

"Mine!" she cries as I pull her panties from the front and rip them the fuck off.

"Guess again." I swipe my hand through her sex and groan at how wet she is.

She moans and rests her hands on my shoulders.

"You're so fucking wet for me," I tease, running my tongue up her neck. "Are you going to be a good little girl and let me fuck you here, against the Chateau Margot?" Oh, the fucking irony.

"Angelo, I'm at work!"

I laugh. "Everyone has left for the day. Nobody can hear your screams. Still, you told me you don't want it…" I pull away, and she immediately tugs the lapels of my jacket and crashes her body into mine. I feel every fine, fucking inch of her.

"*Angelo*," she whispers. "Don't go."

I sink my teeth into her neck and bite it gently, and at the same time, I insert two fingers into her tight little pussy. She makes a sound that makes me want to unzip and shoot my load all over her fucking little skirt and blouse.

"Angelo—" she cries. "Oh God, yes, please…"

"Please what, *Carina*?"

I pump my fingers in and out, making sure the knuckle on my thumb brushes her clit.

I rip open her blouse, and her big, juicy tits stare back at me through the sheer lace of her bra.

Jesus fuck.

"I want you," she cries. "I need you to fuck me, Angelo."

She comes hard and I don't let up, drawing out her every pleasure as she grips onto my shoulders so hard it hurts. She's gonna get bent over that case of champagne, and she's going to be screaming for dear mercy.

I don't even give her a second to recover. I take her mouth, ravaging her possessively, my fingers still in her as she fumbles with my belt and buckle. My cock's so hard I don't know how long I'm gonna last, shamefully quick if she's anything to go by.

I rip her bra down and suck one nipple, trying to get as much of her in my mouth as possible.

She grips my dick once it springs free, and I just about come in her hand.

"Fuck, you're so hot when you're fiery," I grunt as she pulls my cock, gripping it hard.

I can't take it anymore. I turn her around and slap her ass cheek. "That's for defying me." *Whack.* "That's for lying." *Whack.* "And this is for trying to pretend you don't love it when I'm rough with you." *Whack.* I shove into her all the way as she gasps. It's such an erotic sound.

I pull her hips back and she automatically sticks her ass out. Taking her bareback has been a fantasy since that episode in the shower, and it makes me never want to wear a rubber ever again.

"Angelo—" she cries. I slap her ass again and run one hand up her spine, loving how her pussy looks taking my cock from behind.

"Yes, *Carina?*"

"I need it, oh God, I need it—"

I grin, holding her hips so hard I know I'll leave a mark. I bend to her ear. "Are you on birth control?"

She nods, sticking her ass out further, trying to impale me harder—dirty little thing.

I grunt, satisfied. *Good.* I'm going to come inside her, mark her, own her.

Despite what she says or thinks, she is *mine.*

I reach around and pull one nipple with my fingers, making her yelp. "You look so gorgeous taking me like this *Carina,* I might not want to give you back."

I slam into her harder, pumping her, making her feel every inch of my angry dick. She starts to come and I mutter in Italian how fucking beautiful she is, how she's mine, how I'll never let anybody touch her. Then all too quickly, I find my own release.

I spurt violently inside her as I still, a groan sounding in the air that I realize is coming from my throat.

We're both panting and breathless.

"If you lie to me again about not wanting me, then I'll tie you up next time and I won't be gentle about it," I whisper. "You hear me?"

She whimpers as she nods and I hold onto her hair with force. "Yes."

I continue to pump her slowly, feeling my cum dripping out of her, enjoying how it feels and how breathless she is. I bet she's never had an experience like this before in the basement of her workplace. I wish I didn't have to go tonight; I'm fucking pissed about it.

"Good girl," I say.

I can't be sure, but I think we both have an understanding. And it excites the fuck out of me.

The private room at Westmead hospital is like something you'd find at the Ritz Carlton.

If only they could find a cure for cancer instead of spending all this money on decor.

Mario sits up in bed. With the help of a ventilator, he's able to take rapid, wheezy breaths.

His eyes light up when I enter.

"Angelo, my son," he says when I pat his hand, taking a seat on the chair next to his bed. "I'm so pleased to see you." It takes about five minutes for him to get all of that out.

"Mario. How are you feeling?"

He coughs, and I pour him a glass of water. It's hard

seeing him like this. The only man I've ever respected aside from my father. I love him like he is my own father, and in turn, I'm like a son to him.

"About the same. I hear the Petrov's are trying to snake their tentacles through any outlet they can get their hands on."

Good news travels fast. Even though the man's half-dead and confined to a hospital room, he's still on top of everything in the underworld.

"We're stopping them at every turn. They're trying to bribe the already bribed, some greedy fuckers out there who will live to regret that. Word on the street is Petrov got a major cash injection from out of state. Seems they're pretty hell-bent on doing whatever they can to take over, little by little."

"They won't," he rasps. "We're too big. We own too many people."

"That's true," I say, holding the cup up to his mouth. "However, one thing you taught me well was to never underestimate your enemy, no matter how weak they may appear. They've been working the underground gambling and prostitution rings behind closed doors by men that pay me for protection. That won't go unpunished, but first, I need to find out why."

"Power. It's all about power, money, and prestige. You give any one of these bastards an inch, they'll take a mile. You, of all people, know that Angelo. I taught you every-thing I know, and there is nothing more you have to learn. You're most vulnerable when you're predictable. Petrov and Rombaldi will strike when you least suspect it, be ready for anything."

"He already knows we've squashed one of Rombaldi's bookies. I slit his throat. He was employed by the good Senator Mendes. Illegal prostitution and child trafficking are amongst many of his crimes. He likes underage girls. I already shut down one skanky club where girls were being lured. I can't let that go unpunished. I won't."

He nods. "I know how you feel about that. There's a lot of fucked up shit we indulge in, but there's no place for that in this city. All it does is spawn more illegal operations and devalues the drug trade. You'll do what you have to do, and you'll show no mercy. Someone has to be made an example of, and they'll respect you for it in the end."

My father rescued my mother from an illegal sex trafficking ring before I was born. She was poor and homeless, a migrant who was promised a new life in America and was sold to the sex trade instead. He didn't intend to fall in love with her, but here we are.

The one thing you can't fuck with is women and children. I tolerate almost everything except that.

Sometimes I think a twisted part of my soul makes up for the things I let slide, like when I find men who work for the likes of Mendes and Rombaldi. The truth is, I enjoy making them suffer. They don't deserve to live.

"I'll always do what's best for the family, first," I say after Mario's done coughing again. "You not only taught me how to be a brute but also how to get people to respect me for it, crave it even. Nobody fears a man more than one who has the control of the city in his palm."

He smiles, looking up at me with pride. "You're a man of honor, Angelo." He pats my hand as he holds onto it. "I'll be gone soon, and when I am, remember this one thing: a man can only be measured not by the bodies he counted or the souls he took but by the people around him who stood by his side when the waters were rough. You'll have many more enemies, Angelo. You'll have to have your wits about you and be one step ahead of everyone else, that's why you're the king now. And long may you reign."

I wish it didn't have to be this way.

Mario is the one confident I have, aside from my brothers, who I trust implicitly. He's always direct, even when I don't want to hear it. Losing him will be hell on earth.

He's the only father I've known for so long. I'd give my life for his if I could.

He closes his eyes to rest as I get lost in my thoughts.

No good can come from remembering the past. I, of all people, know that only too well.

15

RAYNE

I DON'T REMEMBER MAKING IT HOME. I DON'T EVEN NOTICE the traffic, or parking my car, or drawing myself a bath and drinking a bottle of wine.

If only I could wash away everything. All the sins. All the lies. The secrets.

Hearing my sister's voice brought it all flooding back. How much I have to lose and how much I will do to get her back.

I allowed Angelo to take me in the loading dock at work – I don't even know who I am anymore.

I hate *loving* what he did. The way his hand fit around my throat as he told me that I was his. How I needed to hear it.

I hate him. It's true. I hate all of them, but most of all, I hate how he makes me feel alive in all of this mess.

Then there's the Dane situation that I don't even want to think about. Angelo took care of it. Though, he would probably bathe in his blood if he felt so inclined.

I'm halfway through soaking my sorrows away when he

texts me, telling me he's downstairs. I'm stunned for a moment. *He's here?*

I gulp down the last of the wine and jump out of the bath, wrapping myself in a toweling robe.

I buzz him up and run a hand through my wet hair.

I've had a little too much to drink. Had I known he was coming over, I wouldn't have.

When I open the door, he's standing there in the suit he fucked me in earlier, his top button undone and his tie loose at the nape. He looks so delicious, forbidden, and sexy that I stare at him like a total buffoon.

"Do you usually open the door to strange men?" he asks, cocking an eyebrow.

"I wouldn't call you strange," I reply as I let him in the door. "A little rough round the edges perhaps, but definitely not strange."

He looks a little tired. The great king himself is ruffled and looks out of place, and I've no idea why.

He follows me down the hall into the expansive living room. "What brings you out here so late at night?"

He laughs darkly. "What brings me here?" He pulls at the belt around my robe as I turn to face him.

"You did a very bad thing to me at work." I poke him in the chest and he watches the movement, the corners of his mouth turning up like I amuse him.

I've had a whole bottle of wine, sue me.

"You liked it." He pulls the belt loose and lets the ties fall down to my sides.

"I hadn't had sex for a year before you came along," I blurt out from nowhere, and I immediately slap my hand over my mouth.

His eyes go wide. "No other man has had your pussy in a whole year since that ungrateful asshole you were married to?"

I shake my head as he comes closer and pushes my robe open, baring my body to him.

"Is that a yes or a no?"

I nod. "Oops, sorry, I meant yes."

He narrows his eyes. "How much have you had to drink?"

I snort a laugh. "Umm, a little bit."

He reaches in my robe and cups my breast, running a hand over my nipple as it puckers under his touch. I resist the urge to moan out loud as my head falls forward to land on his chest.

"You can't just touch me and make it all okay."

He kisses my hair. "Make all of what okay, *Carina*?" He tilts my chin up to look into my eyes, then he slowly steers me back toward the couch and I'm forced to sit on the arm when my legs hit the back of it.

"*This!* Whatever *this* is. You make me come undone."

His lips twitch. "Is that a bad thing?"

"I honestly don't know anymore," I whisper.

He crouches down in front of me. I open my legs and pull the robe back, exposing everything to him. "This is what you want, isn't it, Angelo?"

"Yes, I do want it, you're fucking gorgeous, but you're also drunk, *Carina*."

I'm aware of all the stupid things I'm saying and doing, but I'm helpless to stop it, and why the fuck does he care if I'm drunk or not?

That's got to be better than this. I can handle anything, *except* this. I don't need him to be nice.

I don't want honesty or him looking at me like this, like I'm something to pity. It makes me feel weak. I only want to forget.

"I'm not drunk!" I protest.

"You sure about that?"

"Would you like a glass?" I offer.

He shakes his head.

"What do you need, Angelo?"

"That's surely a rhetorical question."

My craving for him isn't normal. It's sick, but I still need him nonetheless. Only he can quench the thirst.

"Tell me."

"You, *Carina*. I need you."

I bite my lip and then shrug my robe down my arms.

His eyes dip down my body; the fiery look he gives me makes my toes tingle. There is no man on the planet capable of making me feel like this, that is for sure. And I want to revel in it for just a little longer. I should know the rules about playing with fire, but I'm so far into this twisted, sick deal I've been bribed into that reality and fantasy are starting to look the same — the lines are well and truly blurred.

"Then come and take me," I tell him.

Every time I let Angelo take me, I lose a little bit of my soul. I tell myself that it's because I have no choice, but that's a lie. All of it's a lie.

"Not like this, Rayne, even I draw the line somewhere."

I look at him, confused. "Right, you're a man of princi-pals, aren't you?" I can't hide the sarcasm in my voice. "It's all for the greater good."

"You say that like you don't believe it." He tilts his head.

"You're a mob boss. You own this town."

He stalks over to me quickly, cupping my face with his hands, the movement so sudden that I jump back in fright. "That's the first time I've heard you say it."

"You kill people," I whisper.

"Only those who deserve it, yes."

"You choose who lives or dies. You play God."

He pushes my hair back off my face. "Does that make me a monster?"

"I… I don't know, Angelo."

"You don't ever have to be afraid of me," he says with conviction. My heart races at his words. He really, truly, fucking means it. I swallow hard. "You know that, don't you?"

I nod. If anything that came out of his mouth were true, it's that.

He picks me up and cradles me in his arms. "Which bedroom is yours?"

"Last door on the left," I say, as he strides down the hall with me in his arms.

When we get there, he places me down on the bed, and I reach for his jacket and pull him down to me. It takes me a second to realize that he's not kissing me back.

"I'm not drunk," I reiterate.

He grins and pulls the duvet back. "Climb in, princess."

I sigh haughtily, growing a little frustrated and confused with his actions. He can't just act like a brute one minute and then a sweet, caring man the next, I'm getting whiplash.

He looks down at me, sizing me up. He shrugs his jacket off, folding it over the back of my desk chair right behind him, then he starts to kick off his shoes, pulling off his socks and unbuttoning his shirt. "Strip," he orders.

I glare at him, who the hell does he think he is? This is my apartment!

I make an exaggerated movement of stripping my robe off, lifting myself up to throw it down on the floor behind him; I kneel in front of him with my hands on my hips.

He reaches for his belt buckle and unzips his pants, shrugging them down. He keeps his cotton boxers on. I glance down at his arousal straining through the material and take him in, in all his gloriousness.

"Get in." He nods to the open space where he's pulled the covers back, unperturbed by my nakedness in front of him. I wish I could say the same.

"You're so bossy." I sigh flopping down onto my bed, letting my head hit the pillows.

He comes in behind me, spooning against my back as I snuggle into his warm body. "Rest, princess, you just need to rest."

Words form in my throat, but they don't leave. Emotions swirl through me as I try not to drown in everything Angelo.

Who is this man?

Just when I think I have him all figured out, I realize that I don't at all.

He came here just to sleep. To hold me.

I feel like an idiot getting teary because of it. It's the alcohol, that's what it is.

And it can't help but think; who is the real monster here?

The darkness in my room tells me it's still nighttime when I rouse. I glance at my side table and realize it's three in the morning. With a slight jolt, I feel a hand on my hip and a warm body pressing into my back.

I slowly turn around to face Angelo. He's sleeping soundly, his chest rising and falling in a calming rhythm.

Even in his sleep, he's sexy as sin, so damned beautiful, his dark hair crushing into the pillow.

My fingers reach to lightly touch his skin. He's warm and seems softer while sleeping, though everything about him screams the exact opposite. He's not a man to be crossed.

I trace his skin tenderly. He has a small smattering of hair on his chest; I trail my fingers down to his belly button and just below to the trail of hair that leads downward. He cracks an eye open suddenly, even though I barely touched him.

"You feeling me up in the dark?" he mumbles, his voice still thick with sleep, dark and husky.

"No, just seeing how far I can get," I whisper, sliding my hand down and wrapping it around his cock.

He glances down to where I have a tight hold. "That's quite a compromising position you've got me in."

I stroke him up and down, and he closes his eyes momentarily. "I didn't think you'd mind if I woke you up."

"You can wake me up like this any time."

"I want to taste you," I murmur, pushing my body towards him, my hand moving slowly up and down his length. He reaches for my breast and pinches my nipple, watching me stroke him, as his hips start to move to my rhythm.

"That feels so good, *Carina*," he rasps. His eyes dance with amusement. "You gonna suck me off, baby? Then I want you to climb on top and ride me."

His bossiness makes things all that much sweeter.

I reach down to kiss him, and he cups my face, deepening the kiss with his tongue.

When I break free, I move to his neck and inhale his beautiful masculine scent.

When this is all over, I will remember this most of all, no matter how it ends. I'm allowed that one luxury, surely. I'll never forget.

I trail kisses down his neck and move to his chest, stroking his cock as I slide my body down and waste no time swirling my tongue around his salty tip. He hisses and it only spurs me on, plunging my mouth straight down and taking him as far as humanly possible without choking, my tongue swirling and my lips pressing tight against him.

"Oh, fuck yeah, baby." His hips start to move, and we find an incredible, frantic pace as I grip harder and suck him hard. "That feels so fucking good."

I can't talk with my mouth so full, but some sadistic part of me is glad that I'm pleasing him. I feel him watching me, it's so erotic, so wrong, but oh so right. I suck and swirl and pull him tighter as I cup his balls.

"Baby, I'm not gonna last," he breathes. "I need to be inside you."

I free his cock with a pop and travel back up to the top of the covers, pushing him on his back and sliding over his body, and lining him up with my entrance.

No words are needed, I know what I do to him and it gives me a sense of power, no matter how fleeting.

I grip him and brush his large head back and forth at my wet center, spreading my arousal over my swollen, sensitive clit. He pinches both my nipples at the same time and reaches forward to take one in his mouth, sucking and flicking with his tongue. He hasn't even penetrated me yet and I can already feel myself unraveling. This is what he does to me.

"Oh God," I moan. "Oh God, I'm coming..." I cry out my release as he shifts my hips and I sink straight down onto him, still in the throes of my orgasm. We both curse at the same time.

He sits up, so we're face to face as he pumps me hard, furious, it's so damned erotic as our skin slaps together.

I ride him fast as he squeezes my ass, his eyes burning like wildfires as my orgasm keeps going and takes me to another place.

Our hands entwine as he loses himself, pushing up into me hard as he stills, clutching my body flush to his as he empties himself inside me, his dick pulsing until he's spent.

"Fuck, fuck, fuck," he calls as I flop down onto his body.

My sentiments are much the same.

"You're gonna be the fucking death of me," he pants, a grin spreading across his face.

I lay down on top of his chest and let him hold me. He wraps his arms around my back, and we lay there for several minutes in a tight embrace.

He kisses my shoulder. "We're so fucking good together," he murmurs in his raspy voice, trying to get his breath back. "I'm glad to see my instincts aren't getting rusty."

I have this deep knot in my stomach that tells me to blurt it all out to him.

Confess everything. Maybe he can help Mia… he has connections.

Then I remember that I'm betraying him, and I'm no better than his enemies who all want a piece of him. And I've helped create that.

I don't say a word; I just breathe in his scent, committing it to memory.

After all, I'm going to the pits of hell with my eyes wide open.

16

ANGELO

I feel like I'm losing my fucking mind where Rayne Michaelson is concerned.

I leave her apartment after a shower the next morning. I actually slept for once. Insomnia has been a friend of mine for years. Though spooning a woman isn't usually part of my repertoire, with her, it feels like the most natural thing in the world.

I'm meeting with my brothers later today to discuss the Russians and the Rombaldi mess. I got word that the bust for human traffickers is going down Thursday, so we're sitting tight and laying low until it blows over. Meeting up at Ma's place for dinner and a catch up with my cousins seems like an opportune time to do so.

Ma has a large, gated property next to Marco's place, he has a zillion-acre fucking castle. We bought the land years before and built her the house of her dreams where she could live her own life but still be close to us. It's somewhere that always has security, and she knows she's safe. Pa would have wanted that; he would have been proud of us.

I meet up with Enzo and we venture to the gym at Fortress because I need to get some shit out of my system.

"We gotta go through those figures later," I tell him as we spar around the boxing ring. I get a jab in here and there, but we're both pretty good fighters, we're not here to kill each other.

"Know it, bro, things are going from strength to strength. There's nothing to worry about."

He's been handling all things security for years, even though I oversee it, he's my right-hand man. Enzo is the only one who knows about Rayne and the level of my involvement with her, however, it won't take my brothers long to find out since I haven't gone out with them in weeks.

There's something deep and twisted within me that wants her to be mine. To possess her, make her look at me like I'm her everything. And I haven't felt that in a long time. I've never cared. *Could I teach her?*

Is it possible for a woman to fall in love with the devil? I consider it as Enzo snickers at me.

"This Rayne chick has me on the fucking hop," I say, as he tries to right hook me. Luckily, I dodge in time.

"The gallery girl?" Enzo laughs, not easing up one bit, trying to back me into the corner.

I duck and fight my way out of it. Unlucky for him, I know his moves well.

Enzo's been married before, but it didn't last too long. He spends his life much like the rest of us, going from broad to broad, yet nothing ever seems to stick. "Why do you say that, because you've had dinner with her once?"

"She spent the fucking night," I bark, like that explains everything. He knows exactly what I'm like with women, and they never stay over. "Then I dropped in on her last night, like a fucking lap dog. She was drunk, and I ended up falling asleep there. Best fucking night's sleep I've had in years."

He does a double-take and then laughs. "Fuck, Angelo, you've got it bad if you ask me."

"I didn't ask."

He chuckles. "What do we know about her?"

"Gus did a sweep, but I've asked him to dig a bit deeper; she seems a bit clean, except some people aren't all from the sewer like us. She moved from New York not long ago, escaping a shitty husband, bad divorce, and all that shit."

"You think it's wise fucking a girl from the gallery?"

"Don't you start." I uppercut him twice just to prove my point and he steps back, fast on his feet, but I'm that little bit faster, and I clip the side of his jaw. "The gallery is one thing, but it's like she's put this spell on me. I can't fucking concentrate."

I don't even believe the crap coming out of my mouth these days. I sound like a pussy, although I know I can say this shit to Enzo, and while he'll rib me about it, at least he'll listen.

"You going soft?"

"Nah, it's not like that, but this girl…fuck me."

We slow down our sparring.

"I can't wait to meet the girl who has finally got you in a spin with your balls tied up," he cajoles. He's known me long enough now to know how I roll, and this isn't my normal behavior. "I'll shake her hand and give her a pat on the back, then wish her well, she's gonna need all the luck she can get."

"That's just it, imagining anyone, even you, putting your hands on her makes me want to commit murder."

Enzo smirks, ripping off his headgear as we come to a stop. We're both beat. "And here I was thinking it was

Jonas who had to be told who he can and can't lay his hands on."

Jonas is the man-whore of all of us, our younger cousin with the babyface and a penchant for undesirable women.

"Ain't that the truth."

"So, what are you gonna do?"

I shrug. "Date her, I guess."

He side-eyes me. "Fuck, man, you do have it bad."

I shake my head, shoving him in the shoulder as we go to the adjoining locker room to clean up and ride straight over to the warehouse. Fuck knows what I'm saying anymore.

My mind is on the new property we've finally acquired, and thanks to our substantial contribution to the mayor's upcoming campaign, we now have the permits to start the process of building; it took long enough. Then the casino will be finally ready after almost three years of hell.

Outside of business, I'm well aware I've been ignoring Tiffany's messages again to meet up with me, and then there's Allegra still wanting to do lunch. I've enjoyed fucking Tiffany in the past, there's a mutual attraction there, or should I say *was*. However, we're only compatible on a physical level, something that never seemed to bother me until now.

I don't know why this feels so different with Rayne. I want to taint her for all others.

"The prodigal son returns," Marco quips, using my line when I enter the building.

Loosening my tie, I nod at Darko and Dom standing in the doorway, keeping tabs as we arrive. I think back to finding and stringing up Rayne's ex the other night. It was good fun hauling him in. And despite her pleas, he did get roughed up, but we kept him alive.

I don't want any more complications this week. It's

been arranged with the Police Commissioner that the trafficking bust will be hijacked as soon as the boat docks. I know it will set the city alight and everyone will be circling. Let them. I want the fucking world to know that nobody comes into my town and tries to sneak underworld shit under my nose.

I own the underworld, and it's up to me who I let in. I don't employ an army of soldiers to keep watch over Boston for no good reason.

Rombaldi has no idea what's in store for him, and I would personally love to see the shock on his face when this goes down.

"You seem chipper," I say, as I give my brother a chin lift. I take a seat opposite him. Enzo walks over to the makeshift bar and pours us both a whisky.

He gives me a shit-eating grin. "I could say the same about you."

I flash him a grin. I'm planning on inviting Rayne to the Gala ball next week, so they're going to know about it soon enough.

I motion over to Dante, he's sitting next to Fynn, playing cards. They're a few drinks down, by the looks of it. "What's up with you?" I nod to my little brother Fynn.

"Need to get to Ma's. She's making meatballs, and I'm fucking starving."

"You fucking serious?" I grunt. "You called me all the way over here for an emergency."

Enzo passes me a whisky and snickers.

"This is an emergency! I haven't had a decent home-cooked meal in weeks."

I could ring Fynn's fucking neck sometimes. "Get your head in the game, Fynn. What you got for me, really?"

He puts his cards down and pushes a manilla folder across to me. "Dante and I have been tracking Senator

Mendes. Everything you need is right in there, the question is, after the raid, how are we gonna take him down? He'll still be at large while everyone else gets arrested."

The question he should be asking is *where.*

I open the file and take a quick look through the photos. I'm sure his wife would be only too interested to see what he gets up to in his spare time, none of it is very tasteful. In fact, it turns my stomach.

"You seen this?" I ask Santino and Jonas; they are sitting at the other end of the table. San hates politicians even more than I do.

"I can't fucking look at that shit," Santino says, disgusted.

The women, if you can call them that because they're just girls, don't even look legal. All of this shit affects Santino the most, I wouldn't say he's the most sensitive, but this crap just seems to do a number on him. His teenage sister, my cousin Bria is around the same age as some of these girls. It hits home.

All I see when I look at the black and whites—taken of him escorting girls here and there, sometimes in the back of his car, primarily different hotels scattered across the countryside where the girls get delivered to him—is my mother.

My sweet, beautiful Ma was used and abused in a small but deadly syndicate early on in her life. She originated from the same village as my father growing up. Though they never knew each other, she migrated with her parents as a child– they both passed away early on in her life, leaving her with poor relatives. She's a survivor if I've ever met one.

It's what keeps my head in the game, it reminds me of what I'm doing all of this for, and some wishful part of me hopes my father's looking down, seeing that I'm taking over his legacy, carrying on the family name.

Some say I'm an anti-hero, but that just makes me laugh.

I still control the drugs. I control the sex and strip clubs. I control gambling. I control who comes and goes in this city, that doesn't sound too saintly to me.

"Are we gonna put a bullet in the back of his head or string him out?" Enzo throws back his shot and winces as he slams the glass down. I down mine, too, with the same reaction.

"I wanna play with the fucker first, wait until after the raid. I'll decide then."

"I hear the Royale is almost ready?" Santino nods, referring to the casino Marco will be running. "About time."

"I'm on it with the contractors," Marco says. "Should all be underway in the next couple of months once the fit-out and landscapers come in, it's one hell of a job."

"Sure is an iconic building," Jonas comments, he's the wild card in the family, and the reason he hasn't had any major responsibilities in the family business just yet, organizing contractors with Marco is about the extent of it.

"You think you're just going to be screwing around with the showgirls?" I eye Jonas and then Fynn, as he's not much better.

Jonas' wide eye grin tells me all I need to know.

"Women are trouble, especially the help," Marco quips.

Enzo's eyes flick to mine, I ignore him. Rayne is not hired help if that's what he means. Plus, I make the fucking rules around here.

The gallery is a non-issue, it makes us money from the wealthy executives buying overpriced ridiculous pieces of art, and I have very little to do with it.

"C'mon, Angelo, showgirls get lonely too," Jonas says, giving me a wink.

"Best keep your brother under control." I eye Santino. "He's too pretty for me to fuck up."

I hear snickers around the table. Jonas, however, is entirely unperturbed as he flips me the bird.

I sit back and try not to think about Rayne and how I left her this morning; curled up in bed after I fucked her like a savage. Nothing can beat a morning like that.

At least I don't need to keep tabs on her. Keeping track of this lot is bad enough; sometimes I feel like I'm running a freaking circus.

———

"Word on the street is my big brother has a hot new piece of ass," says my sister, Valentina. She's a five-foot-six diva-princess with a smart mouth. Being twenty-three years old, she, of course knows everything.

It can be difficult not only being the head of a family like this but keeping my sister out of trouble proves to be more of a challenge each year she gets older. It doesn't help that she's stunning with dark hair down to her waist, olive skin, and deep blue eyes.

She's also a hundred miles a minute.

"Wash your mouth out, Valentina," Ma scolds from the stove where she's stirring the pan of meatballs and gravy.

"What I'd be asking is what you mean by 'word on the street'?" I give her a pointed look.

I give Ma a chaste kiss on the cheek as she turns to me and says, "What's this she's talking about, Angelo?" Though my mom has lived in America for over forty years, she still speaks as if she just left Sicily.

Each of my brothers follow suit greeting her as well as Enzo, but she keeps her piercing eyes on me.

"Nothing, Ma, she's stirring up trouble, like always." I give Valentina a glare.

"Don't shoot the messenger," she spouts with a cheesy grin.

I give her a withering look. "You talking crap about me again?" I turn towards Marco, because I know he's the instigator in all of this.

He holds his palms up in surrender. "I haven't said shit, just you didn't turn up at the club the other night, so it had to be about a girl."

"Fuck off," I bark.

Ma clips me around the head. "Language, Angelo!"

I kiss her on the cheek again. "Sorry, Ma."

Santino and Jonas arrive; they stampede the kitchen like bulls in a China shop.

"What's cooking, Mama M?" She smacks Jonas' hand that goes straight for the simmering pan on the stove.

"It's not ready yet and you haven't washed up," she admonishes.

"C'mon, Mama, I'm starving here," he says.

"Dinner's up in five minutes. Jonas, you can set the table since your mother will be here any minute."

Oh brilliant, Aunt Voula's coming. He does as she says, punching Fynn in the stomach as he passes by, catching him off guard.

"There are too many boys here," Valentina complains. "Why did you have to have so many boys, Mom?"

"Because I knew a girl would come along eventually." She winks over at Valentina, and they share a little smile.

It's good for Ma to have Valentina around so much with us boys always being so busy, it makes me feel less guilty about not seeing her all the time.

Valentina has her own interior design business, so she can work from wherever she wants to and whenever she wants to, although sometimes I wonder if she does anything at all. We've got her designing the new casino's decor and it's a massive job. It should keep her out of trouble for a while, at least.

"That's funny though, Angelo, because a birdie told me you cooked for a girl at your house the other night when you were supposed to be at the club." Valentina grins at me like a Cheshire cat.

"Yeah, where'd you hear that, Val?" I move into the dining room, hoping I can escape this whole fucking line of questioning. This is exactly what happens when you don't show up one time on poker night.

She taps her nose, telling me to mind my business as I give her another glare.

"Well, a man has to eat, doesn't he," I mutter.

"Yeah, he was eating alright," Dante mutters out the side of his mouth with a grin, and I elbow him hard in the ribs.

"Eww, I heard that." Valentina pulls a repulsed face.

I give Dante a slap upside the head.

"You cooked for the gallery girl?" Marco splutters on his beer. "And she survived?"

"Don't insult Nona's secret recipe, it worked like a charm."

"Double eww," Valentina complains again. "Save your sexcapades for your poker nights, I don't want to throw up before eating."

We part for Ma as she moves to the table and puts a basket of garlic bread in the middle, eying my sister.

"Valentina, who taught you to talk like that? That is not the talk of a young lady," Ma scolds.

Valentina points at me. Then Marco. Then Fynn. Then Dante. "Every last one of them, Mama. The first words they taught me in Italian were all the swear words, remember?"

"Hey, I want to get back on the subject of Angelo doing the hired help." Fynn laughs as all eyes fall on me. "Didn't you write a clause in the employee contracts about fraternizing with the staff, and we all had to sign it?" fast.

I point at him. "Shut it, shithead, or you'll be on shoveling duty for the rest of your natural life."

"Angelo!" Ma scolds again. "That cussing. I didn't bring up any of you with foul mouths, and here you are swearing and carrying on like you were brought up in a bar."

My phone rings just at the right time as I fish it out of my pocket and take a few steps away from the family shit show. Fuck knows how Valentina's caught wind about me cooking, good news travels fast.

I see Gus' name flash up on the screen and quickly swipe across.

"Gus."

"Boss," he pauses, "sending over the rest of Rayne Michaelson file that you asked for."

"Took long enough," I grunt.

There's a long pause. "Boss?"

"Still here."

"I have that meeting set up for you for next week."

The Russians, how pleasant. "Good. Give me the details later."

"And the summer house is ready to go," he adds.

"Excellent." I hang up abruptly and take a moment to stare out of the big back windows onto the vast field behind us. Littered with red maple trees, it's particularly stunning at this time of year, like something out of a storybook. It makes me proud that our mother is happy here.

I wonder how my little *Carina* will react when I ask her

to the ball, then take her to my home and spend the weekend there.

It crosses my mind that I'm breaking all my own rules, but I choose to ignore it like most things these days.

I've got a family dinner to get on with and then, God willing, a woman to attend to.

RAYNE

When I wake up, he's long gone. Only the creases in the pillow are any indication he was even here, well, that and his masculine scent still lingering.

I'm sure he's all too used to slipping away in the wee hours, never to return. An occupational habit, I'm sure.

When I finally roll out of bed, it's to go in search of aspirin because I have a Mariachi band playing in the back of my head.

I made a decision last night; when I was soaking in the tub consoling myself with wine, it came to me.

I'm like a cat on hot bricks because if Mia's captors find out what I'm planning, this could be very bad, but I don't know what else to do. I can't just sit around like a damn victim and let them control me and hurt my sister. I mean, what are the chances these bastards are really going to let her go after I get whatever information I can on Angelo, and realistically, what else can I possibly get on him? The process is slow. Sure, I know he's probably going to invite me to the ball, but then what? His place is like Fort Knox, it isn't like he's going to let me anywhere near his Fortress or the warehouse he's rumored to have, and I fear, pretty soon, they're going to realize that too. I have to take matters into my own hands.

I ventured to a shady part of the city that evening, walking into a downtown bar and asking around for a private investigator. It's the only thing I can think of to do. At least if I know where Mia's being held, I may be able to hatch a plan. I don't know what, but I feel like a sitting duck. Sitting ducks get nowhere. Sitting ducks end up dead.

Don't slip away from me, Mia. I'm coming...

This city is full of stinking sewer rats and I have to think like one of them.

I take a cab to the same neighborhood. I figure Sunday might be a little less crowded.

I meet him at a bar in a suspect part of town. Since I couldn't be sure I was not being followed, I took the subway, then two different buses to get here. I'll get a cab home since there's no way I'm doing that again.

I wear as best a disguise I can without looking like a complete weirdo. I glance at my phone and check the time. Nine o'clock.

Dirty Habits Saloon, at least the name is fitting.

It's one of those places that makes you want to disinfect yourself the minute you step inside. I don't even want to drink from the glass that I'm presented with after I order a glass of wine, and the man pours it from a cask. I sit at one of the tables in the better-lit area of the bar. There's no need to tempt fate.

My phone chimes as soon as I sit down.

He's here.

The only reason I haven't gone to a reputable P.I. is the fact that since Angelo owns most of the high-profile politicians and police, I don't know who I can trust. Nobody here will know me. Not that I intend on giving him any information other than the fact my sister is missing and I'm trying to find her. Surely, they have access to security footage from when they snatched her outside of her work. There has to be some trace, and I'm going to find it.

A few moments later, the chair next to me moves, and the man I'm paying an astronomical amount of money to help sits next to me…he's… not what I expected.

For one, he's a little too smartly dressed to be in this place. If we were trying to look inconspicuous, then we both failed. He's handsome, a little older than me, with short blonde, trimmed hair and attractive features. He's wide-set and appears more like a bouncer than a P.I. He has piercing, almost bronze-colored eyes and a dark, heavy-set brow.

"Jessica?" he says, his voice quiet.

Yes, I gave a fake name.

I nod. "Hello, Mr. Russo."

He glances around, a frown on his face. "I understand you need my help?"

I nod. "I'll cut to the chase. I've reason to believe that my sister's in trouble —" I mean, *do I just blurt it out?* I guess it's best to get straight to the point. "Which is why I'm here, in this charming place."

His lips twitch. "Nobody here talks, which is why it's the best place to not be seen or heard, which is what you said you wanted."

It's a real slice of Americana and I want to be out of here.

"I don't know who else to turn to," I admit, unsure if I can fully trust him despite his credentials.

As if reading my mind, he gives me a chin lift. "Whatever you say to me is held in the strictest confidence, but if you want my help, I will need your sister's name and some details about her, where she lives, works, where she was seen last, that kind of thing. Any small thing you can think of can be of help."

I close my eyes momentarily and breathe deeply. "How does this work?"

"I get the 5k now, and the rest when I find her."

My eyes go wide. Not at the 5k but his admission. "You think you can find her and yet I haven't even told you anything about her or the situation."

He sits back in his chair and smirks. "None of those details matter. I find people who don't want to be found, it's what I do. There isn't a stone in this city that I can't get under, behind or over, so the logistics aren't for you to worry about. That's my job."

I go to get the envelope out of my bag. I had to withdraw most of my savings, and I'll have to sell the earrings Angelo gave me to pay the rest until my divorce settlement comes through. My hands shake even though I feel strangely at ease with this man. He doesn't even look shady.

He shakes his head slightly. "Not now. When we part, I'll take the cash out of your purse without anyone seeing."

"Okay." I nod.

He gives me a level gaze. "So, where do we begin?"

I give him the details, starting with her name, address, cell number, where she works, and then where I believe they snatched her from. All the while, I try not to fidget and act nervous, though my heart is racing so fast that I'm almost certain he can hear it.

He doesn't even jot it down.

I take a couple of deeper breaths then he asks, "Have the kidnappers given you a ransom amount and a timeframe?"

"It's not quite that kind of situation," I say, clutching my glass vigorously.

"Okay, so explain that to me. What do they want?"

Obviously, I need to tell him I'm being bribed, I get that. But I can't tell him everything. I still have to be careful. Everyone knows Angelo Medici. *Everyone.* He could be in his pocket, too, for all I know.

I clear my throat. "They wanted me to get information from a certain person of interest to them. A work colleague..." Seems plausible. "And in exchange for the extraction of information and intel on him, they said they'd let her go."

I'm not telling him where I work. *This is going to be fine.*

He nods. "Who is this person?"

I close my eyes. "I can't tell you that."

He frowns. "Without a name, I'm flying blind here, Jessica."

Shit.

"They're high profile. I can't tell you right at this moment who he is. Maybe in time when I get my head around it and am able to..." I pause. *What have I really got to lose here?* "Trust you," I add.

"You're not making life very easy, but I understand if they're high profile and you want to protect yourself."

I almost sag in relief. "Uh, they are wealthy and affluent, and I'll be frank – I don't know who I can trust, so I'll give you the basics first." *I've gotta lie better.*

He nods in approval. "What have they asked you to get so far?"

"Just the colleague's schedule, diary entries, appointments, this person's general day-to-day activities and where they go, where they'll be this week – those kinds of things. It's not like they've asked me to bust into the safe and steal the crown jewels or anything."

He frowns. "Forgive me for saying, but it seems a little extreme that they'd kidnap your sister and then hold her to ransom for some information on a work colleague. This will make things exceedingly difficult if I don't know all the logistics."

I swallow hard.

"I don't mean to be rude, Mr. Russo, but I can't give you any more information without incriminating myself further. All the details I've given you are what I know so far. My sister's captor telephones me once a week for an update from an untraceable number, and I email my findings to a no-reply email."

"I'll need a copy of that email address and your phone records. Have you spoken to your sister at all in this time?"

I nod. "Once, but only for a few seconds."

He looks slightly relieved.

I watch him carefully. "I need to know…"

He takes a sip of his drink and then meets my gaze. "If I think they're going to kill her?"

I bite my lip, tears forming in my eyes. "Yes," I whisper.

He sets his glass down and leans forward as his elbows rest on the table. "It depends on who I'm dealing with, and I don't know that right at this moment. It could be petty criminals — though it seems odd that they'd go to these lengths — it could be mafia, underworld figures… If I knew your colleague's name, it would make things easier."

I shake my head. "No, not until I feel I have to. I'm sorry, but it's the only bargaining chip I have left, and I don't mean to be rude, but we're meeting in a shady bar in a suspicious part of town I didn't even know existed. This could get me killed, and Mia…" I trail off, unable to finish.

He gives me a crooked smile, but I stand my ground. He can make a cute face all he wants, I'm not changing my mind. I'll give him more when he gives me something. For now, he can concentrate on tracing Mia's last known steps, that's enough to go on for the moment.

"As you wish," he says, tapping the rim of his glass with his fingers. "At least I've got somewhere to start, but I am going to need a few things from you in return."

I reluctantly take a large gulp of my disgusting, cheap wine. I need something to steady the nerves. "What do you need?"

"A trace on your phone, for one, when he calls again, I can try and trace the call and get a location."

My eyes go wide. "Are you serious? I thought you couldn't do that with private numbers?"

He chuckles. "Why would you think that?"

My heart accelerates at this information. "Anything for a price, right?"

He taps his nose. "Now you're getting the gist of it. I should be able to get some footage if she was snatched in a public place. That will be the crucial turning point, they obviously bundled her into a car so I'll need her work address as well as home. The way the city has cameras everywhere, I doubt they're smart enough to evade all of them, even a partial plate number can be instrumental."

I grip my glass again, unafraid that it may shatter at the sheer force hold I have on it. That is meant to be good news, but I feel like hurling at imagining my sister being snatched off the street. I truly hope I never get to witness that footage.

"Okay." I nod. "I'll agree to the trace. If it's going to help...I just want my sister back...I... I have to get her back, Mr. Russo." My voice cracks, and he looks up at me with sympathy. I need to be strong, just for a little longer.

I don't care how desperate I seem or sound, I'll do anything to get Mia back, *anything.*

He nods to my phone on the table, and I hand it to him.

Whatever he does next, I don't even want to see. I don't care if he bugs my fucking phone, he can take any means necessary.

About five minutes later, he tells me the software has been downloaded and the bug is in place.

I can't help the tremble in my hands when I slip the phone back into my purse.

"I have to go," I say, wanting to be out of here. "I'll get that information to you tonight."

He nods. "I'll call you on a secure line with any updates. If you think of anything, anything at all that may help, then here's my card." He reaches into his swish-looking jacket's inside pocket and pulls out a card. I take it without looking.

"Okay. Thank you."

"We'll stand now, and you'll embrace me like we're old friends and I'll take the envelope."

Holy shit, this is so cloak and dagger.

"What assurance do I have you're not just going to scam me?" I say, as he starts to stand.

He gives me a look. "You don't. But right now, I'm your only option, and I want the rest of my money, doll. I don't like working for free."

His word needs to be good enough, though he wrote nothing down and clicked around with my phone. Probably to see where I live so he can come and murder me later; so much for my fake identity. I realize it's stupid and probably futile, but I have to try. I'll die trying.

I follow his lead as we embrace for a split second. I don't even feel his hand slide into my purse, he's so quick and silent that I don't feel a thing.

"I'll be in touch."

"Thank you," I whisper, but I don't think he hears me. I

watch him disappear across the dull, lit bar and out of sight.

I quickly make for the door, lowering my head and walking briskly until I get as far away from the bar as possible. While the street is well lit, there are unscrupulous people everywhere and I don't wish to meet any of them. I manage to hail a cab pretty easily and only when I'm safely in the back, clutching my purse to my chest, do I let out a rush of air in my relief.

What the ever-living fuck am I doing?

Do I even know anymore? Have I completely lost my mind?

Insanity and desperation clearly tick all of those boxes.

I stare out the window as the driver leads me away from this stinking part of the city.

I just want to be safely back at my apartment, so I can think about what the hell I've just done in the privacy of my own four walls. I don't see how I had any other option, and time is ticking while they are doing God knows what to my sister. I mean, what are the chances they are taking proper good care of her?

I want to be sick thinking about some of the possibilities. I push that as far from my mind as I possibly can. If I go there, I will never come back out again and that's not going to help her or my nerves in the process.

I rest back on the headrest. The cab seems to move in slow motion. I just feel so weary, and I want all this to be over. *When is it going to be over?*

One thing that kind of gave me some hope was that the P.I. seemed to know what he was doing at least, even though it crosses my mind that there's a very good chance he's a professional con-artist. However, when I put the word out and did some research, his name came up more than once. I'm flying blind, but my options are minimal, all I can do now is see what he comes up with.

I reach into my pocket absently and pull out the business card he gave me, staring at it like a lifeline, and really right now, it's my only one.

His name and contact details are written in tiny scriptwriting, simple and straightforward, much like our conversation in some respects. And while I'm not mildly confident, the way he held himself and the way he seemed quite unphased by the sketchy details I gave him, gives me the hope I need to hang on to, no matter how futile.

I immediately punch his number into my phone, so I'll know it's him when he calls.

Maybe he's the one who's going to save us and blow this whole kidnapping to smithereens, wouldn't that be perfect. And I know I'm counting on him way too much to come through for a guy I've just met. My eyes flick down to the card again as I read his name in fancy writing.

Enzo Russo.

My savior or my swindler. I don't know which.

18

ANGELO

I swirl the remaining whisky in my tumbler before necking the rest down. The burn hitting the back of my throat feeling extremely similar to the way I felt when I left Rayne sleeping in her apartment. Everything about her makes me burn.

I have more on my mind than I know what to do with right at this moment, yet it doesn't stop the ache to feel her, smell her, be inside her.

Unfortunately, duty calls and my mind is on the job. The days that follow only fill me with more angst than ever before, reminding me that this is the life I chose.

The raid is all over the news. I sit back and watch with my scotch in hand, contemplating the fickleness of life. One moment you can think you are on top of your game and that you're in control of the world around you, the next your empire goes up in smoke, much like Rombaldi's right now.

We saved him for ourselves, that was always the deal, and I'm reveling in the massive paycheck that has just landed in our account for this latest sting from certain politicians. Sure they're dirty, but at least they're not child molesters. I share the cut around; we all have our parts to play, and this is still a business after all.

The clubs I run don't employ trafficked women or obviously children. The women who strip and work in the sex clubs are not there by force, nor are they high on drugs, and they're paid well. I may not be a saint, but I do have principles. I still want to be able to look my mother in the eye and not feel like a total scumbag.

Aside from keeping my businesses flowing and bringing in more money, it also sends a message that I won't tolerate anyone going against my rule in this city.

If they want to try, they better have one hell of an army.

If Petrov and his underground betting and gambling operation think they can better me and the Medici crime family, he's sniffing up the wrong tree. I have a thirst for blood and a reputation for vengeance, and I won't tolerate anyone trying to take or change what I've got.

His time will come, and soon.

Rocco and the soldiers brought the kingpin in themselves, taking down Rombaldi's guards in a sniper-style situation, leaving just him standing. He had nowhere to go, and boy, it felt good finally getting him where we wanted him. I didn't hit the final blow, but I witnessed it once we got back to the warehouse. He deserved everything he got; jail was too good for him. He could've bought off too many people, and then he'd be back out on the street again, ready to lead his filthy, rotten army of sewer rats. Pricks like him never stay down for long.

Senator Mendes is next, and I plan on playing with him just a little bit first to see what else he may be hiding. We have enough on his sex trafficking preferences to nail him for the rest of time, and I do want him exposed and shamed for what he's done, but I also want more names.

This is just the tip of the iceberg because there are always more of these scumbags lurking around in plain sight, pretending to be a family man with Christian values. What a fucking joke.

Rombaldi and Mendes had it coming, and I don't mind spreading the message of what's tolerated and what isn't.

My phone pings as I tear myself away from the CNN afternoon bulletin, it's Enzo, again. He's been trying to reach me all afternoon. I know it can't be anything to do with the raid because I've seen it all on TV, and it's going down as one of the most biggest busts in history.

The truth is, I don't feel like conversing with anyone tonight, not my brothers, my cousins, or Enzo; I want my girl.

While bringing her into this life is selfish and wrong, it won't stop me. Nothing can stop me. I'll protect her. I'll kill for her.

I get up to pour myself another shot, ignoring my phone. I shouldn't get shitfaced if I plan on paying her another visit tonight, we're supposed to be laying low after all.

I know everyone is over at Fortress, yet I am here sitting alone.

I walk over to the large sliding glass doors, loosening my tie so it hangs around my neck. I smirk when I think about using my tie to keep Rayne trussed up to my bed so she can't move. I'd maybe gag her too, then have my cock in her balls deep so she can't cry out as I punish her over and over. That might teach her to get too drunk to fuck when I visit her late at night. I need to feel her taut body against mine, her soft lips, her touch...I need her so fucking bad.

I decide to have another look at the profile Gus sent over to my email.

Rayne June Michaelson. It has her date of birth, education, current address, social security, police check, and marital status. Everything important, including family, deceased and living.

I stare at the last line.

Siblings; Mia Jayne Michaelson, born February 2nd, 2002

I read it again.

I swish the drink and my brow furrows, if I remember correctly, her sister died in a car accident the same night as her parents. I look at it now, wondering if I just dreamt it up, though I rarely get these things wrong. Maybe it's a stepsister or something.

I'm not sure why I didn't notice it before. I guess I was more interested in her marital status and getting that idiot ex-husband away from her.

Rayne doesn't have a social media profile, I already checked, but this new piece of information has me beat. I grab my phone and type Mia's name into the Instagram search, it brings up everyone with the same name, of course. I click on a few profiles before finding what I may be looking for. The beautiful young woman has dark shoulder-length hair, which is cut into a blunt, long bob, but she has the same green eyes and pretty skin. I stare at the profile.

New Yorker through and through, fashion mogul, lover of Starbucks, and six-inch heels.

It's not that which grabs me though, it's because I can see Rayne in her smile straight away. As I scroll down through some random photos, I see a picture of them together, a selfie; they're outside Café La in New York. Rayne has her sunglasses pushed up on top of her head, her golden locks a little shorter than she wears them now, and they're both laughing in the picture taken six months ago. Rayne's eyes are lit up, she looks really happy. And she's fucking gorgeous, the caption *just hanging with my sis* below it with a love heart emoji.

To say I'm confused would be the understatement of the year, there aren't many photos of Rayne on her sister's profile, I take a screenshot and decide I'll ask her about it later, or maybe do some delving of my own first. *Why did she lie to me?*

I dial Gus and look out to the fading light of the day.

"Boss."

"Did you get everything on Rayne Michaelson?"

"Everything you're looking at. The girl's clean, not even a parking ticket."

"Hmm." I stroke my chin as I think.

I always know what to do in any situation. No point asking him to dig deeper, he did that already. I guess I have to go straight to the source. I have an unsettling feeling in my bones, which I've felt here and there, but haven't paid much attention to. Now my interest is piqued, and I need to know why she told me her sister was dead when she's clearly not.

There's a part of me that knows nobody is this perfect, there are skeletons in every closet. If she knew the real me, she would run as fast as her heels could carry her.

I sigh, downing my whisky with one throw. I don't even feel the burn.

I should have been at Fortress hours ago, but sometimes I need to take a moment to myself after a kill to wash my hands of my sins.

I need to message Rayne and ask her to the Gala this coming weekend, or maybe I'll just show up at her place again, and this time I'll shove her down on her knees to take my cock while she explains why she's made a very grave decision in lying to me.

That's when I glance at the message from Enzo and narrow my eyes.

Pick up the fucking phone! We've got a big problem.

I sigh. A man can't get a fucking break without someone interrupting. I'm about to dial back when my doorbell rings, and I frown. I'm not expecting anyone.

I look at the security camera on my computer screen and I see Allegra on my front doorstep.

I've been an asshole and not even messaged her back about going for dinner before she leaves the country. I can't exactly help it if my cock's been busy this week.

My housekeeper, Sophia, knocks on my open door a few moments later and pokes her head in.

"Mr. Medici. I have Allegra Medici here to see you."

I feel somewhat irritated. I don't have time for this shit. While I like Allegra, and she's a part of the family, I've got important shit to do and now I'm going to be late.

I interlink my fingers as she waits for my answer. "Thank you, Sophia, send her in."

"Can I offer you something to eat, sir? Or your guest?"

I give her a rare smile. "I meant no the last five times you asked me, but I appreciate that you don't want me to starve, and she won't be staying."

"Very well, sir."

Sophia takes her leave and a few moments later, I hear the click-clack of heels down my marble floor and then Allegra appears in my doorway.

As usual, she's stunning. Dressed in a tight-fitting black skirt and a lacy-fitted blouse synched at the waist. Her dark hair is shining like she just stepped out of a runway magazine.

I stand. "Allegra, to what do I owe this unexpected visit?"

I move around my desk as we embrace. I kiss her cheek

on each side as she clutches a black Chanel purse and stands back to assess me.

"You look tired," she says. I notice she's holding onto a takeout bag that smells distinctly like my favorite tacos.

"Thanks, nice to see you, too."

"I was in the neighborhood, and I thought you may like a little snack." She waves the bag at me.

"I have a personal chef and you're bringing me Richie's tacos?"

She grins. "I bet you haven't eaten yet, though, have you?"

I shake my head and take the bag out of her hand. "You know me way too well."

"Just looking out for you. Somebody has to."

She takes a seat in the chair opposite.

"Would you like something to drink?" I ask.

"Whatever you're having."

I give her a look. "You want a straight bourbon?"

She shrugs. "It's been that kind of day, Angelo. Trust me, I don't want to rehash it."

I walk over to my liquor cabinet, conveniently located in my study. I top up my glass and pour another.

"So, this is just a social visit?" I muse, walking back to my desk and handing her the glass.

She takes a sip, her eyes on me as I round the desk again and take a seat.

"Fine. I confess, I was worried you were still mad with me, and you know how I hate bad blood between us."

I frown. "And this is because…"

She rolls her eyes. "I spoke with your new squeeze, remember, and you weren't happy about it."

"My new squeeze?" I give her a pointed look.

"I just worry about you, Angelo, I always have. We've

always been close, ever since... before Roberto and I got together, when things were simpler."

I don't want to cast my mind back to when Allegra and I had a brief dalliance. It was a long time ago, before Roberto. I never outrightly told him, but I'm sure he guessed. The trouble with me back then is I could never commit. Allegra wanted the things most women wanted and I couldn't give those things to her. I only ever wanted that later, with Lucia.

We were brief, and it was over long before it ever began. We're too alike. Allegra is sharp and cunning, a lot like me; she'll do whatever it takes to be the best. There's nothing wrong with that, hell, I respect it, she's done well for herself. But I want a woman who is my equal, not someone craving power, wanting more, never being truly happy. I don't want any of that.

And that's why we'll never work. I couldn't do it, not after Roberto...

"I don't remember things being simpler, but I do remember us being better off as friends."

I study her as I take a long pull on my bourbon. *Why is she here?*

She stares back at me, and something hits me in the chest. Is she actually here to...?

"That's because of Roberto," she says simply. "And we'd feel guilty if we were to start something again."

I almost splutter my drink. Is she mad?

She's a beautiful woman, I can't deny that, but we're never going to be a couple. She was married to my cousin! Last time I checked, he's still dead in the ground.

"Allegra, what are you trying to say exactly?" I sound annoyed, even to my own ears.

She levels my gaze. "I'm not trying to say anything. I

came here to say sorry and feed you your favorite takeout, not to get into a fight." She's been drinking, I realize.

"Do you think I'm not with you because I'd feel guilty?"

Her lips twitch into a half-smile. "Aren't you?"

I lean forward, my elbows hitting the desk as I deliberately meet her gaze.

"No, Allegra, I'm not. You were married to my cousin, one of my best friends. It wouldn't just be an insult to his legacy, it would bring shame on the family, you know this. You're like a sister to me…"

"We fucked," she reminds me curtly. "We fucked a lot before Roberto. We had something, Angelo."

"*Had* being the operative word, Allegra. You need to drop it, this isn't good for either of us."

"Why? I'm just telling you how I feel, like we've always been able to do with one another."

I run a hand through my hair. "Why are you bringing this up now?" I demand, my temper flaring. "You're trying to stir trouble where none needs to be stirred, and I don't like it. You don't need to complicate things."

"I'm not trying to complicate things, Angelo. I care for you. I guess seeing you with…that woman from the gallery brought it all back up, and I began to wonder," she says, her lip trembling slightly, and I know I've upset her. I don't mean to, but she can't talk like this. I won't allow it. She's Roberto's widow. I almost shudder at the thought of it. "You've been single a long time, so have I…."

"What do you think Mario and the family would say?" I bark as she flinches ever so slightly. "Do you think that's respectful to your dead husband and father-in-law?"

"Angelo, don't act like you're on some kind of high horse. You wanted it as much as I did, and I know we still have a spark. You can't deny it. We're one and the same."

I take a sobering breath and try to calm myself. "The

spark we had was back in college, before you met Roberto, and I was young and reckless. I'm not the same person I was back then. I won't piss all over Roberto's memory, Allegra, and you shouldn't, either."

Her eyes narrow. "You just won't admit it."

"I admit you're a very attractive woman, but be smart, we can't go there, Allegra. I will *never* go there. You need to accept that once and for all if we're ever going to have any kind of friendship."

She stares at me unmoving. "Fine. If that's how you feel."

"That *is* how I feel. It's probably best you leave, I've got work to do."

She looks crestfallen, but I find it hard to reach out to her. She's clearly taken all of my rare bouts of kindness and concern with her as something else. I have never, ever hit on her after she was with Roberto or after he died. She's family. I had no fucking clue she was still hung up on me, I thought that ship had sailed a long time ago.

"Angelo, don't leave things like this. I wasn't trying to stir trouble." I go to stand, but she remains seated. "Don't be mad at me, I couldn't bear it."

I don't return her smile as she reluctantly stands.

"I'm not mad at you. I'm just confused. I don't want there to be this strange thing between us."

She reaches for me, brushing her hands up to the lapels of my jacket. "You always looked good in a suit."

"Looked?" I note. "Past tense."

She rolls her eyes. "You can't blame a girl for trying, Angelo. You're a handsome man, it would take a strong and competent woman to be able to give you what you need." Her hands still rest on my chest.

She smells so fucking good. Like a rich woman. Like a woman who could take any man she wants, maybe we could have been something in another lifetime, but it won't be in this one.

"After all, we're cut from the same cloth, aren't we?"

Something about the way she snakes her body closer to mine makes me recoil. My body stiffens as she moves her lips to my ear. "We both have needs that other people could never fulfill, Angelo."

I swallow hard. "You're making a mistake," I mutter, my jaw clenched as her lips graze my jaw… "Allegra…"

"I don't bite," she whispers. "Let me show you how good it could be, don't throw away our chance together because of what other people might think. Fuck me like one of your whores if you want to, bend me over the desk and punish me, it'll be our dirty little secret."

She rubs her pussy into my thigh as my heart races at her intrusion.

I don't fucking want this.

"We don't even have to talk."

"Stop it."

"What if I don't want to?"

"Allegra…"

She laughs, but it sounds cold. "Hurt me, Angelo, do it. I want you to. I want you to fuck me like you hate me."

I shake my head as the realization hits and she presses her lips into mine. I grab her wrists and shove her back.

"Allegra!"

"Angelo, what are you doing?"

"I said stop. You're crossing a line. Listen to me! I don't fucking want this, do you hear me?"

She steps back and rubs her wrists where I grabbed her. "Angelo…"

"For fuck sake, we can't do this. Get out."

She looks hurt as confusion crosses her face, but I'm not playing games. I'm done.

"I thought…I thought you…"

"Please, just go before you do any more damage. You've been drinking, this is obviously an error of bad judgment on your part."

Anger flashes in her eyes, followed by humiliation. I never meant to hurt her, but there is no way to gently let her down.

She swipes her purse off the desk and stomps to the door. "Your loss, Angelo. Don't come crawling back to me when you need something."

I shake my head at her retreating figure.

This is precisely what I don't need.

19

RAYNE

When I fish out my phone from my bag and see the No Caller ID, I want to faint. I try not to freak out, but this is always the part that makes me the most anxious.

I wish Angelo were here.

I internally kick myself. I've no idea where that thought came from or why I would wish it. Nevertheless, he's the type of person who would know what to do in this kind of situation with Mia.

I know he could help me.

As strange as it is, in the times we've been together, I've felt safer with him than I have with anyone ever before. How I let myself get involved to this degree shocks me. There's no reason to feel safe with someone like Angelo, none at all, but that's exactly how I feel.

I stare at the phone, and hope blooms in my chest when I think about Enzo Russo and the fact that he may be able to get a trace on the call or IP address, or better still that he's already found something.

I flick the screen across to answer.

"Hello?"

"Change of plans, Miss Michaelson." The words hang like dread in the pit of my stomach the second they are spoken.

I swallow hard. "What do you mean?"

There's a long pause. "I no longer need information."

If this is meant to be good news, then why does my heart rate kick up a notch?

I wait, afraid that one breath out of place will change the outcome.

"What you've provided isn't enough."

Panic swirls through me as one hand reaches into my hair. "I've got more. I'm getting closer every time –"

"It isn't enough."

"Please," I beg, "I'll do anything…"

"I want him dead."

I blink once, twice, then clear my throat. "Did I just hear you right? You said you want him –"

"I'm not in the business of repeating myself, but you heard correctly. The stakes have changed and I've no choice, which means *you* have no choice, that's if you ever want to see your sister alive again."

I feel like I may actually faint for real. *Dead?* They can't be fucking serious.

I stand there frozen in between my dining room and the kitchen. "Dead?" I whisper. "I can't do that."

I can't kill Angelo Medici. What kind of drugs are these people on?

"Then I'll tie her hands and feet and toss her into the Charles."

I fist my forehead trying to think, but it's hopeless. They have me. They have me at every turn.

"Why do you hate him so much?" I half shriek. "Why can't you get someone else to do your dirty work? I'm not a fucking assassin!"

A soft chuckle sends a shiver down my spine. "No, which is exactly why it's perfect. He won't be expecting it, it'll come out of left field. Since he's so taken with you, it seems I've chosen well."

"I need to talk to Mia." My voice sounds strangled. "I need to talk to her now."

I can't do this.

"You're in no position to make demands…"

"Fuck you!" I spit. "You keep changing the rules to suit your own selfish needs. I did everything you said. I continue to do it and put myself in danger every single day. And now I have to kill him?" I know I sound hysterical, but this just went way past complicated.

"I can change the rules as I see fit," the voice tells me. "The game has taken a new turn. He's no longer useful to me and my cause, and once you take out the captain, the crew will shortly follow."

I swallow hard.

This is all they want; power, domination. It's all based on money and greed, and it makes me sick.

They want me to kill the head of the Boston Mafia. Could this bullshit get any more surreal?

"I need Mia," I repeat, trying not to lose it. "I need my sister…"

"Your needs are not my concern."

"If I don't get proof that Mia is still alive, then the deal's off," I say, except I've no idea where that outburst comes from. "You can say and do what you want, but I'm the only person who can do this for you, and we both know it."

I'm insane, but calling their bluff may be the only thing keeping me in the game, and I'm running out of options.

I think the caller has gone, but then I hear, "I will send you a photo of your sweet, dear little sister unharmed with a short video. You'll receive instructions on what you're to do next with no questions asked. Once your task has been completed, we will leave Mia in an undisclosed location."

"Alive," I reiterate, like I have any say in the matter. "She gets delivered unharmed."

"As you wish."

The phone goes dead.

Just like that, I'm left hanging. I grip the wall and I think I'm going to faint or just shrivel up and die.

I want to vomit thinking about what they're doing to her and how scared she must be. I will find this asshole if it's the last thing I do. I will hunt them to the ends of the earth and kill them with my bare hands. I will avenge her. The more the days go on, the more this inferno inside me builds.

I scream. The only thing that stops me from throwing my phone and smashing it into a million pieces is that it's the only connection I have to my sister.

I'm in too deep, way over my head, and I've nowhere left to turn.

Kill Angelo Medici?

Holy shit. I'm many things, but I know that I'm not a killer. I can't do it. And even if I could, how the hell would they expect me to carry out such a task? He'd see it coming a mile away.

I need to talk to Enzo. He's my only hope.

I move to the bathroom, splash some cold water on my face, and stare at my reflection. I don't even recognize the person who looks back at me. She used to be full of life, her eyes used to sparkle, and she was pretty and ambitious. Now she just seems lost. How fucking pathetic.

My phone pings again, and I glance down as I pat my face dry with a towel.

It's a photo of Mia blindfolded and tied to a chair; she's

holding a piece of paper with today's date. I zoom in on the picture and nearly gag.

She's alive. Thank fuck.

I can't take any more. My stomach heaves, and I just make it to the toilet, where I hurl into the bowl until I've nothing left to vomit. It's all just too much.

When I'm done, I sit down on the cold tiles and rest my head back on the wall. I click out of the message and flick my phone to Enzo's number, dialing him with a shaky hand.

I need to get a grip.

He answers pretty quickly. "Enzo Russo."

"It's me….. umm…. Jessica," I whisper, unsure why I'm whispering in my own house, but it somehow seems safer that way.

"Ah, Jessica, are you all right?"

"No, I'm not. They called again, just now."

"I'm on it, I've got my guy tracing –"

I panic. Everything has me jumpy and on guard. "I thought you worked alone?"

"I have an IT guy. Trust me, if it can be traced, my guy can find it. He works for me exclusively."

I swallow hard. "I have an even bigger problem; the demands are getting um … much worse than I could ever have imagined."

"Worse, in what way? Actually … don't tell me over the phone, I'll come meet you. Where are you?"

"I'm at home, but I can drive downtown."

"I'll meet you at the Esplanade Harbor View in an hour."

"Okay," I puff out exasperated. I've no idea how I'm going to pull myself up and get off the floor to drive downtown, but somehow, I have to. Enzo Russo is my lifeline.

"We're going to get this fucker. I promise you, I will do everything in my power to help you."

"Thank you." I know I sound defeated and less than enthusiastic, but I don't rightly give a fuck given the circumstances.

I've no idea if Enzo is taking me for a ride or if I can trust him, but I guess I'm about to find out. "Do you think you can find them?" I ask though I'm dreading the answer.

"This isn't my first rodeo, kid, just sit tight and let me deal with it. I'll see you soon."

We hang up, and it's only then, due to my foggy brain, that I realize he didn't answer the question.

I don't know what the fuck I'm going to do. Scream. Panic. Beg for mercy?

I don't care what it takes, I'll do it.

Even kill him? Well, I can't fucking do that. I'm not a murderer.

If I hadn't applied for this stupid fucking job at Fortress Galleries, we wouldn't be in this mess now. If only I had known it was owned by the mob back then, I would have thought twice about it.

I dress warmly in sweats and a baseball cap; I don't bother with the wig anymore. In fact, I don't give a flying hoot what I look like right now. The world can go to hell.

I feel like I'm going into combat, a battle that is so far out of my league that it doesn't seem real.

Then there's the daunting task of having to tell Enzo about Angelo and how I'm now supposed to kill him! There has to be another way.

Angelo is a mass of contradictions.

All the things I thought I knew about him, and yet I know that he's nothing like the ruthless barbarians that have Mia. He couldn't come close to that because at least you know exactly where you stand with Angelo.

I slip out of my apartment building and take a cab to the Esplanade, my heart racing the entire time.

It's late in the evening, and all of the restaurants surrounding us are winding down for the night. He's not hard to find, sitting on a bench under a southern live oak that looks like it's stood the test of time. I wish I could say the same.

"We meet again," he says, looking a little grave when he greets me, which does nothing for my nerves.

"Thanks for seeing me so late," I reply, having no idea why I'm thanking him. He's being paid rather handsomely to be here after all.

"Take a seat." He gestures to the bench next to him.

I plonk myself down. "Did you find anything yet?" I ask quickly.

"The call came through encrypted, Jessica, it's very difficult to –"

"So that's a no." I put my head into my hands. I can't even hide my grief and sadness anymore; I take a few deep breaths before losing it altogether. "My name's not Jessica, you know, but I bet you already knew that."

I don't have to look up at him to know he holds a knowing expression on that immaculate face, he seems way too handsome and sure of himself to be in this line of work. Like he should have a desk job, as a banker or stock-broker. Not a P.I. who may or may not be set out to rip me off.

"I had a hunch," he says quietly. "Plus, I followed you home."

That makes me sit up and take note. "You followed me?" I gasp, though I am not sure why that surprises me.

"Look ….. uh, Rayne, that's your name, isn't it? You know it's hard to help you when you won't help me and tell me basic information, such as your real name. Lying to me only hinders this whole operation. We could have cut several corners if you'd have just given me the truth and not just some version of it."

The next sound out of my mouth sounds like a strangled cry. As if this wasn't going to be a problem. I'm such an idiot.

"I need to know it all from the start. God knows how long this has set us back. How can I find any trace of your sister when you don't tell me the truth, or tell me the simple details of your colleague?"

I swallow hard. So many lies. "I'm sorry, all right, I wasn't thinking straight since my sister has been kidnapped and is currently tied up, God knows where, and I can't even help her. Nobody can help me. I'm fucked. And now the demands are just getting stupid, now I have to ki–" I stop in my tracks.

"Now you have to what?" he repeats.

Tears start to fall down my face; I can't stop them anymore. I'm at everyone's mercy except my own.

A strange thing happens at that moment. I feel his hand on my back, comforting me, and I welcome it because I am fucking human after all. It's a soft gesture and it has a calming effect.

"I have to kill him. My… colleague. They sent a photo of Mia tied up. He said they'll throw her into the Charles if I don't do it…"

He frowns. "The stakes have definitely gotten higher."

"There's a file coming through tonight with all the details. I don't know anything yet of how or where or when."

He nods like he understands, but he has no clue about my dilemma right now. How can he? He's a P.I., not a cold-blooded would-be murderer. "Show me the photo."

I reach for my phone in my pocket and hold it toward

him, I can't even look at it, or I may throw up again, and I really don't want to do that in front of him.

He looks sympathetic, at least. "Despite how horrific this is for you, showing you some proof is a good thing, Rayne. They want what they want pretty desperately."

"Meanwhile, Mia is still alone and suffering." If my mind wanders for long enough, I may just will my heart to stop beating right now.

"I'm sorry, I really am. Obviously, the situation has escalated much quicker than I anticipated," he says. "This person wants revenge in a big way, and what alarms me even more is they haven't asked for money."

"I don't have any."

"No, but clearly you could get it if you work together." He looks deep in thought.

"What else do you need from me?" I swallow down my fear.

He glances at me. "Everything. We need that file; the contents are crucial. I think we should go to the diner around the corner and have a coffee to discuss everything. You can tell me about what happened from the start. And no more secrets."

I nod. It's more than reasonable.

"If you're honest with me, this will be a lot easier on the both of us," he adds.

"I understand, I'm sorry, Enzo. I'm way out of my league here, and it's not like I've ever been in this kind of situation before." I've no idea how to tell him that the 'colleague' is the head of the Boston Mafia, and the man I'm also falling for.

But it has to come out, all of it. I can't do this on my own, I'm going to have a nervous breakdown.

He gives me a kind smile as I wipe my tears with my sleeve.

"You know the red kind of suited you," he says, gesturing towards my hair, as I realize I have a messy bun sticking out the back of my baseball cap.

I laugh a little despite myself, glancing up at him. "Now, who's lying?"

He chuckles. "Let's get you that coffee."

I wipe my eyes. "I think I need something a little stronger than that."

"I know it's easy to say, but I know you're gonna get through this." He stands and I follow suit. Relief pours through me, even though that's naïve since he hasn't given me anything I can work with yet. At least he's willing.

"You're a fighter through and through, I can see that. I'm good at reading people, I have to be in this line of work. I know you'll do anything for your sister, and right now, we need that strength. Can you stay strong for just a little bit longer?"

I take a deep breath and close my eyes. *Of course, you can do it. Use that strength, the rage, the hate...* I know I have to; my sister's life depends on it.

With renewed vigor, I hold my head high. "I'll do it, Enzo. I'll do anything you say to get my sister back."

"Good," he says. "The first thing I need to know is who it is. Who do you have to kill?"

I steel myself, swallowing hard as I follow him down the deserted walkway. "Angelo Medici," I reply, my voice barely a whisper. "Head of the Boston Mafia."

20

ANGELO

I TRY TO SHAKE OFF THE UNPLEASANTRIES WITH ALLEGRA while driving over to Fortress.

I have to meet with my brothers and Enzo. I have no fucking clue what's gotten into her and why all of a sudden she's accosting me at my house and coming onto me. It's been so long since the days we were in college that I hardly even remember them. Maybe after so much time on her own, she's losing her shit.

I've never honestly thought of her in *that* way since she married Roberto, it would be so wrong.

I dial Rayne on the way, hoping for a distraction, but she doesn't answer. I should pay her a visit tonight, but it depends on how things go down at Fortress when I get there.

I think back to her file and the new information I learned about her very much alive sister. My hackles rise when I think about why she would say her sister was dead when she so clearly isn't.

Maybe they have a strained relationship, maybe they've

fallen out of touch …but still, it seems extreme and doesn't explain the photo I saw of them taken just six months ago.

I know I should have cut her loose by now, that isn't even a question. A quick, hot little love affair could have done me just fine, yet she's gotten under my skin in a way that no woman has been able to do in a long time. I wish I could shake it, shake her, but the more I try, the more I fail, and I don't ever fail at anything.

I arrive at Fortress thirty minutes later, tapping my fingers on the steering wheel while impatiently waiting for the huge, heavy gates to open.

My brothers are all hanging out when I arrive. There's a buzz all around from the raid. It's good for us all to be low-key and here in one place together. The boys are playing a round of pool when I notice Enzo's absence.

"Where the fuck is E?" I ask Marco, who's resting on his pool cue.

"Beats me." Marco shrugs. "Though he did say he'd be back in an hour or two."

"He only called me *fifty* times today. I still don't know what's going on with him, any of you guys got any fucking clue what's up his ass?"

"I assume he and Rocco have some business downtown." Fynn shrugs. "Where've you been all night, anyway?" he asks, taking an impossible pool shot and pocketing it.

"Balls deep, little brother, not that it's any of your business." I lug the shot down. Of course, that's untrue, but it's the best thing I can come up with rather than lying about Allegra paying me a visit to rehash old times.

"So, let me get this straight, we're all hiding out here all night after the raid, and yet you're out there getting pussy?" he snorts.

"Watch your fucking mouth, Fynn. I'm warning you."

"The gallery girl again?" Marco grins. "Quite taken with her, aren't you?"

"Why don't you two quit asking me about where my dick's been and someone fill me in on what there is to know. Dante, you're looking a little quiet over there." Anything to take the heat off me right now is welcome.

"Nah, man, nothing to tell. Ma came over with food, that was about it."

"Ma's been over?"

"You know what she's like, she didn't want her boys starving to death." He grins.

"Valentina?"

"Staying at Ma's. She went over there not long ago."

I'd go over and see them, but it's a little late tonight and I really need to see what Enzo was so urgent about earlier. I have a feeling it isn't good.

"They all good?" I ask.

"Ma's fine. Security is extra tight, so you don't need to worry," Marco informs me. "Gotta be."

"Good," I mutter.

I throw back another scotch, knowing that's not a good thing when I'm feeling a little agitated. I decide to get out of my suit and take a shower while we're waiting for Enzo's grand entrance.

"Oh, and the drop's done," I inform my brothers on the way out, meaning payday for us all has come around for this latest hike all over the news. It's currently being taken care of by the company accountant.

"Nice fucking work," Dante quips as I leave the room and head towards my quarters. I have a stash of stuff here; I could stay here a month without leaving and not run out of anything.

I dial Rayne again on my way to the shower to see if she answers and to make sure she's okay, but it goes straight to voicemail and I hang up even more frustrated.

A little visit will be on the cards at this rate, and a late-night spanking to go along with it for not answering her fucking phone. I don't like to be kept waiting.

After I freshen up, I wrap a towel around my waist and walk over to the window to our forest of a backyard that stretches for so many acres I lose count. It doesn't displease me at all the exorbitant amount of money we all just got paid, this last account was profitable and well earned, although I wonder what it all means sometimes.

I acquire more money, more cars, and more gadgets than I know what to do with. I own all my own houses, my mother and sister are taken care of, and will never have to struggle in their lives. To say I'm well off would be more than an understatement.

However, there are times I wonder when the madness ends, and at the end of the day, I still sit here alone.

My mind flicks back to Rayne and the way I've felt with her in this short period of time.

I want her so fucking bad. I want to make her mine and have her in my bed every single night.

She courses through my veins like sweet poison, and up until this point, she's captivated me, seducing me with her hot little body and her sexy smile.

I love how we are together. I love how we fit so well, and I love she's not afraid of me.

I want to be the only thing she ever needs and craves. She doesn't know this yet, but I would give her everything; she would want for nothing for the rest of her life. What's more, I barely know her.

I contemplate that exact notion while I dress, and Enzo finally decides to show his face.

I'm past the point of entertaining my brothers when he

walks into the informal parlor straight off the back entry-way. I pour us a whisky and pass it to him as he runs his hand through his hair and takes a long breath. He does look a little worse for wear which is unusual for him, but he doesn't appear to have been drinking.

"Why the fucking long face?" I ask him, throwing the amber liquid back in one mouthful.

"Wait till you hear where the fuck I've been," he says not looking at me.

"Well, out with it, why call me nonstop all evening and then disappear?"

"I'm gonna need another few rounds, and then some, for this," he mutters.

"I'm fucking serious, Enzo!"

"So am I!" he shouts.

I stare at him in disbelief, something sinks in my chest. Come to think of it, he's looking grave as fuck, like some-body died or something.

"Fuck, is it Ma or Valentina?"

He shakes his head momentarily. "It's nothing like that ….. it's …. oh, Jesus fuck, Angelo …. I don't know how to tell you this."

My patience is wearing thin and this isn't like him at all. What could be so difficult to tell me where the hell he's been and why he needed to speak to me so urgently?

"Do I have to shake it out of you?"

He looks down at his feet. He doesn't look me in the eye; I don't understand his demeanor at all. "It's Rayne," he then says quietly. "I was with her just now."

I stare at him dumbfounded. "What the fuck did you just say?"

"There's something going down, Angelo …"

I don't even give him a second before I'm on him, grabbing him by the throat and pushing him backward into the wall behind him. "You fucking messing with me, Enzo? Is that what this is?"

He pushes against me, shocked. We've never come to blows before, not outside the ring anyway.

"It's not like that," he manages to choke out with the bit of breath he has left. "What the fuck, Angelo!"

"You better start talking some sense," I bark, throwing him back into the wall. "Because I will god damned choke you to death if you're fucking with me."

By now, my brothers are making their way down the hallway to us, and Marco is there almost immediately, probably hoping to break us up.

I hold my palm out to him to stop him in his tracks.

"Angelo, calm the fuck down!!" Marco yells.

"Don't fucking tell me to calm down!" I punch the wall right next to Enzo's head, the wall taking my fist easily. Thank God it's not made of stone like the exterior, but it still fucking hurts like a bitch.

Enzo is as strong as me, but I can take him, we both know it.

We stare each other down in the dark. "I tried to call you all afternoon, didn't I? I said it was urgent, but you were too busy in pussyland or whatever you were doing to bother with taking it seriously."

"Call me? That's fucking rich coming from you. If it was that fucking urgent, you should have said so. Allegra came over to the house just as I was leaving. I had more pressing matters than you whining about everything."

He runs a hand through his hair, something he only does when he's very nervous. "Angelo, I was with Rayne…"

"Yeah, I gathered that, fuckface."

"I meant, she hired me."

I stare at him, stunned. "She hired you? What the hell are you talking about?"

"We better sit down, brother."

"I haven't got all night."

I take a few steps back, and we walk over to the wing-backed chairs, my brothers hovering away from direct earshot, but I'm aware they can hear every word. I plonk down heavily and feel the dread inside me, knowing that somehow it was all too good to be true.

I look him square in the eye as we sit opposite each other.

"You better start making some sense, E."

He holds his hands up, "Firstly, I'm insulted that you'd think I'd fuck your girl behind your back."

I growl. "Don't fucking even go there."

I want to stand up and punch his head off his shoulders for even being with Rayne behind my back, and I still have no fucking idea what he's talking about.

"Angelo, cool it, for Christ's sake," Marco says from somewhere behind me, because he knows me only too well. "Let the man speak."

"Stay out of it, Marco, this is between me and him and nobody else," I bark back over my shoulder.

"You think I would do that to you? After how many years we've known each other. We signed a blood oath, that means something to me. If you let me explain –and believe me, you'll want to hear this– you'll understand where I've been and why I tried to call you a million times."

I turn around and tell my brothers to fuck off. They slowly, but reluctantly leave, Marco muttering under his breath. My heart is racing with what he's about to tell me, and I need to digest this first before they know anything about it.

I lean back in the chair and try to regain some kind of composure, the one I'm used to. "So, talk."

He nods. "Earlier in the week, I had a meeting with

Rayne, only I didn't know it was her then. She went by the name Jessica, and we met up in a seedy bar where she hired me …. "

I stare at him blankly, unable to believe the words coming out of his mouth. "For what exactly?" My patience is growing thin.

"Angelo, she's in real trouble, you've no fucking idea." I brace myself for impact as he goes on. "She's being black-mailed. It started early on, just after she was hired. I don't know who is behind it yet, but she's just a pawn; she was hired to get information about you."

"What the fuck?"

"They snatched her sister Mia and threatened to kill her if Rayne didn't comply."

My head pounds. He glances at me, but I show no emotion, even though something has caved in my chest, I show him absolutely nothing. I never display weakness to any of my men, but Enzo knows me well.

My eyes drop to the opposite side of the wall. "All for intel?"

A few silent moments pass. "No."

"What else."

"You know what it means, it goes way past intel."

"I want you to say it." The pounding in my head just gets worse every passing second.

Fuck. Me. Dead.

"Angelo…"

"Fucking say it!" I yell at him.

He winces and says, "She's supposed to kill you."

The words come out, but they make no sense.

My beautiful, sexy, strong woman is my silent assassin?

I couldn't even write this script, it's absurd. My mind races to every moment we shared like it's passing in slow motion.

"I don't believe it."

"I assure you, it's all true. And I'm gonna make it my mission in life to make them all pay, Angelo."

"Rombaldi's ilk?" I can see he doesn't know yet, but I still have to ask him.

"I've got one of Vaughn's guys on it," he says. "We're doing all we can to track them down."

"Why didn't you use Vaughn? Everything goes through him."

"Because I suspected something was a little off, and after I followed her home and did a trace on her address; I found out who she really was. Vaughn would have gone straight to you, but I needed more information. I didn't know the target was *you*. She only just told me the truth tonight, after much coaxing. She's scared shitless."

I stare at him.

So, this whole time she's been trying to get close to me for information to give to her kidnapped sister's captors? I guess that makes sense why she was so edgy around the subject and tried to blatantly lie to me, saying her whole family had all died in that crash. But it doesn't explain what has been going on between *us*; the fire and the passion, was it all a lie? To fucking mess with my head? Obviously, that answer is yes.

The simple fact is, she's been lying to me this whole time. She lied straight to my face and has been digging ever since. Something ruptures in my heart, and my black soul begins to take over. I didn't even see it coming, what does that make me? A fucking pussy, that's what.

"Angelo, tell me what you're thinking," Enzo goes on when I don't answer.

I stare over at him, except for the first time in a long time I don't know what I'm thinking. I take a few moments to feel the numbness of it, of knowing things were too good to be true, and why I even care. I meet a hundred broads every week. Why was she any different?

Because she was.

I commit the feeling of her to memory, because that's all she's going to be—a distant memory.

She wants me fucking dead.

I'm pissed at myself more than anything, for wanting her, for wanting more. For opening myself up like a fucking pussy.

"I've no fucking idea," I say blankly. "Do you know anything about her sister's location?"

"Not yet, she's expecting an email with the details. We're hoping to get a hit with the IP address, the phone tracking is taking a lot longer than normal. The encryption so far has been intense."

I sigh and slump down in the chair, not the actions of a true leader, I'm aware of that, but I don't care about that right now. It's just me and Enzo.

"If it's any consolation, she seems like a decent woman," Enzo offers as my eyes widen.

"When she's not out to kill me?"

"She doesn't want to do it, she never had any –"

I hold up a hand. "Don't, E."

"Angelo, just think this through."

"Right, because I haven't killed men for less? You know how I feel about betrayal."

I'd go as far as to say that it's a hard limit for me. I've slit throats with my own knife because of it in the past. She's a traitor.

My eyes brood over the opposite side of the room as I remain silent. It doesn't dull the pain any less. I'm just a commodity. I shouldn't expect that people want any more from me.

"Angelo, you can't utter a word of this, she has no idea

who I am right now in relation to Fortress or to you. We have to play along for the time being. The Gala is in two days, so if I haven't gotten any leads before then I suggest we go to the thing and act normal and play this thing out to the end. She can't know that you know, it's imperative."

"This is my fault," I mutter without hearing him. "She weaseled her way into my life, and what's worse? I fucking let her. I let my guard down, I dropped the fucking ball."

Enzo shakes his head. "She's not a fucking criminal mastermind, Angelo. She's petrified and lost. If she weren't involved in trying to knock you off, I might even feel a bit sorry for her."

I narrow my eyes. "Nice to know where your loyalties lie."

He holds up his hands. "I know this isn't ideal, but she's no assassin. She's being bribed. She's not going to do it."

"You'd be surprised what people would do for the ones they love, E," I reply. "I'd kill for any of my brothers, for you. She's not to be underestimated. How do we know that she's not just acting with you? Fuck knows she could get a goddamn Oscar for her role in this so far."

"She's not acting."

I snort. "I feel so much better knowing that the girl I'm infatuated with has been bribed into spending time with me to gain information, including my darkest secrets that will ultimately lead to my death, so that she can save her own ass."

"It's not her ass she's saving," he corrects. "It's her sister's."

I glare at him. "I don't know why you're defending her; anyone would think you quite like the idea."

He gives me an eye roll. "I like the idea of finding out who sent her so we can string them up and cut their tongues out."

Now that sounds like a plan I can get on board with.

My jaw ticks, so my little *Carina* thinks she can fuck with me, does she? I've got news for her, and it's all merciless.

She thinks she can just walk into my life and turn it upside down, spending time in my bed, pretending to be interested, using me for information to feed back to my enemies?

It's all so fucking perfect.

She's so unsuspecting. So innocent, yet she's been playing me this whole time. The rage inside me begins to boil. I know it'll turn nuclear before long if it's left to fester, and fester it will.

"By the time I'm done with them, they'll be wishing they never heard the name Medici. I want every last one of them."

Thinking of all the ways Rocco and I can torture them makes me feel slightly better, but it doesn't numb everything.

Enzo cracks his neck from side to side. "You know, that grab by the fucking throat hurt," he grumbles like a little bitch, testing if it's still working.

"Lucky I didn't have you by the balls," I mutter.

"Did you really think we were hooking up?"

I run a hand over my face. "You know how I am." I'm possessive when something's mine. There is no argument. I own them. They say you can't buy people, which is a load of shit; I buy people every day. Police. Politicians. Businesspeople. Everyone. *Except her.*

Then I add, "If another man touches her, I will literally cut off his fucking hand and every single finger that's burned her skin, and then I'll ram them down his fucking throat."

"Save that rage for finding out who's behind this, we

need all the help we can get because these guys know about covering their tracks. Like I said, our hacker is having a hard time getting any kind of trace. Whoever it is, has gone to an extensive amount of trouble to encrypt everything."

I've always had targets on my back doing what I do, that's nothing new but never like this. This is something else.

"Look, I've got a plan if you wanna hear it," he continues.

I nod at him, resigned to the fact that I don't see what choice I have in the matter.

I'm still digesting the information and working out what to do with it. More to the point, being able to look her in the face again and not flinch.

Having to act like I know nothing will be a testament to how much Mario has trained me to remain composed over the years. To show nothing, not even contempt, that'll be the biggest test of all.

I need to put my mask back in place.

I need to play the game.

"Let's do what needs to be done." I run my fingers through my hair. At least that statement is spoken like a leader, I can't say much else for the rest.

21

RAYNE

It pains me more than it probably should to pawn the jewelry Angelo bought me at the auction. I take a final look at the pieces before going and getting ready for the Gala. Today is the day.

Escrow, unfortunately, is taking too long to settle with the Dane situation, and I need to pay Enzo for the rest of his services. It saddens me because Angelo's face lit up when he saw me wearing the diamonds.

I feel like a cheap whore more than I ever did before.

The bittersweet truth that I've betrayed him rings true more than any emotion I've ever had.

I'm all nerves and don't know where to put my restless energy. Melody, bless her heart, treats us both to a salon visit straight after work, so I get my hair washed and styled before having to get ready for tonight. I think she notices I've been visibly off in my own world for the last few days, but she's polite enough not to say anything about it.

I'm walking on a tight rope right now, juggling balls in the air, and if I drop one ball, the whole lot will crash.

I pawn the jewelry straight after the salon visit and go

home to get changed, feeling like shit but better in some ways because I have the cash for when I need to run.

I reread the email in the cab ride; a drop will be made tonight before the Gala starts, and a syringe will be placed in my clutch bag when I visit the south side ladies' room at precisely 9pm. I have to leave my purse on the counter, go into the stall, and wait for exactly three minutes before coming out. Then I've got forty-eight hours to kill Angelo Medici.

Yes, that's right, I'm supposed to poison my mafia king by lethal injection. According to the instructions, the poison is undetectable and will simulate a heart attack.

I have no intention of jabbing Angelo with anything. As the hours and minutes pass by, I

have faith that Enzo is going to come up with something, *anything*. He has his guys trying to encrypt the high-tech security blockers on the IP and the mobile devices, but it's taking longer than expected.

If that fails, I will risk my own life and tell Angelo everything. I have no choice.

I sit down at my coffee table in my robe and decide to write every confession down on paper. I finger the gold edging around the linen stationery I bought as I think about what to tell him. I know that if things go bad tonight, and by that, I mean if something happens to me, then I want him to know the truth.

He may be a lot of things, but he deserves that from me. He's not the monster I thought he was.

While I know that I'm a plaything to him, my own feelings have come front and center, and I shouldn't have let that happen.

I didn't want to get my heart involved. It was just a business transaction, a means to an end; it was supposed to be simple, get the intel, and my sister goes free.

I didn't imagine things would get this messy or for them to keep changing the rules. And I certainly didn't plan to fall for the head of the Boston Mafia, but it appears I have, and I'm not sure what will be left of me after this whole thing goes down.

There was no way we could ever be more, it was never going to play out that way, but the

dark and dangerous way he has about him lured me in, like a moth to a flame.

I shouldn't feel secure in his embrace, except that's the only place I've ever felt whole in this mess. Like I'm untouchable, which is, of course, completely untrue. I'm not safe anywhere.

There has been more than one occasion where I've forgotten myself and the task at hand and actually enjoyed it and let him give me pleasure. And what pleasure he gives. I can still feel him everywhere...

It all comes pouring out as I write. He has to know.

When I'm done, I seal the letter inside the envelope and get dressed, knowing that when he reads it, I'm a dead woman.

I wear a figure-hugging black dress with cut-outs all through it, so parts of my skin are exposed, it has a plunging neckline and a large gold collared necklace. I strap on some heels, forcing one foot in front of the other.

I stare at my reflection, happy with what I see because I look like the perfect, soulless monster that he'll remember me by.

I haven't seen him since the night I got drunk and he texted me saying he's been busy, but he'll pick me up at eight.

It's better this way. Please, Enzo...find something...

True to his word, Angelo texts me when he's downstairs.

I glance at my appearance in the hall mirror, my makeup is heavier than normal with long fake lashes and red lipstick. I almost don't recognize myself, though that's nothing new. I don't know who I've become since all this began. I stopped seeing *me* some time ago.

My inner turmoil is so palpable, that I'm certain Angelo is going to see straight through it. I just hope I don't blow my cover acting like a nervous, blithering idiot. I just have to get through tonight.

If Enzo can't crack the code, then I'll have no choice but to confess to Angelo and suffer my fate in his hands. I can't kill the guy, no matter what is at stake, and I know he'll have my head for this betrayal.

If I run, Mia is dead. I tremble at the thought because I'm stuck between a rock and a hard place.

When I step out of the foyer, he's leaning back on the limo door facing me.

I hug a faux fur shawl around my shoulders as he takes me in with his penetrating eyes; hungry and dangerous looking. He has a glacial stare as I glance up at him as I approach.

"Hello, Angelo," I say. He looks sexier than a man has a right to in a tux and bow tie, I just about melt on the spot. "You look amazing."

He grins and pushes off the door to reach a hand to my waist. His lips find my neck, and he kisses my pulse point. So much for my reservations about him seeing straight through me. "You look good enough to eat, Miss Michaelson."

He guides me into the waiting limo with a hand on the small of my back.

We ride in companionable silence while he pours me a glass of champagne. I sit opposite him as I take in how dashingly handsome he is. He's shaved but still has a small amount of stubble on his face, his hair is gelled back and his skin is tanned like he just got back from Mexico.

For as long as I live, I'll never want a man as I want him, and I'm already secretly mourning the loss. Nothing could ever fill the void; I know that now.

He sits back in his seat with one leg crossed over the other, assessing me and watching every move I make, like a predator stalking its prey.

"Are you okay?" I ask him, taking a sip of the bubbles and feeling nervous at how he's looking at me.

"Just taking in the view," he says, his voice low. "Your fucking breathtaking, Rayne. I like how you tease me with bits of flesh on display. Is that to give me easy access?"

I bite my lip and laugh under my breath, "If you play your cards right."

He licks his lips and grins. "The only reason I'm not gonna take you now is because I don't want to ruin your hair and makeup. It's a pity, the just fucked look really suits you. It'd give the old cronies something to talk about tonight."

"Has anyone told you how incredibly sexy you look in that tux?" I fire back.

He downs his shot of whisky, his eyes sparkle dangerously as he reaches forward and nuzzles into my neck, softly biting the flesh at my pulse. "You smell so fucking great," he growls. His hand snakes into my dress, and he finds my breast easily and tugs on my nipple. "Want to fuck these tonight, you're gonna be wearing my cum all over you, so any man who dares to fucking come near you knows who you belong to."

My eyes go wide. He's been possessive before, but this is something new.

My heart races in my chest.

"That's very alpha of you, Mr. Medici," I whisper,

playing along as he tweaks my nipple hard and I press my legs together. He snakes a hand up my leg, pushing my thighs apart and brushing my panty line. He hisses when he finds I have no underwear on.

"Fuck," he mutters. He pinches my clit as I open my legs for him, letting him run two fingers through my wetness, but he doesn't penetrate. "Wish I had time to fuck you hard and fast."

I run my hands through his hair, pulling tighter as his kisses on my neck become wilder, nipping, flicking, sucking. Like he really is marking me.

"But," he goes on, pushing the gap of my dress to one side so my breast pops out freely. He grasps it and bends his head to suck me, then laves me with his tongue. His eyes close, his fingers are still rubbing me while I try to seek out my pleasure. I'm so close…. "I think I like you panting and frustrated better than I like you sated."

"Fuck," I whisper. "Angelo, please."

He tsks, biting my nipple as I mewl and feel moisture pool between my legs while he pinches me again. "Patience, little one. Every time I look at you tonight, I want you to picture this. My hands on your body. My head between your legs. My cock inside you. Me keeping you right on the edge. Your body is mine, do you understand? *Mine.*"

I nod.

"Answer me!"

"Yes!" I cry out.

He squeezes my breast as his eyes come to mine, and he tongues my pebbled peak. I reach for his cock, but he knocks my hand away. "Patience, *Carina*," he mumbles, withdrawing his hand as I groan out loud in frustration. "I'll fuck you when I choose to, when you least expect it. And you'll love every minute of it when I do."

His dirty words go straight to my core as he pulls my dress back together, and I stare at him wordlessly.

"Angelo, you can't…"

He grins like the devil. "Oh yes, I can. That pussy is mine. Only I can give you what you truly crave, and I will, if you're a good girl for me tonight."

Even now, knowing what I know and what I've done, I still cannot resist him. He can take me. My heart. My body. My soul. It's his.

I'm so sorry, Angelo. You've no idea how sorry I am…

The car comes to a stop just in time before I jump his bones. Angelo helps me out of the limo and takes my hand, leading me to one of the VIP entries. There are paparazzi taking photos of everyone walking up the red carpet, including us.

"Is this for real?" I murmur to Angelo.

He chuckles darkly. "We're going to be the talk of the town, you know, being seen like this."

"Do you care about that?" I ask him honestly as he leads me through the barrier and into one of the vast ornate tents where a huge bar has been set up, offsetting the main marquee. There's a runway for the fashion show and a dance floor adjacent.

"A little late for that, don't you think?"

I smile up at him as we walk to the bar. Angelo nods greetings to several people along the way, and I swear every pair of eyes in the room turns to look at him.

Of course, I don't know anyone, although Patricia and some of my colleagues, including Melody, will be here.

"My brothers and Valentina will be here tonight," he tells me. "You'll get to meet them."

I frown. *This wasn't how I had this planned out in my head.*

"They know about me?" I ask as he gestures to a stool at the bar. He orders two martinis and then turns to me.

"They know enough." He nods at the bartender and hands him a large bill.

"And what is that exactly?" I've no idea why I'm choosing now to ask him this, with so much at stake. At some point tonight, he's going to end up reading that letter. I can feel it in my bones.

A part of me desperately wants to know what I am to him, if anything.

"What do you want it to be, *Carina*? You tell me."

"I didn't know there were options, I thought we were just … you know." I look around to make sure no one can hear us since the place is fairly crowded already.

"Fucking?" he finishes with his eyebrows raised. He stands with one hand leaning on the bar, commanding authority, while the other touches the skin on my back through my dress. His eyes bore into mine, the darkness lingering as I sip my drink and I'm tempted to down the entire thing.

"Well, yes, that."

"Is it really just fucking, *Carina*?"

We stare at each other, and his eyes remain cold, sending a shiver right through me.

"I think you know it's not, Angelo," I whisper. My hands begin to shake, so I set my drink down. Nerves are getting the better of me.

He leans down and kisses my neck again as I bury my face into his shoulder. This is the third time he's kissed me anywhere except my lips. He seems…off, somehow.

Suddenly, someone slaps Angelo hard on the back and my eyes snap open. I'm faced with a tall, dark, and extremely handsome man with very similar colored blue eyes to Angelo, a careful smile on his lips.

He doesn't quite have that penetrating Angelo-stare

that makes you shake in your boots, but it's there all the same. His dark hair is gelled back off his face.

These Medicis are not playing around with the gene pool. He's fucking hot too.

"Well, well, Angelo, is this the girl you've had stashed away for none of us to see?"

Angelo rolls his eyes and turns to face him. "Cool it, brother, you don't need to scare her off. Rayne, this is my brother Marco. Marco, this is Rayne."

He takes my hand as if to spite Angelo, and kisses the top of my knuckles. "Nice to meet you, Rayne. I'd love to say I've heard so much about you, but Angelo keeps his cards close to his chest, and on this occasion, I can clearly see why."

Charmed, I'm sure.

"Nice to meet you, too." I smile back.

"You should get to meet the rest of the family tonight, they'll all be here." He gives me a sly wink.

"Don't you have somewhere to be?" Angelo snaps, his eyes like thunder.

He's jealous of his own brother?

This man has a temper like no one I've ever met.

"Actually, nowhere at all," he replies cheerfully. That is until we both glance at that God-awful woman I met at the cafe the other day. The one who told me about her and Angelo being fuck buddies. *Allegra.*

I glimpse beside her to see Patricia and Melody, and they're all in deep conversation. Melody laughs at something she says, then our eyes meet, and she waves over at me. I wave back, avoiding looking at what's-her-face.

"Fucking, Allegra," I hear Angelo mutter.

"It was lovely to meet you," Marco says. "I should do the rounds while everyone is still sober."

Something passes between Marco and Angelo that I can't decipher.

"Lovely to meet you, too," I reply as he makes his way around the room.

"Don't worry about Marco," Angelo says when he's gone. "He's usually extremely uptight. Must be the easy flow of cocktails going around."

"He has the Medici charm down to a tee."

"That he does." His hand lingers on my knee, tracing the skin with one finger. Every single touch sends fire right through me.

Losing him is going to be like torture.

His scent. His touch. His presence.

Suddenly, he pulls me off the stool and clasps my hand in his. His touch is demanding, not like he was a moment ago, and as we steer toward the marquee, his fingers tighten around mine. We don't get far. Literally, out of nowhere, a girl comes bounding up to us like she's on a mission. Angelo leans down to whisper that it's his sister, Valentina.

She doesn't even stop to find out who I am, instead, she barrels into me and hugs me with all her might, then stands back to assess me from head to toe.

"So, this is the mystery woman!" she cries with glee.

"Valentina!" Angelo scolds.

She's taller than me, has long dark hair down to her waist and, unsurprisingly, she's blessed with the same gorgeous looks as her brothers. Her eyes are a striking azure blue. She is absolutely stunning.

"Just taking a look at the girl who has had you captivated for weeks. We knew someone had to tame the wild beast sometime!" she says behind the back of her hand toward me.

"For fucks sake, Valentina." Angelo looks mortified.

"It's nice to meet you," I say, smiling back. At least the family seems to be friendly.

"It would be lovely to get together sometime." She beams at me.

I don't know what's more astounding, that his sister thinks I tamed 'the wild beast' or that she seems pleased about it.

"We're mingling," Angelo says, sounding annoyed. "I've got some important people to talk to tonight, it isn't all playtime for some of us."

"All work and no pleasure," she giggles.

Angelo looks at her more closely. "Who did you come here with?"

"Nobody."

He frowns some more. "You know you can't lie to save yourself."

"I'm with some friends." She waves behind her, but Angelo isn't buying it. Before he can say any more, she adds, "Ooh, there's my friend Alison. I'll see you two love-birds later…"

She dashes off, giving me a huge grin as she passes. I can't help but smile. She reminds me of…

"And that was my annoying little sister, Valentina," Angelo says, turning to watch her dash across the floor. He shakes his head. "And the reason for my many gray hairs."

I can't help grinning. "She seems lovely."

He turns to look down at me, his hand gripping my hip. "Let's dance."

"I don't really –"

He pulls me out onto the dance floor and into his arms. The band is playing a slow, sultry song as he pulls me flush against him. I feel his hard cock press into my stomach, and it makes me swallow hard.

He leans down to my ear. "You get me like this so fucking easy, *Carina*."

His eyes are dark and heated when I look up at him as we begin to slow dance.

"Angelo–"

"Shhh," he says. "Every pair of eyes are on you tonight."

"I only have eyes for you," I tell him truthfully.

The corner of his mouth turns up. "Is that right?"

I nod, unsure of the predatory way he's looking at me – he's different tonight, rougher somehow.

"Yes," I murmur, looking down at his fingers as he tugs my nipple and smooths his hand back down to my waist.

"You asked me not long ago what I would do to someone who betrayed me."

Oh shit.

"And the truth is, I'd show them no mercy."

"I don't doubt that," I whisper, though I don't even know if he hears me.

The song ends, and it's time to excuse myself to the lady's room before I panic completely and blow the whole thing. I have to go and collect the package. What I do from here is anyone's guess.

He kisses me on the cheek.

"I'll be right back," I say, giving him a smile as he watches me.

I scramble my way to find the south side bathrooms. Everything depends on this moment in time. If I can secure the package, then at least that part is out of the way.

I text Enzo as I walk. He tells me he's got someone discreetly staking out the ladies and following me. The bathroom is off of the main building and I can see why they chose this spot, it's dark and secluded.

I look around as I enter the opulent restroom. My heart is beating so hard in my chest.

I don't want to do this, but it's all part of the show, make them think they have the upper hand and that I'm going to kill him …. how wrong they are, so very wrong.

But all I can think about is Mia, so I press on with a heavy heart and more anxiety than I've ever felt in my entire life.

I'm running on adrenaline now, it's all I have.

I take a big breath, push the door open and step inside.

ANGELO

When she leaves the fashion show, I wait a good five minutes before making my own exit to get to her, and I know exactly where to find her.

Enzo and the guys also know to follow whoever is making the drop; I hope they enjoyed their life up until now. It will be the last breaths they take.

Enzo filled me in on my impending demise, lethal injection. And I'm keeping it to myself for the moment, my brothers will know when I choose to tell them later tonight.

One thing is for sure, it's going to be interesting if she does attempt to use that thing on me, and now would be a perfect opportunity to test that theory.

I find the south side ladies'. Most people are watching the show and nowhere near this end of the building. Perfect.

I've been like a cat on hot bricks all night, trying to keep my calm, but my rage knows no bounds. She acts like she's some kind of fucking saint.

Enzo can tell me all he likes, but I have to hear it from her. I have to fucking know for myself.

I stand outside the ladies' like a fucking stalker and wait for her to come out.

I shove my phone back in my pocket as the door swings open, and Rayne runs straight into my chest. She looks up and literally screams from fright.

"Jesus, Angelo." Her eyes are wide like a deer caught in headlights and her hands are visibly shaking. "What are you do–"

I cage her in against the door and push my body into hers.

I reach down and take her hard with my mouth as she gasps. Yeah, she's gonna see the wrath of me when I fuck her against this door, not caring who sees us. "Couldn't wait, baby, especially feeling you up on the dance floor. Perfect timing, though, we're all alone."

"Angelo, not here, we can't–"

I push the ladies' door open and glance over her head. "There's no one around, and I'm so fucking hard for you." I pull her hand to my cock, and she bites her lip as I hold it there, moving it over my length.

"In the ladies' room?" she stutters.

I grin like a hungry panther. "Yeah, this is as good a time as any to rip that dress off you and fuck you over the sinks."

She looks up at me with such an internal dilemma that if she weren't trying to kill me, I might feel sorry for her.

I edge her backward through the door and she pulls on the lapels of my jacket. I move inside quickly and lock it behind me.

"Are you sure this is hygienic?" she whispers as we kiss wildly, her hands grabbing and squeezing my ass.

I ignore her, my eyes eating her up as I move the strap

of her dress down her arm and reach to kiss her again. I'm rough as our tongues collide. I unzip her dress to her lower back and roughly shove it down to her waist.

"I love no fucking underwear." I pull her up to me so she can wrap her legs around my waist. I dip my head and suck on one nipple as she throws her head back, clawing her hands in my hair. I sit her ass on the marble counter, pulling the bottom of her dress up to her waist.

She puts her clutch purse down next to her and wraps her arms around me, pushing her tits into my face. I reach my hand up her thigh straight to her wet center and a growl involuntarily leaves me throat.

"You do this for me, baby?" I whisper against her skin. I move to work on her other nipple while she reaches down for my belt buckle. She's such a good girl, she knows what I want.

"Yes, Angelo, I knew you'd want to fuck me in public," she whispers. "I know how your dirty mind works."

Fuck. If only she really did know how my dirty mind works.

I watch as she undoes my belt and fly, and I help her by tugging my pants down to my thighs. I pull her hips forward so I can tease her with the tip of my cock. Her fingers dig into my shoulders as I brush through her wet folds.

"Remember when I said I was gonna make you beg me to let you come?"

She whimpers as I rub her clit with my tip, I want to cum all over her, marking her as mine, but I need to be buried deep inside her one last time.

I stop just as she tries to quicken her rubbing, and I see the frustration in her eyes when I don't let her.

"You don't come till I tell you to," I whisper in her ear, and for the first time, I don't make her come first before penetrating. This isn't about her anymore, it's about me.

I line up and plunge my dick straight into her wet pussy, making her scream out loud.

I'm in full tilt, grasping her hips as I show her absolutely no mercy while I bang my hips back and forth like a man possessed.

I'm primal and hungry with need. I completely lose all control; all the pent-up frustration, anger, and betrayal go into every thrust.

I can see in between my rampant thrusting that she's completely let go of her purse. So, the traitor doesn't plan on jabbing me right this second? How comforting.

"Yeah, baby, you like that, don't you? You like being fucked without any mercy." I glance down to where we're joined, and I close my eyes as her pussy swallows my cock.

She moans so fucking loud it only spurs me on. I feel my balls tightening and I'm so close to blowing but I want to give her something to remember me by.

"Don't come yet," I warn her. "Or I'll keep you in here all night."

I lean her back a little, so her pelvis tilts and my shaft runs over and over on her clit, knowing I'm hitting everything from this angle; her face is red and flushed.

"Angelo…" she cries.

"Angelo, what?" I bark.

"Please!"

"You fucking tell me how much you love it, Rayne, how much my cock owns every inch of your pussy."

"I love it!" she screams, "Please, Angelo, oh God…please don't stop…I need it…"

Our eyes meet as I bang her harder. "Come for me, *Carina.*"

She cries out as I thumb her clit, and she comes long and hard.

I stop abruptly and pull out of her, giving her no time

to recover. She stares up at me, breathless, with sweat beading on her forehead.

"You want it harder, baby, is that what you want?" I pick her up and move over to the smaller marble table just below a massive full-length mirror at the end of the row of sinks. I shrug out of my jacket and throw it down on top. "Kneel, ass out," I instruct. Her eyes go super wide, but she complies. It's so fucking hot watching her with her dress pulled down to her waist, tits out, and the other end of her dress rucked up to her hips. "Gonna take you from behind, don't take your eyes off that mirror."

I bend down and part her ass cheeks with my dick, rubbing her through her wet folds up to her ass as she cries out. I do it again, reveling in how wet she is for me.

She braces her hands against the mirror as I stroke myself and line back up. I grunt as I enter her again, grasping her hips roughly as I pull her back closer to me, impaling her.

I stare back at her in the mirror as I move my hips, my cock sliding in and out of her as I quicken my pace again, watching her every move. I slap her ass as she gasps, it's such a fucking turn on that I do it again, reveling in her the way her skin pinks so quickly.

My dark eyes lock on hers, lust filling them as I fuck her hard. My impending death is on ice until she gets her next orgasm. And boy, is she gonna get one.

Her tits bounce up and down as I reach my hands around and squeeze them. She watches me in the mirror and squeezes her eyes shut as I reach one hand down to rub her clit.

"Come for me again, baby. I wanna hear you scream louder this time." I slap her ass again as she squeals then she detonates as she squeezes my dick for all its worth. I begin to cum, groaning violently, finding my own release as I call her name over and over.

Our eyes never break, she's so damned sexy.

I still as my body spasms, and I know in this moment I've never loved anyone in my life other than Lucia, but I fucking love this woman with any amount of heart that I have left. It shocks me to my core. It shouldn't even be humanly possible after what she's done.

I pull out abruptly, panting as I run both hands through my hair. Our eyes lock again and the corner of my mouth turns up, satisfied. She begins pulling her dress back together as I pull my pants back up.

"You get cleaned up, *Carina*, I'll wait outside."

She nods as I make my leave.

"Don't forget your purse," I holler behind me. I can't help the smirk that crosses my lips.

I take a few moments to gather myself and how fucking good that felt. Seeing her taking me like that, up on all fours with her ass in the air and her tits out. Jesus Christ. I could die a happy man.

She appears outside a few moments later. I take her hand and lead her back inside to get some food, there's complete and utter silence the whole way. I would pay everything I currently own to hear her thoughts right now.

That fuck was brutal and so damn hot. I purposely keep my mouth shut. She brought out the beast tonight, and the beast is who she gets from here on in.

We stop by the food marquee, and I tilt her chin up with my hand. "You look a little shaky there, *Carina*. Everything okay?"

She nods. "Everything's perfect."

Liar.

I smile back at her. "Do you like mirrors, Rayne?" I

prompt, guiding her towards the buffet with the palm of my hand on her back.

"I do now," she whispers, avoiding my gaze.

I snort, moving my mouth to her ear. "I've got so much more planned for us later."

She bites her lip.

I stare at her. "I want you on all fours again, impaling yourself on my cock."

She swallows hard.

"You want it like that, don't you?" Teasing her like this could become my new past-time.

She nods. "The filthier the better, Angelo."

Touché.

I see my sister waving madly at us as I inwardly groan.

"You two, where have you been?" Valentina gushes like she's known Rayne her whole life.

You don't want to know, little sister.

"I'll grab us a plate, I'll be right back," I whisper, knowing I'm leaving her hanging and well aware I'm about to be an absolute asshole, but it needs to be done.

I've spotted Tiffany over by the buffet and I head towards her. I didn't even know she was coming tonight, I'm also well aware Allegra isn't too far away at the champagne bar, but I try to avoid that. It's only as I walk closer that I see Senator Mendes standing right next to Tiffany.

I don't fucking believe he's even here after the rough week he's had. This is all I fucking need tonight, yet, once again, all plans fall into place as they're meant to.

"Tiffany." I reach down and kiss her cheek, knowing full well Rayne is watching my every move.

"Angelo," she gushes, clearly surprised to see me kiss her in public. "Have you met Senator Diego Mend-"

"Of course." I stick my hand out to his, although what I really want to do is have him strung up by his balls. Oh, but

I've got something so much sweeter planned for him later tonight.

My lips twitch with satisfaction.

"Likewise." He reciprocates the handshake. "I'm surprised our paths haven't crossed before now. Your reputation proceeds you, Mr. Medici."

If only you knew our paths are going to cross much sooner than you could ever imagine.

"Likewise, how are things in the political world?" I ask, like butter wouldn't melt in my mouth.

"It's been a crazy campaign," he replies in his thick accent. "Nonetheless very rewarding. I'm a lucky man to have such wonderful supportive friends and family."

I can see why people would think he was a nice enough guy at the outset. He's polite. Smiles at everyone. Kisses fucking babies on the political campaign trails. But not every monster looks like one, some hide in plain sight.

I tip my drink to him. "Truer words have never been spoken." I let the words hang. *How much underage sex have you paid for this week?* I wonder.

He excuses himself as I turn to stare at Tiffany.

"What the fuck are you doing here with Mendes?" I bark when he's out of earshot. Usually, I wouldn't give a shit who she's with, but I have to draw the line somewhere for her own good.

"Hold your horses, Angelo. I'm not *with* him, we just got talking."

"Well, just be careful around him. He's bad news."

She looks confused but knows better than to question me. "You miss me or something?" She pokes me in the chest.

I move in and put a hand on her hip. "Settle down, I just came to make sure that fuckface wasn't stepping over the line."

And also to see my sweetheart's reaction. She's still watching us.

"You up for it later?" She goes straight there. "I need a Medici fuck."

I turn briefly and look over to the buffet where Rayne is still standing, watching us. My sister of course, is blabbing away with Melody in her ear. The look on her face says it all.

"I don't think so, honey. My date might be a little pissed." I nod over towards Rayne, and Tiff follows my drift.

She pouts up at me. "Seriously, Angelo?"

I feel like an asshole for openly flirting with Tiffany, but it's the only way I'm going to know Rayne's reaction to me flirting with another woman right in front of her. The fucker in me has to know.

"Don't fucking start." I pull her to me before she knows what's happening, and we embrace. Though it pains me, I add, "Keep your ass on ice."

"Promises, promises," she muses as I let her go and stalk towards the bar.

I see Allegra from across the room, she looks away the minute I see her. This is going to be awkward at our family get-togethers from now on, but she'll get over it. I order three glasses of champagne and take them back to Rayne, Melody and Valentina.

I throw the entire glass down my throat as Rayne watches me. "Not thirsty, baby?"

"We need to talk," she says, her voice shaky. "In private."

I turn to Valentina. "Just going to get some air," I tell her. I give Melody a curt nod.

She nods as Melody smiles, and I lead Rayne out to the double doors, holding her elbow.

"What are we doing here, Angelo?" She shrugs out of my grasp the minute we're outside.

"With what, *Carina?*"

"Angelo, you stalk me to the bathroom, ravage me senseless, tell me all those sweet nothings, and then go and eye fuck the first available woman who comes your way."

I laugh. "Me, playing games?"

She starts to stumble a little, and I reach to steady her; she looks up at me with wide eyes. "What's that supposed to mean?"

What she doesn't know yet is that I just slipped half of a roofie into her drink and I'm delighted that it's taking an immediate effect.

"You sure you've got nothing to tell me?"

She frowns as my grip on her wrist tightens. "Angelo, you're hurting me."

I lean toward her ear. "I know everything, Rayne. The question is, why didn't you jab me with the needle while I fucked you one last time?"

Her lips quiver as her wide gaze meets mine. She opens her mouth and then closes it again.

"Mia?" I prompt. "Kidnappers. Ransoms. Oh, and I thought you might like these back."

I reach into my pocket to pull out the Harry Winston box with the earrings I bought her that she pawned. I bought them back.

She gasps as I hold them out in my palm.

"They are rather fetching on her, aren't they, Enzo?"

She pales as Enzo walks up behind her and comes into view. Their eyes lock and he forces a smile.

"It's not what you think," he says when her eyes go wide.

She squints at him, like she's seeing him for the first time, "What are you do–"

"No time for that," he replies as she stumbles. The drugs are starting to take effect.

Good. We need to get out of here as discreetly as possible.

She turns to me. "I never meant to hurt you, Angelo. I wouldn't have done it, I swear, it's my sister," she pleads.

"You know, I think I've heard enough."

"*Please,*" she begs.

"Don't worry, *Carina,*" I whisper as I let her fall into my arms. "Your secret's safe with me, at least for now, anyway."

She tugs onto my suit jacket. "Angelo, my sister…Mia… *please…*" She tries to struggle but it's fruitless. She's no match for me, or Enzo.

I pull her close to me, her body limp and almost lifeless. "Shhhh," I say into her hair, "the time for talking is over."

"I hate you," I'm sure I hear her mutter into my chest before she loses consciousness completely.

I pick her up in my arms as she goes as limp as a ragdoll. "If only that were true," I mutter.

I carry her around to the waiting limo. I place her on the back seat and stroke her hair out of her eyes; she's out cold.

A mixture of emotions runs through me; I feel guilty, angry, and frustrated all at the same time. But I have to believe this is for her own good.

Enzo's face is ashen as the door closes, and I turn to look at my *Carina,* lying on the seat, lifeless.

"Don't look so sad, E. She'll come around in no time."

He regards me coolly. "You've got that look about you."

"What look?"

"That look that says all bets are off."

I smirk. "Take her to Falmouth," I tell Gus over the hood of the limo.

"Yes, Mr. Medici."

I tap the roof of the limo as I watch him drive off. I keep her purse tucked under my arm for safekeeping.

Enzo meets my eye. "It's better this way," he says, trying to reassure me. It's fruitless. There's no hope for me now.

"Better than me being dead, you mean?"

How we got here isn't necessary, all that matters is where we're going.

And so, let the games begin.

2 3

ANGELO

"WHAT THE FUCK?" MARCO SAYS, HIS FACE PALING WHEN I tell him the details back at Fortress, where we've gathered within the hour.

I left the particulars out from my brothers earlier; I didn't want their coldness toward Rayne to give anything away. Fuck knows it would have.

"So, she's been sent in…as an assassin? "Marco's disbelief almost has me smiling.

"For want of a better word, yes," I reply, running a hand over my face.

He stares at me, waiting for the punchline. "You're fucking kidding me?"

Nobody is more shocked than I am.

"I wish I were. The whole thing was a fucking setup. Send in the femme fatale, the oldest trick in the book. Simple yet effective."

This not only reflects poorly on me personally for being weak, but on the whole organization as well.

Fooled by a fucking broad.

To think I'd even considered a future with her, that I,

somewhere, in my dark and twisted heart, thought that we had a connection. This is precisely why women make men fucking weak.

"This is pretty fucked up," Enzo says. "Even by your standards."

"Thanks for the vote of confidence," I mutter.

"If it makes you feel any better, she wasn't going to go through with it," Enzo tries to reassure me.

"So that makes plotting my murder somehow romantic?"

"That's not what I meant. She was a fucking mess when I met with her…"

"That doesn't make any of this okay."

"I know it doesn't, but what would you do under the same circumstances?"

The truth is, I know why he's saying this. He wants me to fucking spare her, and I want to hear him say it.

"You got something to say?" I prod. "Then just come out, and fucking say it."

"We don't kill innocents, Angelo," he says. "I know a killer when I see one, I know cold-heartedness when it rears its head, and she doesn't have any of it. You know probably more than I do that she doesn't have the killer instinct."

I laugh in his face. "You know that do you? Like you're some kind of fucking expert?"

"I know manipulation when I see it. I saw how unsure she was, how she told me repeatedly that she didn't want any harm to come to you…"

"Save it." I shove him and step back, running a hand through my hair to try and compose myself.

Marco grasps my shoulder, but I shrug out of his reach.

This is the price I pay. For everything.

This is how I must live, and I was a weak fool to think it could be any different.

That I could live any other way except always looking over my shoulder, keeping the women in my life at arm's length, I dropped the ball with Rayne Michaelson. She got right under my skin, an itch I couldn't scratch.

The thought of her curled up, drugged, in the back seat of my limo has me seething as well as hard.

Even after all of this, that fucking traitor…she has the ability to undo me. The hole in my heart doesn't grow bigger, it fucking shrivels up into nothingness, because that's all I really am when it all comes down to it. A cold hard shell of nothing.

I'm empty inside, there's only darkness.

"Someone better tell me that they got a lead on the guy who made the drop," I mutter.

I feel like killing someone tonight, and maybe I will.

The only way I know control is by taking it. Grasping it in my hands and molding it into any fucking shape I like. And I thought I was good at it, until this moment.

"Rocco and Santino are watching him as we speak," Enzo goes on, straightening out his tie.

"And?" I demand.

"He went into Russian territory. They have him under surveillance," he says. "They'll bring him in without detection."

"The trouble with that is he'll be missed if he doesn't report back," Marco interjects.

Enzo nods. "Got it covered. They'll grab him when he's off the hook and heading home, no one will be any the wiser."

I walk across the open space, trying to make sense of my next move.

I've let my purpose slip by the wayside. I've let my feelings get away with me.

Well, no more. It ends here.

If this whole experience has taught me anything, it's that there is no one I can trust outside of my immediate circle. The one thing that Mario taught me long after my father died was to keep your friends close, and your enemies closer. No truer words were spoken. I just never figured he meant women in my bed too.

"I need to talk to Mario," I mutter as Marco nods in agreeance.

"What are you going to do with her at Falmouth?" Enzo pours us all two fingers of scotch into crystal tumblers as I turn to face him.

I've got ways of making people talk, but never in my wildest dreams did I ever imagine that I'd be using the powers of seduction to subdue an enemy. And I never imagined I'd be using them against Rayne.

She's at my mercy now, God help her.

I'm not like Enzo. There are no second chances. There are no words that can make any of this better.

Rayne Michaelson will pay... even as I think the very words, my insides curdle at what I know I should do.

Enzo crosses the room and hands me my glass.

He frowns. "I know that look."

I smirk, throwing back my scotch, reveling in the feeling when it burns the back of my throat.

I swear, I get my best ideas when I'm under siege, and I don't know why it didn't occur to me sooner.

And then I laugh, tipping my head back as I pinch the bridge of my nose. My voice echoing across the room and off the thick, cement walls.

I see Enzo and Marco exchange glances.

"Fucking brilliant," I mutter more to myself than anyone else.

"He's finally cracked," Marco mumbles, throwing his scotch back, sensing the storm brewing.

I pace the room again, my back to them.

"I know what I have to do in order for the little fish to catch the big fish."

"Aside from stringing her up and torturing her?" Marco's frown deepens.

"That would be pointless," I reply. "She doesn't know who they are."

"Vaughn's traced the cell back, but it seems they use a new burner phone for every call," Enzo puts in. "This motherfucker definitely covers their tracks. The best bet we have is nabbing the associate who did the drop, and finding out whatever he knows."

I flash him a wicked smile. "Looks like it may be time to wake sleeping beauty."

"Wait, what the fuck are you laughing and grinning about?" Marco calls as I slide my tumbler onto the marble countertop. "Is that it? We need to work out the strategy before you go completely off the rails."

I give him the finger as I stalk off. "You'll find out soon enough!" I call back. "And I think the rails left the track a long time ago, brother."

"Shouldn't you wait for the others; we've got to hatch a plan!" Marco tries again, exasperation lacing his tone. "Angelo!"

"I've already got a plan. Get everyone together, I'll call you when I'm at Falmouth."

I slide into my Aston Martin and slink back into the cool leather and try and contain myself.

I live for this shit.

The threat. The lure. And then the kill. It's what I do.

And while the betrayal seeps through my bones like an unwelcome visitor, I push it down. I can't let the bitterness inside me cloud my judgment for what has to be done. And even though I shouldn't give two fucks, Rayne's sister is innocent, and she's still being held hostage. If I'm honest with myself, aside from the fact that Rayne is trying to kill me, I might be mildly impressed with her efforts to get this far undetected.

No one else has gotten this close to me. If this weren't my life on the line, I might even offer her fucking promotion. Maybe not as an assassin, but I can see her tied to my four-poster bed while I ravage her body and take back every single fucking feeling I had for her and show her no mercy. That sounds like a much better plan than torture.

My palms sweat with the plan swirling around in my head.

It's fucking perfect.

My cell phone rings; not the distraction I need, but I answer anyway, seeing as it's Dante.

"Just heard that Senator Mendes had a heart attack," he says.

"Is that so?" A slow smile creeps across my face despite my current predicament. So, I'd had enough of him after all. With my meeting with the Russians next week, it was time for Mendes to go. One less headache to deal with.

"Dropped dead at the Gala, in front of his wife and his mistress."

"Such a shame," I muse. "Can never trust a man who dibs his nib with the nanny."

I guess they don't call me a ruthless bastard for nothing.

Extinction is the best route for these types of men. There is no redemption, only in hell may he see the error of his ways.

I've got all I need from the bottom dwellers underneath Mendes, and while I would have enjoyed playing with him for a little while until he broke, he's too high profile. People would notice his disappearance and investigate. While I can control the feds, it's less of a headache if I keep them out of it. Favors are all well and good, but I need to use them wisely.

And sometimes, let's face it, you just gotta take out the trash.

If Rayne thinks she's the only one who can go around trying to poison people and make it look like an accident, then she severely underestimated me.

A heart attack is nice and neat, even if I would've preferred his heart on a platter.

I drive out of town and through the nearly deserted freeway to the country.

"I guess there are worse ways to go," he replies.

"Why aren't you at Fortress anyway?"

"Why are you going to the country?" he counters.

We never say Falmouth or give away our location over a cell phone. With the amount of de-tracking devices on all of our phones and devices, it's unlikely anyone would ever encrypt it, but I never take the chance.

"I've got to deal with an urgent matter."

"Of the blonde female variety?"

"Very much so, yes."

"Might I remind you they're out for your head, and they won't rest until they've got it, if Ma gets a hold of this..."

"Ma isn't to know anything just yet," I bark back at him. "I have security tight, and Valentina is with Ma at Fortress.

They think it's to do with the raid, so better for them to keep thinking that."

"This is some serious shit, Angelo, even for you."

He's right, but it's typical of Dante to worry.

"There's nothing to stress about, I'll be back in the morning. Rocco and Santino are taking care of the location. And I've got soldiers here, Lenny on the gate, Darko and Dom at the house. Nobody knows where I am aside from you guys."

"You of all people should know that nothing's a secret in this town," he reminds me.

"I'll talk to you tomorrow." I need time to think and the less chatter going on while I figure things out, the better.

His voice lowers. "Is it true she tried to poison you?"

"Goodbye, Dante." I hang up and run a hand through my hair. By now, they'll all know.

This is so fucked up that it's not even funny.

I think back to the brief quality time I had with Rayne and feel like an even bigger fool.

I also feel something in my chest for the second time tonight. I should want to rip her fucking vocal cords out so she can never utter another lie again in her life. I should lock her up, chain her to my fucking basement and never let her out.

Letting her go is inconceivable, but so is killing her.

Oh no, Rayne Michaelson, I've got far more despicable things lined up for you to keep me occupied, and none of them are good.

The betrayal, more than the 'killing me' part, is what trickles into my blood faster than the poison ever could, it seeps into my very core and turns my soul black.

I've never understood disloyalty, not in my past and certainly not in the present day. It doesn't compute in my brain. You're either in, or you're out.

Enzo wants me to go easy on her, but she has to know the consequences of what happens when you double-cross a Medici.

And she will know.

She has no idea who I really am.

Now she is going to fucking pay.

I pull into the high gates surrounding my expansive beach house late into the night.

The full moon is hung high in the sky, creating an eerie backdrop, menacing as much as it is enchanting. I can't decide which I prefer.

My hideaway house, surrounded by the Saconesset Hills, is the least used of all my properties, but it's the only one that brings me the most peace. Nestled high on the edge of a cliff, the elevated peninsula boasts views north of Buzzards Bay to the Little Sippewissett Marshes in the west.

Fuck knows why I brought her here, there are plenty of holding cells at Fortress, yet a part of me wants to do this without my brothers around, without the watchful eyes of my soldiers, and not because I'm soft, but because I want complete control over what I do next.

I don't want any distractions when the time comes to talk to her.

If I know my brothers, cousins, and best friend by now, they'll be assembling more security to send to Falmouth, so I figure I have a couple of hours to get what I need out of Rayne.

The house is dark, just as I instructed Gus to keep it. He's good at staying out of the way, as are my guards.

None, except the one at the watchhouse at the gate, can be seen.

I park in the underground garage and shut off the engine.

My heart races in my chest like it never has before. I learned long ago, when my father and Mario began to train me in the business, to keep my emotions in check.

Never wear your heart on your sleeve, fuck, I don't even have a heart anymore. Not like I did back when I still believed in more than darkness and destruction.

Your enemies should never know your next move, and that's what she is right now, *my enemy.*

I punch in the code to the side entry that leads through a secret passageway and into my study.

This place always fascinates me. The architect who built it and remodeled it was slightly mad, so paranoid that he had a panic room cellar and an underground bomb-proof shelter built in case of doomsday. He couldn't have known before his untimely death just how thankful I would be because of his foresight and ingenuity. It's like this place was made to be mine.

The house is still and smells like pine needles and cognac.

I cross the expansive rug and see everything is in its usual place.

I pay a housekeeper handsomely to keep my place dust and dirt free. Since I never know when I'm going to be here, she comes once a week without fail, and when I'm in residence, she'll clean after I've left, leaving no trace that I was ever here.

I loosen my tie as I decide to take the steps, instead of the built-in elevator, up to my bedroom, because that's where I told Gus to keep the traitorous woman I've no idea what to do with.

She should be locked in a fucking dungeon. Or at the least, the guest suite, not that that's punishment. But no. I have her close to me, even when the cold darkness swirls around me like a snake. I have to be there when she wakes.

I want the first thing she sees when she comes around is my face and the wrath I intend to inflict on her staring back from my eyes.

Lucky for me, I don't have to wait long.

I enter my bedroom through the double doors, and the first thing I see is Rayne lying on my bed on her side, her long, golden locks spread out like a fallen angel along my silk pillows. She's still in her dress from the Gala, of course.

For some reason that I can't explain, I reach down and pull a throw over her body, covering her. I cross the room and pour myself a scotch from the tray on my bookcase as I turn to stare at her. After a few moments, I move back to the bed and sit on the edge, my fingers itching to touch her, to know what it feels like to feel the skin of the woman who lied to my face and tried to ruin me.

A strange thing happens, however.

Instead of the bubbling anger that I felt when I almost punched Enzo, and the rage that consumed me as I drove here plotting her death, I stare down at her now, and all I feel is…*pity.*

What would I have done in her shoes? What if it was Valentina?

Would I give a fuck about the person I was betraying to get what I really wanted? If my own flesh and blood were kidnapped and they were being threatened, could I honestly say I wouldn't do the same?

The fact is, I know I would. I would do whatever it took to get my loved ones back. She's no exception.

I close my eyes. I don't know when my feelings turned

to more than just lust, but even my heart – as blackened as it is – knows that what we shared was something more than just sex.

It was fucking perfect, if I'm honest with myself.

And it was all a lie. All outlandish lies.

But was it, though? A part of me wonders what if….I guess we'll never know.

I get up and walk to the window, the night sky is too alluring for me not to seek solace in its blackened abyss. It lures me in like the darkness always can, and for a moment, I realize that I had the light for a while, like a beacon. She lit up my soul like an angel would, not the devil's mistress that she turned out to be. Taking me to places I never dreamed possible. *And I let her.*

She let me fuck her in the bathroom stall, knowing all she knew. *Why?* One last hoorah?

I wonder…Would she have waited for me to fall asleep after the Gala? Long after we tousled in these very bedsheets? Wrapped up, in her arms, sated and satisfied?

All of it breeds a new form of anger inside me. One that fills me with bitterness as much as it does lust. I still fucking want her. My body betrays my mind on every level.

I run a hand through my hair and stare down at her form.

She's so fucking beautiful.

That in itself just goes to show you how far gone I actually am. I still hold her beauty in as much esteem as I do my life. No wonder Marco and Enzo looked at me like I'd lost my mind. Maybe I have.

I sip my drink and turn back to her as I hear her murmur in her sleep. Curious, I saunter around to try and make out her taunted whispers.

Her eyelids flutter and her chest moves rapidly as I watch with fascination.

"…..*No*….*please….*" she murmurs softly, then, "*Angelo.*"

My name on her lips jolts me like I've been struck by lightning. There has never been such a sweet sound, it's like a siren's call. Even if I am a fucking fool, I afford myself this last little luxury.

Without thinking, my hand moves to her face as I caress her cheek with my knuckle. My hand then moves over her hair, smoothing it down as my throat thickens.

She bewitches me at every single turn, even unconscious. And the sight of her here, in the shadows, all alone with me in my house with nowhere to run to, sends shivers down my spine.

She's mine now. To do what I want with, she's at my mercy.

I smirk, a cold reverie running through my bones.

She's the fucking devil.

2 4

RAYNE

WHEN I WAKE, THE FIRST THING I DO IS BLINK MY EYES rapidly, and a searing pain shoots through the back of my skull almost immediately.

The Gala.

Music.

His touch.

My betrayal.

Angelo.

My hand flies to my throat as panic washes through me.

Where am I?

I scramble to sit up, and all the blood rushes to my head. I groan, lowering back down as I rub my temples.

Holy shit. I feel like I've been run over by a bus.

I glance around the darkened room, and the first thing I notice is the cool of the silk sheets beneath me as I try to grasp what happened and where the hell I am.

The last thing I remember is being herded out of the Gala and Angelo wrapping his arms around me, the back of the limo…That's how I ended up here…wherever I am.

I look down at myself and see that I still have last night's clothes on, my shoes have been removed, and there's a throw blanket over my body.

There's a stillness in the air that doesn't feel real, like the calm before the storm. And my instincts are exactly right.

Movement from the far corner of the room has my eyes darting in that direction as I sit up on my elbows.

It's him.

I swallow hard as I see his silhouette. He's sitting in an armchair by the window, the gleam of the moon shines through the glass accentuating his body, but it doesn't quite touch his face, keeping him in the shadows. His hand clutches a crystal tumbler, and if it weren't for the slight movement of his fingers tapping against the glass, I wouldn't have known he was there at all.

His voice breaks through the eerie silence. "Sleep well, princess?"

My throat feels like I've swallowed razor blades as I scramble to pull myself together, my brain foggy.

"Angelo..."

He raises his hand, and I stop in my tracks.

One thing I do know is, that there's no way out of this. I'm trapped. He won, and I lost.

I wait for the sob to rise in my throat, thinking about my sister and the fact that I may never see her again, but it never comes. I'm in too much shock for any of this to register properly, or maybe I've just been so good at masking my feelings since she got kidnapped that this is who I am now.

It confounds me as much as the alarm bells ringing in my head.

Acceptance replaces sorrow. It feels different from how I thought it would feel. I know this is my fate, there is no point denying it. If I have to fight, I will, even when I know it's futile, and I can't win, that doesn't matter. I will never give up. *Never.*

My sister is all I have. She's the only family I have left after the accident that claimed our parents; she's everything to me, my best friend. And even though my fate is bleak, I won't stop, *I'll never stop.*

So he can do whatever he wants to me; I'll face it head-on. I've come this far, and I've no intention of giving up. I doubt I can escape, but I'd try, not that I've got anywhere to go or even have my phone to make contact, but I'll die trying.

This is my new reality, and I have to adapt. I *have* to try and find a way out. If I don't, I'm dead anyway.

"I want you to know something first," I manage when he doesn't rush to fill the void with words. It unsettles me more than I care to admit.

I can't see him properly, but I can imagine him raising his eyebrows. "So speak."

I wince at his tone, but I can't expect anything less.

I clear my throat. "I don't want to insult you by saying that I wanted things to end this way, but for what it's worth, I never would have attempted to kill you, Angelo. I did what I had to do, and that doesn't mean that it didn't rip me apart in the process."

He scoffs. "Yet, you went to the drop. You put the poison in your purse, ready for the kill."

I know he's testing me. Baiting me. And who can blame him? I would too.

"I had to, Angelo. I had to make it seem like I was still playing the game. I had to stay one step ahead."

"And just what game do you think we're playing here, *Carina?*"

The way he says my pet name is like poison rolling off

his tongue. It's changed, no longer laced with a warmth I once knew.

"I don't know anymore," I whisper.

He uncrosses his leg from his knee and leans forward. "Well, lucky for us both, I *know* the game. I live and breathe it, just as well as I know how the next part will play out."

My heart races so hard in my chest I'm sure he can hear it. "And that is?"

He tsks. "Patience, my dear little fox. First, I need to tell you the new rules."

My eyes dart around the room, only one way in and one way out. He probably has the place surrounded, probably has guard dogs for all I know. My eyes land on the pitcher of water on the bedside table.

"May I?" I ask, nodding to the glass that sits next to it.

"Of course."

I pour a glass and quickly drink it down. It feels like I haven't tasted water for an eternity.

When I'm done, I place the empty glass back on the side table.

"Rule number one," he says as my eyes land on him again. "If you try to escape or attack me in any way, I'll kill you."

My eyes go wide as I realize we're not in Kansas anymore. My worst nightmare has come true, and he means business.

This is the Angelo Medici you don't mess with. The tyrant I've never known.

"You can't get away anyway because we're secluded, so save yourself the trouble. I took you out of the city," he goes on. "Two. You will not speak unless spoken to, and you will not try to explain yourself and make excuses for what you've done. My patience is waning, and my temper is barely hanging on by a thread."

"Did you find the letter?" I blurt out, ignoring his rules.

I guess not. If he did, he wouldn't show it anyway. Anything that we ever had is gone. I betrayed him – in his eyes, I'm a traitor.

"You're already breaking rule number two, *Carina*. I'd watch that mouth of yours."

"I need to find my sister," I whisper-shout. "If you feel the need to punish me, hurt me, keep me captive for the rest of my life, you can do it, but I have to get her back. She's innocent...she's lying there somewhere, probably being raped and tortured. Hell, she could be dead by now!" A shudder runs through me at such a thought; it's quickly replaced by anger.

"What makes you think I won't kill you first?" he muses.

My heart races at how he would do it.

A crime of passion? Would he place those large hands of his around my neck and squeeze?

Would he use a blade, slice across my neck, and watch me bleed. *Or would he just shoot?*

I should feel terrified.

It's not like I've ever been in a situation like this before, yet there's a sense of calm in the room. Like when the hunter has caught the gazelle, and he's just playing with it for a while before striking. I know he will do it. That's how he operates. I just don't know how.

Instead. I taunt him. "You would have done it by now," I retort. He's my only hope; there are no two ways about it. "And I don't really think you want to do that, do you, Angelo?"

It's like I can feel his fury from across the room. Like he's a volcano, simmering and ready to erupt any minute.

"Rule number three. You will do every fucking thing I say, without a debate, without so much as a blink of an eye or any backtalk. If you think you can sit here and outsmart me and keep me talking while you try to figure out what move comes next, you're done, Rayne. We're at checkmate. You lost, and you're mine now, and I'll do whatever the fuck I want with you. Do you not understand? There's nowhere else to run."

I fold my arms over my chest. "And if I refuse?"

"You say that like you have a choice."

"You won't hurt me," I whisper.

He places the crystal tumbler on the side table as I inadvertently scrunch the sheets under my fingers.

Please don't come over here...please don't come over here...

"You really don't want to test me."

"Have you killed a woman before?" I ask, trying to meet his gaze, but I still can't see his eyes.

"You know the answer to that, and you're forgetting something; I'm the only person who can help you find your sister, and it's still debatable if I'll even do that."

"You bastard!"

He chuckles. "That hurts, and here I was thinking we shared something special."

I feel my eyes pool with water and swallow hard to stop the tears. I'm at his fucking mercy, and I don't care.

"I'll do anything," I cry. "I will do *any* fucking thing you want, Angelo! But I have to... I have to..."

"Kill me," he says helpfully. "Funny thing about that when my heart's still beating."

"Tell me what to do, and I'll do it. I'll fucking do it," I beg.

He tsks again. "You don't take direction very well, do you, little fox?"

"Why do you keep calling me that?"

"Because that's what you are. Sly. Cunning. Disguised well, yet flawlessly beautiful."

"I don't know who took my sister," I fire back angrily. Fury rises through me. I may have hurt him, and gotten closer than what I ever intended, hell, I fucking enjoyed it, but I'm no killer. That's why I hired Enzo… "Enzo…"

"Ah, yes. You see, *Carina*, Enzo has been my best friend since we were in diapers, he told me everything. Do you know how hard it was to fuck you knowing you hate me?"

"I don't hate you," I whisper. "One thing I never did was hate you."

"You can't even say it, can you?" he taunts.

My mouth goes dry again. I open and close it again. I hear him snicker.

I'd like to think that Angelo appreciates strength over weakness, and I can't show him just exactly how weak I really am.

"I can say it, but it doesn't mean anything."

"So say it."

I steel myself. "Kill you," I say, the words feeling like poison on my tongue. "I was supposed to kill you."

"See, it's not that hard, is it. I have to applaud you, though, nobody has gotten this close to me since…" He taps his chin as he thinks. "My wife," he finally finishes as my eyes go wide. "And we all know how that turned out."

I know I've hurt him. I can see it now, which means he felt something for me.

It's why he's so angry. And it hurts more than I ever thought it could. Like someone has cut a piece out of my heart, and it will never repair. Bile rises in my throat.

"Despite what you think of me, I only did what anybody would do under the circumstances," I bite back. "And do you want to know something else, Angelo Medici?"

"Enlighten me."

"I'd do it again."

I don't even hear him move, but he's at the side of the bed before I can blink, and then he's on me, grabbing my wrists as he pins them over my head. I wriggle instinctively as I try to fight back.

His scent intoxicates me; it always has, always will. Even now, as his murderous eyes finally meet mine, I still want him.

"What's wrong, *Carina?* Do you want to scream?" he taunts, his body pressing against mine as I lay flat on the bed, and he rests all of his weight on me. I feel his hard cock and desire shoots through my body, I can't control it. Being aroused by this man isn't part of the plan, not when I'm supposed to be his prisoner and at his mercy, but this is what he does to me.

He runs his nose up the side of my neck as I turn my head away. "Don't pretend you don't like it," he whispers in my ear. "Or did you fake all the times I made you come as well?"

I swallow hard and shake my head. And for the first time in as long as I can remember, I go with the truth. "No," I whisper back. "None of that was fake, in fact, it was the only thing that kept me from wanting to dive into the Charles and end it all…"

He grunts into my skin, then I feel him lift off me and he reaches behind to his back pocket and pulls out his tie.

I watch with trepidation as he straddles me, then grasps my wrists again and ties them together.

"That's it, little fox. It's so much better when you don't resist."

He knots the tie and then secures my hands to the bed. He sits back on his knees and tests the knot. "Perfect, now where were we?"

"I was disobeying rules one, two, and three."

His lips turn up. "Even now, you're not afraid, are you?"

I shake my head. "I know you won't hurt me. You're not like the other monsters."

A slow grin spreads across his face as his eyes dance. "Don't be so sure about that. Although tied up like this, I've got you right where I want you. At my disposal, to do with as I choose."

"I told you I'll do whatever you want," I whisper.

He reaches a hand to my face and I resist the urge to flinch. "I bet if I reached under your dress right now, I'd find you wet and begging for me, wouldn't I?"

I don't say a word, for I can't disagree. This man is probably going to kill me, yet my body still wants every single inch of him. It's like I can't rest without him inside me; I need him like I need air. It disgusts me as much as it thrills me.

His stern face waits for an answer, except I don't give him one.

Instead, he reaches down my body, and I try to contain the thrill that runs through me because I can't touch him back.

He's not the only one who can play games here, I've been doing this long enough that it almost feels second nature.

I want him to touch me.

I wait with anticipation as his hand makes its way under the hem of my dress and he bunches it up so I'm exposed, then he slips his fingers through my folds, and I try to hide the groan that leaves my lips.

Of course, I don't make a liar out of him. I'm wet, and as his fingers brush my clit I let out a gasp. His touch sears every part of my soul.

"Even now," he muses. "Your body defies you, doesn't it, *Carina?*"

"No," I fire back. "My body knows exactly what it needs."

I feel him grin against my neck as he tenderly nips it with his teeth, all the while his fingers skim my pussy and circle my clit, teasing me in the most delicious of ways.

"Was it a hardship?" he bites out. "Having to sleep with me?"

I close my eyes. Even in the dark, where he can't really see my reactions, I feel my face heat.

"I didn't sleep with you because of..."

"Shhh," he whispers. "You're breaking all of my rules, and you know what that does to me."

It feels depraved, but my body has come to crave him. He's like an addiction I may never be able to shake.

"Angelo..." I whisper as he sucks on the skin below my clavicle, his fingers move faster, and I find myself needing to come. I need it so bad that a sense of shame washes over me.

I should hate this man. And I did, in the beginning. That is until I got to know him, until I realized that he wasn't anything like I thought he was. He's a different kind of monster.

"Yes? Tell me, and I might let you come."

"I...I want you to know..." I groan in pants that I can't even control. His fingers start to slow. "That they told me things about you that I know aren't true. They told me you were the one who ran the people smuggling, that you hired underaged girls..."

He falters his ministrations for a moment at my confession. Then, his other hand pulls my dress up to my chin, as if he's annoyed, he rips the top of my dress wide open. I feel his mouth on my nipple as he sucks hard. I feel it down to my toes as I fight off my impending orgasm.

I try to gain more friction by moving my hips, but he stills as soon as I do.

"I won't let you," he whispers as I groan in frustration. "And I can do this all night, my sweet, sweet *Carina*. So, behave, or you will never leave this room."

I swallow hard, annoyed at the hold he has over me and even more annoyed at myself for being so aroused by him, given the fact he has neither confirmed nor denied he may kill me.

An eye for an eye, right?

"It was easier to hate you in the beginning," I go on. A few moments later, his fingers begin rubbing me again. "Even though I acted differently. I thought you were a mindless, murderous barbarian, nothing more. And that suited me because all I wanted was to get close to you so I could get my sister back. Then they said I had to take things further…"

"Sleep with me?"

"Yes, and find things out about you, which I didn't do much of, obviously. Let's face it, you're kind of hard to keep track of and impossible to pin down."

I hear him chuckle, his other hand cups my breast as he shifts, and I feel his mouth on me once more. I almost combust, but I manage to hold on while he works his sweet torture.

"Touché' to the woman pinned down to my bed."

I open my eyes, and when I glance down, he doesn't look up at me. His eyes are scrunched closed as I try to make sense of what the hell this fucked up shit is and why I want more of it.

"I'm sorry," I say. "For what it's worth. I never meant to actually…care about you."

"But, you did?" he scoffs. "Was that not part of your master plan, *Carina?*"

I close my eyes again, his fingers rubbing through my folds as I bite down hard on my bottom lip.

"No," I admit. "It wasn't."

The sensations are too much. I want to lose myself in him so badly that it burns my body like hot embers rushing through my blood.

"How do I know that you're not just saying all this so I'll spare you?"

"You don't," I whisper as his hand reaches up to my throat and he grasps it.

He moves his face to mine, our eyes locking. His dark, blue irises resemble something between rage, lust, and bitterness.

"You'll do as I say, nothing more. You will fucking obey me."

"Yes." As much as it pains me, I will.

"You belong to me now. If you want to keep breathing a while longer, don't test me, little fox."

Warmth flourishes in my chest. *He's going to help me?*

I swallow hard, his hand tightening around my throat, and I feel a rush of wetness between my legs.

I don't make a sound, just my heavy breathing as he moves his fingers over me, then he whispers. "Come for me, *Carina.*"

He watches me as I let go, spiraling out of control as my body shudders and I cry out. The sensation takes me under as he loosens his grip from my neck, where I gasp much-needed air.

"You do that so beautifully," he whispers, reaching up and untying me.

"I want to take care of you too," I tell him, reaching for

his cock, hoping that's what he wants. Instead, he turns away from me and stands before I can reach him.

"You're not going to get any piece of me ever again," he says, adjusting his hard length that bulges front and center. "My body may betray me, but my mind is as sharp as a blade. And I will cut you, *Carina*, even if it pains me."

"Because you want control in all things," I murmur, gathering myself. Unafraid even though he hasn't bothered to pull my dress down.

He smirks. "Oh, that's where you're wrong. I *always* have control in everything I do, including this."

Silence settles between us as I ask him, "What are you going to do?" It's a loaded question, and I think he knows it.

"Easy." His eyes glisten in the dark. "I'll help you get Mia back, but when I do, you agree to whatever punishment I see fit when this is over."

"Agreed," I say without hesitation. My heart bubbles with adrenaline as I scramble to pull myself together.

He stares at me, the devil in his eyes as my heart skips a beat to what he really means…

"What do I have to do?" I question, not truly wanting to hear the answer. But it's inevitable. I'm in this up to my neck, and there is no way out.

It's him and me now, nobody else.

A devilish grin spreads across his face as the serpent shows himself…*And this is why they all fear him.*

Angelo Medici, the King of the Boston crime family.

Time stops as I wait; the silence deafening.

"You have to kill me."

ACKNOWLEDGMENTS

Thank you so much from the bottom of our hearts as we enjoyed our second co-write together!

Thank you to our amazing P.A. team: Savannah and Brianna for all your help with this release.

Special thanks to Savannah for the Medici Mafia covers and as always, your amazing formatting.

Thank you Angie at Lunar Rose Editing for your expertise, patience and guidance during this journey. We've loved working with you and can't wait to bring you more mayhem with the Medicis. Bring it on!

Michelle (The Outgoing Bookworm) thank you again for reading and all your suggestions. Hugs MF!

Thank you to our ARC readers, we hope you enjoy reading about the Medici crime family and can't wait to bring you book 2 in less than a month!

As always, to our blogger friends and fellow indie authors out there who support, share, read, blog and send kind messages or comment on a post. We are forever grateful.

Thank you to our loyal, amazing readers. We hope you enjoyed reading as much as we did creating this exciting new world, you will be hearing from Angelo and Rayne in book 2, and psssst! The series will not be ending there as there are plenty more Medici men to discover!

Keep up to date with all of what we're up to by joining our newsletter below.

Stay tuned for book 2, releasing on 29th June 2022, Fortress of the Queen and the conclusion to this duet and you are in for some surprises!

Check out our links below to follow us on social media and keep up with our latest book news.

Love from Australia, Mackenzy and Dakotah x

ABOUT THE AUTHORS

Mackenzy Fox is an author of contemporary, motorcycle, dark mafia and steamy themed romance novels. When she's not writing she loves vegan cooking, walking her beloved pooch's, reading books and is an expert on online shopping.

She's slightly obsessed with drinking tea, testing bubbly Moscato, watching home decorating shows and has a black belt in origami. She strives to live a quiet and introverted life in Western Australia's North West with her hubbie, twin sister Dakotah and her dogs.

Dakotah Fox is a new author of contemporary, dark mafia and small-town romance. She enjoys walking and hiking, finding new tea haunts, and is a qualified yoga instructor.

When she's not writing she enjoys finding a good book to curl up with, loves watching Beauty and the Geek and is the Queen of planning. You can find her living a quiet, fulfilled life in Western Australia's Northwest with her beloved doggies.

#twinlife
  #indieauthors
  #girlsrule

Please note: This book is a duet and ends on a cliffhanger. Book 2 Fortress of the Queen is the conclusion and will release June 29 2022.

Mackenzy Tiktok: https://www.tiktok.com/@mackenzyfoxauthor
Mackenzy Face book: https://www.facebook.com/mackenzy.foxauthor.5
Instagram Mackenzy: https://www.instagram.com/mackenzyfoxbooks/
Instagram Dakotah: https://www.instagram.com/dakotahfoxbooks/

Don't forget to join my private Facebook Group: The Den – A Mackenzy Fox Readers Group here: https://bit.ly/3dgQfKk

Sign up for our Newsletter: https://landing.mailerlite.com/webforms/landing/g2l8y8

Find all Mackenzy and Dakotah's book links here in one easy spot: https://linktr.ee/mackenzyfox

Checkout Mackenzy's website:
https://mackenzyfox.com

WANT MORE?

Blurb for FORTRESS OF THE QUEEN: BOOK 2

I TRIED TO STAY AWAY.

Even when everything fell apart, when I became his prisoner and my world

tumbled out from under my feet. I didn't know then…

That he would still own my heart. My soul. My very being.

And I want to be his Queen.

The lies and betrayal seem like nothing compared to imagining a

world where he's not in it.

When our paths collided, I kept my true feelings hidden,

scared that my heart would shatter.

But the rules have changed, and now we have to work together.

Everything we hold dear hangs in the balance.

Everything ends tonight.

And Angelo Medici is the one thing I can't bet on keeping.

This book is the conclusion to Book 1 (Fortress of the King) in the Medici Mafia series which is a steamy, suspense filled, dark mafia romance. This book cannot be read without reading book 1 first.

Release date: 29 June 2022, order here:
       https://books2read.com/MediciMafia2